Sacred Monsters

Sacred Monsters

DANIEL FARSON

BLOOMSBURY

ACKNOWLEDGEMENTS

The author and publishers are grateful to the following for permission to reproduce copyright letters in the text: Lindsay Anderson (postcard from Lindsay Anderson to Daniel Farson); Helen Cherry (letter from Trevor Howard to Daniel Farson); Henry Williamson Literary Estate (letters from Henry Williamson to Daniel Farson); Livia Gollancz (letters from Victor Gollancz to Negley Farson); Kathleen Sutherland (letters from Kathleen Sutherland to Daniel Farson); Colin Wilson (letter from Colin Wilson to Daniel Farson).

All photographs in this book were taken by Daniel Farson and are his copyright. Those appearing on pp. 32, 33, 38, 54, 66, 67, 68, 69, 70, 74, 75, 82, 83, 84, 85, 86, 96, 97, 175, 177 are copyright BBC Hulton Picture Library, and the one on p. 161 is copyright Marlborough Fine Art Ltd.

Bloomsbury Publishing Ltd, 2 Soho Square, London W1V 5DE

British Library Cataloguing in Publication Data

Farson, Daniel, *1927-*
    Sacred monsters.
    1. Celebrities, 1920–1986 – Personal
    observations
    I. Title
    920'.009'04

    ISBN 0-7475-0254-4

Designed by Mark Foster
Typeset by SX Composing Ltd, Rayleigh, Essex
Printed in Great Britain by Butler & Tanner Ltd, Frome and London

To Irene, with gratitude for all the years of loyalty

Daniel Farson photographing Dame Edith Evans,
portraying one of the most fearsome monsters of them all:
Lady Bracknell in *The Importance of Being Earnest*

Contents

Introduction

It is hard to decide whether I have collected sacred monsters because I liked them, or liked them because I met so many at crucial moments in their lives – and my own. Either way, the term is one of approval. How does one define the breed? They are more formidable than eccentrics, and more rare. They are the life-enhancers though they may not enhance their own lives in the process. They are larger than life, but so were Stalin and Genghis Khan, so that description is inadequate unless you add the vital element of fun, and that is not necessarily deliberate.

Equally, if they were merely ruthless they could be something in the City, but the sacred monster has a sort of innocence too. Winston Churchill was a sacred monster but he possessed these other prerequisites. I spoke to him only once, when we collided on a secret staircase in the House of Commons where I worked as a Lobby Correspondent at the age of eighteen. I said, 'Good morning, sir,' and he growled back, so that scintillating confrontation is not included here.

There seems some doubt, but I have always believed that the term comes from the French – *monstres sacrés* – applied to matinée idols of a certain age who remained indomitable, and that Sacha Guitry was the prime example. However, Lady Diana Mosley suggested that Sarah Bernhardt had the necessary exaggeration, playing a young man in her eighties, when she had a wooden leg. Such panache is shared by many of the sacred monsters who appear in these pages: Ken Tynan exhorting a college porter on his arrival at Oxford: 'Take a care with that trunk, my man, it is freighted with golden shirts'; Salvador Dali in a boat at Port Lligat, with a stuffed swan in the prow; Brendan Behan dancing drunkenly on stage during a performance of *The Hostage*. Yet sacred monsters are better than exhibitionists, they need to have some value. You will find no TV personalities here (though Gilbert Harding *nearly* qualified) apart from one who is simply monstrous. They are *enfants terribles* who have never grown up.

By chance, this book has developed into a form of autobiography as it became evident that I had the luck to meet my sacred monsters at formative moments, in some of which I actually played a minor role myself. I have resisted the temptation to include those I have not known but regard as eligible: Evelyn Waugh; Wilfred Lawson; Edith Piaf; Nureyev. You will have your own ideas as to who is a sacred monster and, definitely, who is *not*.

I realise my definitions are incomplete – perhaps it is impossible to be definitive – but have you noticed how a rainstorm intensifies before it dies out, and how the sun is especially fierce in the moments before the clouds obscure it? Most of us are drizzle or, with luck, comparatively sunny. Sacred monsters have that extra force or brightness. They are special people – to the advantage of ourselves.

Christmas at the Villa Mauresque

SOMERSET MAUGHAM

Somerset Maugham warned my godmother in Chicago: 'It goes against the grain for me to say this, but I fear that it is not a suitable home for Daniel. It's too immoral for such a sensitive ch-child.' Maugham referred to Pinehill, the house in the Midwest town of Oregon, Illinois, where I stayed with my godfather, Tom Seyster, who was no relation to my godmother. Indeed, Mrs Kellogg Fairbank disapproved of Seyster and seized on Maugham's advice gratefully. I was twelve years old, naïve like many English school-boys at the time, yet I sensed that Maugham's intervention was hypocritical. Certainly Seyster's relationship with Gerald Haxton, Maugham's 'secretary-companion', was peculiar – even I could tell that from their scenes on the staircase – but, if Maugham was correct in condemning the household as immoral, surely he was a part of that immorality?

Now, due to Maugham, I was barred from the house where I was happy.

Arriving in Canada on 3 July 1940, I had been shunted around like a freight car, one of the hundreds of English schoolboys evacuated on the *Duchess of Bedford.* Today I find that evacuation inexplicable. Did our parents want to get rid of us because it made life simpler? Did they believe that Britain had lost the war? Either way, it was an admission of defeat, with the irony that many of our parents housed evacuees from the East End of London for as long as eighteen months, while they sent their own children overseas with the probability of never seeing them again. Curious.

I was head boy of Abinger Hill, a prep school in Surrey; the last head boy, as it turned out, for the school closed down, half the boys returned to their families, and the rest were cast into exile. In Montreal I was collected by a nice alcoholic businessman, claimed like a parcel in a lost property office after he'd seen a photograph of me and my gas-mask in the *Montreal Star.* He said he had known my father, which proved untrue, so the National Committee of Refugees – 'a clearing house for groups of children evac-uated from England' – handed me over. When he disappeared on a drunken spree, his family transferred me to the care of a lonely woman who nurtured some private grief and lived in a silent house where the curtains were seldom drawn. Suddenly, after a flurry of telegrams and phone calls, I was placed on the overnight train to Chicago and took a bus to another station where I must have looked bewildered, for two kindly women bought me a book and saw me safely on a train to Lake Geneva.

I arrived there on a Sunday morning to be met by my godmother, Mrs Fairbank, and her harassed secretary, Miss Cronin, known as 'Birdie', who ran after her, notepad in hand, like a frail dinghy in the wake of a battleship. Mrs Fairbank, a large lady, greeted me with an abrupt embrace and the reproach: 'I've met two trains already. Hurry up or we'll be late.'

If Somerset Maugham was a sacred monster, Mrs Fairbank had her own monstrosity. I was told in her defence that she had been gentler when her husband was alive, but I suspect she was born to be bossy – not to be bossed. Endowed with hyperactive energy, she wrote historical novels under the name of Janet Ayer Fairbank. She took an active part in Midwest politics – *Life* called her 'the First Lady of Chicago' – and she was rich. Dining in the Chicago Club at the Millionaires' Table alongside George Pullman, Marshall Field and Robert Lincoln, the President's son, Nathaniel Kellogg had invented a soap. Now his fortune was dwindling but enough remained for Mrs Fairbank to brook no opposition and to entertain on the scale of Gatsby at the summerhouse on the shore of Lake Geneva built for Nathaniel by the same architect who designed the Club in Chicago.

Butternuts was a dainty name for the most astonishing house I had seen. For a child it was particularly gorgeous, a wooden replica of a Swiss chalet with gingerbread carvings, deceptively compact for it was able to accommodate a house-party of twenty to thirty guests. The atmosphere reeked of wealth: Wrigley of chewing-gum fame was the neighbour, his mansion invisible behind the trees, and there was no right of way around the lake. Trespassers were threatened and manhandled by Mrs Fairbank's sons if they protested. When a stranger with a foreign accent, carrying a small case, dared to walk up the drive early one Sunday morning, he was marched away by the butler who ignored his protestations. As the day progressed, it was noticed that the most important guest, a tycoon with infinite wealth and a famous art collection, had not made an appearance. Finally an angry message revealed that he was waiting for his personal barber who accompanied him everywhere and was staying in the nearby village, the foreigner who had been turned away and now could not be found. After the indignity, and novelty, of having to shave himself, the tycoon emerged at last in a vile temper for the rest of his stay.

Butternuts was a refuge for artists and writers and those seeking escape from the heat of Chicago, like my parents in the mid-1920s: 'Janet Fairbank saved our lives in Chicago,' my father remembered in *The Way of a Transgressor*. 'Her wooden house out at Lake Geneva had defied all the raucous progress of time and mass production. It was almost a museum piece. And her exhilarating house-parties would compensate for purgatory itself.'

Sixteen years later, the ritual of the weekend house-party continued, if more frenetically. Mrs Fairbank led me on to the lawn which stretched down to the wooden jetty which grew too hot to stand on, and clapped her hands for attention. 'Look everyone,' she cried, 'this is my godson, all the way from England.' A murmur of sympathy stirred the guests as they crowded towards the verandah while I stood there uncomfortably, itching in my thick tweed suit bought by my mother before I sailed from Liverpool with no awareness of the summer. 'The son of Eve and Negley Farson!' She turned towards me, beaming with sudden benevolence. 'So let us welcome Dan to America!' The guests clapped and smiled ingratiatingly and, though I was too hungry to be embarrassed, I felt they were clapping her for her magnanimity towards me.

I was unaware how bizarre this situation was, for Mrs Fairbank was the Vice-President of the America First Committee pledged to keep America out of the war which Britain had started. As an English evacuee, I had been paraded as a token salve to conscience and proof of her tolerance.

My one concern was food and I gazed greedily, though with disappointment, at a meal unlike anything I had known as servants appeared in black uniforms carrying jugs of a special cocktail prepared by Mrs Fairbank and named after her, and trays with bowls of popcorn and bits of things on biscuits. After I had tucked in voraciously, assuming this was lunch, the butler announced that the proper lunch was served and the guests filed into the dining-room with wide-eyed anticipation. Mrs Fairbank's food was famous, prepared by a fierce Swedish lady with a moustache, the only servant who was not intimidated. She was paid a huge salary, owned a Buick and a mink coat, and if she was crossed she gave in her notice. I liked her on sight, but with a child's instinct I could tell that the

Outside the gates of the Villa Mauresque, in my US Army greatcoat

English butler was a fake, as he proved to be when he absconded with a suitcase of silver.

That first lunch began with the Swede's speciality, a baked fish rich in cream, onions, and mushrooms, followed by curry with a score of side-dishes and vanilla ice-cream churned interminably in a wooden tub by the hard-worked, well-paid servants, a task which I joined in later for the first scrape of that incomparable taste.

Lunch finished in the middle of the afternoon, followed by mint tea and bitter cookies. Then there was a short respite and a bath before the guests filed down to dinner in evening dress, and to Mrs Fairbank's credit I was allowed to join them in my new blue blazer and white trousers, seated next to some unfortunate guest who was out of favour.

All the time the sun was glaring outside. At least we were able to use the lake for swimming and boating after the guests had gone, but they must have returned to Chicago satiated, like stuffed Strasburg geese.

I was fortunate. Butternuts was full of interest and they were kind to me. The first shock came as we drove to Chicago to attend the Democratic convention and I mentioned Roosevelt admiringly, believing that the Americans regarded him as we did Churchill. Mrs Fairbank turned. 'Never, never let me hear you mention that man's name again. We hate him far more than the English can possibly hate Hitler.' Another time she accused him of 'betraying his class', an equal offence, so this was the start of a strained summer in which I was ordered to remove my British War Relief badge and had to crawl into a car on the drive to hear Roosevelt on the radio, for his voice was forbidden inside the house. When Colonel Charles Lindbergh and Colonel McCormick came to Butternuts for an America First weekend conference, I was confined to the kitchen with the big Swede – which I preferred – in case I staged a protest. Considering their views, this was a wise precaution: the great aviator spoke throughout the country for the America First Committee whose 'first duty is to keep America out of foreign wars'; Colonel McCormick was the rabidly anti-British owner of the *Chicago Tribune*.

It was in Chicago that Mrs Fairbank revealed her true monstrosity, ruthless with anyone who sank to the occasion. When I was fitted for a pair of shoes by a salesman who unwittingly displeased her, she summoned the owner of the store to the telephone and told him to dismiss the wretched man on the spot, which he did. To start with, she took the trouble of taking me to the cinema which was a generous act in view of her hectic schedule, and was poorly repaid by my bad behaviour. 'I have been sorry about the Roosevelt business,' she wrote to my mother in September, 'as it has done Dan out of a certain amount of fun. When he goes to a movie he "boos" Willkie [Wendell Willkie, the Republican candidate] and cheers Roosevelt, so I don't take him any more. I can only make you understand my point of view when I say that my feeling about F.D.R. differs only in intensity from your feeling about Hitler – both men threaten the countries we love. I hope that you will not encourage Dan in what really is a serious breach of manners.'

As a further example of my bad behaviour, she quoted a letter I had written to my grandmother which I was rash enough to show to her daughter-in-law who promptly sneaked. 'Overcome by the pride of authorship, Dan wound up his diatribe in a splendid burst which said, "American men are so weak that they will not fight even to defend their own country." Startled by this, Ginny said, "Dan, you know that isn't true." And he said, "Yes, but it's much more dramatic."'

Mrs Fairbank was unamused at harbouring such an ungrateful child and determined to Americanise me, taking me to the Todd School in Illinois where Orson Welles had been a student, and I was granted a scholarship. To her annoyance, I resisted and returned to Ashbury College in Ottawa and my school friends from Abinger. I accepted my situation with no fear of the future but I felt a fanatical loyalty to the country I had left behind, even though I possessed dual nationality.

There was nothing stalwart in my opposition to Mrs Fairbank, just the narrow-mindedness of a boy of twelve. Abinger had taught me to be self-contained. Occasionally I wonder what might have developed had I gone to Todd. I doubt if much would have changed for I would have returned to England when it was possible to do so. That was where I belonged.

Ironically, it was Colonel McCormick's anti-British *Tribune* which published my first poem, due to a columnist called June Provines who befriended me when I returned to Chicago that winter of 1940 for my school holidays. It was called 'Absence'.

> O, to have a little look
> At England once again,
> To walk once more in London's streets
> Or down a village lane.
> To see anew the little house
> In which I used to live –
> O, only just a little look,
> And anything I'd give.

> DANIEL NEGLEY FARSON JR.

Nauseating and twee though this seems to me now, the sentiment must have seemed genuine for it touched the heart of Somerset Maugham, noted for his lack of sentimentality.

Maugham was in America to present the case for Britain, ostensibly on behalf of the Ministry of Information with the occasional hint that he was working for British Intelligence too. In this respect, he was opposed to everything that Mrs Fairbank represented and might have felt sympathetic to an exile like himself, thrown among such anti-British lions. Mrs Fairbank's views were notorious and he knew her personally.

Tom Seyster, my godfather, phoned me at North State Street where Mrs Fairbank had a small but priceless house, squeezed between two fashionable blocks, to say that Somerset Maugham had invited me to lunch. When I refused, he was startled and sounded vexed, for how could anyone, especially a child, refuse to have lunch with the most successful writer in the world? In fact I was going to meet a school friend from

Abinger called Fodor, and for once I had my priorities right. It was natural to prefer the rare chance of meeting someone of my own age. Perhaps my unexpected refusal appealed to Maugham's dry sense of humour for he asked to see more of my poems, a courageous request verging on masochism, and sent me a handwritten letter which revealed a gentleness which few people suspected:

> I have read your poems. You must expect them at your age to be immature [I was now thirteen], but I who cannot write verse at all envy you the gift of being able to. I hope you will write more; you will find it a constant source of pleasure.
>
> I think the best of the lot you sent me is 'Absence'. That is very simple and very moving, I suppose one always writes best when one is impelled by a given feeling. But the others also have some very good lines.
>
> Bless you.
>
> W. S. MAUGHAM

A few days later, Maugham and his 'secretary-companion', Gerald Haxton, collected me from North State Street to take me to my godfather's home in the typical Midwest town of Oregon. I sensed that Mrs Fairbank was furious, but the poor woman could not tell me why – that the three men were infamous for their homosexuality and the two younger men for their drunkenness too. She could hardly explain this to a thirteen-year-old boy, and her feelings must have been mixed as she saw me go – relief at being rid of me for a few days, anxiety at sending me to the proverbial 'den of iniquity' though Maugham provided a semblance of respectability, at least. She wrote to my mother afterwards: 'It was impossible for me to refuse to allow him to go to Tom's.'

The taxi raced to the station, for we were late, and Maugham who detested haste was plainly cross as we scrambled aboard the silver Zephyr just in time.

The relationship between Maugham and Haxton was surprising. They were opposites, which, of course, was part of the attraction.

Maugham was successful and wealthy. He has been described as 'shy' but this is not wholly true, for he genuinely disliked his fellow-men and flinched at the prospect of someone resting an arm on his shoulder in a gesture of *bonhomie*. Maugham's withdrawal was also due to his stammer, translated as a club-foot in his novel *Of Human Bondage*, but steeliness was part of his nature, due to the loneliness of his childhood after the death of the mother he adored. His marriage to Syrie Barnardo, who became famous as an interior decorator with her all-white rooms, seems to have been loveless on his part if not on hers. She served as a convenient cover for his homosexuality, with the advantage of being an excellent hostess. When she became pregnant it was both the decent and the useful thing to do, to marry her. This makes his obsession for Haxton so unexpected, for Haxton had no discretion whatsoever.

Gerald Haxton was born in San Francisco in 1892 and though he was brought up in England by his English mother, and I assume that his accent was a blend from both countries, I remember him as wholly American.

Despite his being described as slightly built, I remember him as huge, partly because Maugham was slighter and I was even smaller. He wasn't handsome, but rough and ready with immense vitality. An early photograph shows a curious discrepancy in the eyes: the right eye frank and merrily mischievous; the left one threatening. What sticks in my memory most of all from that first impression in Chicago was a large gingerish moustache and a violent temper.

Haxton was twenty-two when he met Maugham in Flanders in the First War when both were members of an ambulance unit, though Maugham's reference to this encounter which changed his life was characteristically terse. 'I had been attracted to him by his immense vitality and his adventurous spirit. I had met him infrequently in the interval. I had found him a very useful companion.'

This was a sliver of the truth. To start with their relationship was intermittent, and this could have been the pattern afterwards except for an unfortunate incident in a Charing Cross hotel when Haxton had the bad luck to be found in bed with another man when the police raided the premises in a search for an army deserter. On 5 December 1915, he appeared with the other man at the Old Bailey on six counts of gross indecency. Six seems excessive, but Haxton was not a man to do things by halves. Well represented legally, the two men pleaded not guilty and were acquitted, but Haxton was under suspicion on other charges and the police took the surprising step of having him deported as an undesirable alien when he returned to England four years later. This is why Somerset Maugham made his home in France at the Villa Mauresque on Cap Ferrat.

Was Haxton really as bad as people made out?

Syrie said, 'He drinks like a fish and lies like a trooper and if one has any sense one doesn't leave one's bag out of one's sight for a moment if he's in the same room, but he *is* very attractive.'

Robin Maugham, the nephew, said, 'He had an air of dissipation and people who didn't like him said he looked shifty.' But they were rivals in some respects, and Haxton made Robin his heir.

Beverley Nichols was the most vituperative. 'Although he was careless of the conventions (he used to pick his very white teeth with some ostentation), he was a gentleman and he was no fool. For example, he translated many of the Master's finest stories, and André Gide, who presumably knew what he was talking about, once told me that his French was impeccable. There was only one thing wrong about Gerald, and it can be put quite simply. He stank. He had about him an aura of corruption.'

But Beverley was a rival too. He ground his axe vigorously in a scurrilous yet entertaining book, *A Case of Human Bondage*, after Maugham reviled Syrie in his dotage in an even nastier book of his own, *Looking Back*, published in America but only serialised in Britain, in which he cast doubts on the legitimacy of his daughter. Beverley Nichols seized his retribution when he described a weekend at Le Touquet when Syrie Maugham gave a lavish weekend house-party in a misguided attempt to effect a reconciliation, an unlikely outcome as the guests included Noël Coward, Beverley Nichols, her husband and Haxton who seems to have behaved caddishly from the outset, telling 'the most revolting story of an incident on his last voyage with Willie . . . about a twelve-year-old Siamese girl whom he had seduced in return for a tin of condensed milk'.

To lend the house-party a semblance of respectability, other guests included Kruger, the Swedish match millionaire; Gertie Millar, the musical comedy star who became Viscountess Dudley; and Lord and Lady Plunket who were killed in a car crash shortly afterwards. Even so it was an impossible situation.

When Syrie made her appearance, 'all in white . . . exquisitely made up', at noon on their first day, she advanced on Willie with outstretched arms wanting to be kissed as she exclaimed, 'Darling!' With calculated insult, Maugham turned away. Finally she moved towards the drinks tray where Haxton was standing 'very dissolute but perversely pretty' and blew him a kiss too – 'Darling!' The humiliation became too painful and she returned to England with Beverley Nichols before the weekend was over, leaving her guests behind. Nichols was particularly sickened by 'something very disagreeable' which had taken place in 'the small hours of the morning' after Haxton returned from Le Touquet's casino where he had gambled with his usual verve. Hearing moans from the next room Nichols put on a dressing-gown and went to investigate. He was shocked by the sight of 'Gerald on the floor, stark naked, *covered* with thousand-franc notes. Never seen so much money in my life.' Haxton was trying to be sick while Nichols stood there feeling inadequate, when he heard a noise behind him and faced Maugham looking as livid as his bright green dressing-gown.

'What are you d-d-doing in G-G-Gerald's room? Did-d-did he ask you to c-c-come to his r-room?' Nichols denied this indignantly but Maugham gripped him by the shoulders and shouted, 'Get out!' Which Nichols did, 'leaving Willie, not for the first time, to clear up the mess'. One is left with the impression that what really riled Nichols was the scale of Haxton's winnings – '*covered* with thousand-franc notes'. His italics, not mine.

Plainly, Haxton was a rotter. Maugham recognised this himself, disguising him, thinly, as a gigolo called Paxton in his play *Our Betters*. Finding him with her friend, Lady Grayston, the Duchesse de Surennes calls Paxton 'a liar, a gambler, an idler, a spend-thrift. He's a thorough wrong 'un . . .' The point is that Maugham liked 'wrong 'uns', as he wrote to an American friend who was having similar problems with her young man: 'You must expect to pay something for the amusement you get out of knowing wrong 'uns.' In *Of Human Bondage*, Philip Carey, based on himself, derives an almost masochistic pleasure from his humiliation at the hands of Mildred, the ABC waitress – the bondage referred to in the title. Above all, and this was far from destructive, Haxton was the vital catalyst. Maugham was extraordinarily lucky, as he acknowledged in *The Summing Up*: 'I was fortunate enough to have on my journeys a companion who had an estimable social gift. He had an amiability of disposition that enabled him in a very short time to make friends with people in ships, bar-rooms and hotels, so that through him I was able to get into easy contact with an immense number of persons whom otherwise I should have known only from a distance.' Haxton may have provided a frisson of danger – there were hints of blackmail and violence – but his hail-fellow-well-met personality, so alien to Maugham's, proved invaluable.

Imagine the excitement of the scene! Those voyages in the East, sometimes adventurous but more often on crowded ships where Haxton heard the late-night confessions at the bar as he swapped yarns with his fellow-passengers, a man's man in every capacity. Imagine him bursting into their cabin: 'Listen, Willie, there's this scandal in Singapore, this woman, well-known wife of a government official who shot her lover dead, not once but several times, root-toot-toot – but there was this *letter*.'

Maugham acknowledged his debt: 'With his vitality and good humour, Gerald knew everybody on board ship before we had been twenty-four hours at sea. But for him I should never have got the material on our journey to the South Seas that had enabled me to write the short stories . . . called *The Trembling of a Leaf*.' These included 'Rain', depicting the struggle between Sadie Thompson, a woman of easy virtue, and the missionary who has her removed from the boat they are sailing on. Sadie emerges triumphant after the man of God cuts his throat: 'She gathered herself together. No one could describe the scorn of her expression or the contemptuous hatred she put into her answer. "You men! You filthy pigs, dirty pigs! You're all the same, all of you. Pigs! Pigs!"

'Dr MacPhail gasped. He understood.'

Those last few lines of Maugham's famous story, and the last two words in particular, illustrate his craft as he reaches his denouement and thrusts his point home. The same applies to 'The Letter', when Leslie tells the lawyer that although she does not love her husband she will never let him know this. 'That will be your retribution,' he says. 'No, my retribution is greater. With all my heart I still love the man I killed.' Melodramatic, but splendid stuff. And Haxton was the constant inspiration. No wonder, as a guest recalled (the writer and broadcaster Arthur Marshall) of a visit to the Mauresque, that Maugham's face lit up when he saw Haxton coming through the trees to the tennis court: '"O, look, good, here comes Master Hackey." It was said with love, you know, and deep affection.'

'I have most loved people who cared little or nothing for me,' Maugham admitted. And, on another occasion, 'I've never been good-looking and I know that no one could fall in love with me.' At least Haxton enabled him to love, however unrequited, and it must have been good at the Villa Mauresque in the summers between the wars when the house was filled with entertaining guests and the pool was full as well, except for the night when Haxton staggered back from the Cannes Casino and dived into it, unaware that it had just been drained. 'I should have added more water!' he gasped as he was taken to hospital with a broken neck.

They stayed at the Mauresque when the Second World War was declared, though after the fall of France Maugham had to escape on an overcrowded cargo boat in conditions of exceptional discomfort. Haxton stayed on, presumably with the immunity of an American citizen, to hide and pack their possessions as best he could, until he was persuaded to leave. Maugham had flown to America on 2 October 1940 with a phial of poison which he broke dramatically on his arrival. Haxton joined him in Chicago in December and it must have been shortly afterwards that the three of us headed for the Zephyr's restaurant car on the way to Oregon. By then Maugham was in his mid-sixties and

Haxton nearing fifty. That is hardly old by today's longevity, but Haxton's ravages were starting to show. There had been a short ride on the wagon, to everyone's relief, but now he was drinking again, if more secretly, and this is another proof of the strength of his hold on Maugham who detested drunkenness to such an extent that he disapproved if a guest dared to suggest a *second* cocktail before lunch. As he wrote to his old friend, Barbara Back, 'I cannot spend the remaining years of my life acting as a nurse and keeper to an old drunk.' Yet he continued to do so, for Maugham was a self-deceiver. 'I have a great tolerance for the follies of the human race,' he declared. It could be said that the opposite was just as true. Anyhow, the tension between them was evident on the silver train.

In the blessed age before television, even Maugham was not as recognisable as he would be now and we must have looked an odd trio – the urbane, immaculate, though sometimes inarticulate author telling me about the book he was writing called *The Razor's Edge*; the tough braggart, Haxton, who appeared to be sulking; and me with all the gaucherie of an English schoolboy, speaking in an accent which would have sounded like an alien drawl to our fellow-passengers.

For such an inveterate traveller, Maugham made few concessions, insisting on his afternoon nap regardless of spectacular scenery, exploding with anger on the Blue Train from the South of France when told there was no orange juice for breakfast. Apparently he was speechless with rage as he jabbed at the menu which promised it, and shockingly obscene when he was able to utter a few words. Now, as the train approached Oregon and we were back in our reserved seats, he discovered he had left his wallet in the restaurant car and screamed at me when I hesitated to run back through the train, terrified of being left behind for I had no money, no resources, no addresses, and no idea where the Zephyr was heading. However, his rage was so alarming that I charged headlong through the corridors, retrieved the wallet and jumped out at the other end of the station to be greeted by Maugham with utmost courtesy, now fully recovered.

The Seyster house, Pinehill, was impressive, but not particularly lovely and, though Thomas Seyster billed himself as 'Landscape and Garden Architect' on his letterhead, the surroundings were bleak, but of course it was winter. Yet I grew to love Pinehill over the next few days due to a rose-coloured porthole which overlooked the neglected garden with shivering shrubs which might have been dead apart from the odd, courageous Christmas rose though even that was forlorn. I looked through that porthole as if to another world; probably it was the strangeness of a porthole in a landlocked house that enchanted me, the peaceful antidote to the violent scenes inside.

I can only guess at the relationship between Haxton and my godfather. Certainly it was close. Tom Seyster was a handsome man with the rapidly ageing and taut looks of someone who had once been pretty. Years earlier, he had broken down one night in Spain and confessed his homosexuality to my parents, appalled by the guilt of it. According to them, they were terribly understanding.

Maugham lent a veneer of respectability to the household while my godfather and Haxton raged on the staircase with raised voices and raised fists. Seyster's mother, a beautiful woman who was adored by everyone, had died but old Mr Seyster appeared each morning on his way to the bank, which he owned, a tiny man with a face like a peanut. Presumably his meals were served in his room for he remained upstairs when he returned and I cannot remember him addressing a single word to any of us. Surprisingly, I do remember the kindness of Haxton and Seyster in their sober moments, driving me in a splendid open car to the local cinema, feeding me with bags of popcorn, waiting uncomplainingly though they must have suffered agonies of alcoholic withdrawal and, possibly, sexual frustration too.

The two men did their best to make me happy throughout, and succeeded. Their arguments resembled charades though I could sense the embarrassment on our first evening when my godfather led us proudly to see the new bowling alley he had bought his boy friend. This was a small Midwestern town as narrow-minded as only the provinces can be, and if we had looked unusual in the train our appearance at the alley was bizarre – Tom, besotted with his dark young friend; Haxton hardly able to stand upright; and Maugham, who must have been desperately bored unless his writer's instinct was aroused. I trailed behind, totally uninterested in bowls. The tough boy friend could hardly look us in the face though he shot me a glance of fierce dislike, mystified by my presence, acutely aware of his friends who watched our entrance.

With the humility of a long-suffering Christian martyr, Maugham did his best to retrieve Seyster's tarnished reputation, agreeing to a signing session of his books the following afternoon. For a moment, during that ordeal, he allowed himself a truly crocodilean smile when one lady, more brazen than the rest, produced a massive bag filled with his collected works. 'My husband was so *furious* with me,' she confided archly, 'when I brought these home, even though I'd bought them at a special price. He said it was a horrible waste of money, but if you sign them he'll think I've got a bargain and forgive me.'

Always respectful of commercial flair, Maugham understood and signed the books obediently, with a chuckle of appreciation. Otherwise, he played patience interminably, scarcely speaking to Haxton on the journey back to Chicago where he telephoned Mrs Fairbank who asked him to dinner. 'Just the family,' she informed me brightly, 'I think he'll prefer that.' Knowing the family, I doubted this, and when he surveyed the table with deepening gloom my doubt was confirmed. He told 'Aunt Janet' that if I were more observant I might become 'a good journalist', and took her aside to advise her that Seyster's home was unsuitable, so I was denied the one place where, perversely, I had felt at ease.

I returned to school in Ottawa and further shuntings in the holidays, including a visit to a family devoted to Moral Rearmament in Virginia, until Alexander Woollcott, the inspiration for 'The Man Who Came to Dinner', and yet another godfather, saw a photograph of Mrs Fairbank on the same platform as Colonel Lindbergh who was giving the Hitler salute, and decided that *her* house was unsuitable for an English refugee and cabled my father accordingly. Woollcott invited me to New York for my second Christmas, to be looked after by *his* secretary-companion: 'I could provide you with a room and latchkey and tickets to all the theatres and hockey games you wished to see.' Then the secretary fell ill and a visit to Alice Duer Miller was substituted. As the author of the sentimental poem 'The White Cliffs of Dover', which caused a surge of pro-British feeling, Woollcott thought she would prove a suitable 'antidote' to Janet Fairbank. When she was carried off to the Roosevelt Hospital with pneumonia, he wrote with some impatience, 'This is the effect you have on people,' and I received an alternative invitation from June Provines who had published my poem in the *Chicago Tribune*. 'A countrywoman of yours was my house-guest last weekend – Jan Struther. She wrote *Mrs Miniver* which sold 250,000 copies. Would you like to come to us for Christmas? I'd love to have you. The only thing is I couldn't spend as much time as I'd like because I'll be working terribly hard for the new *Chicago Sun* – and you might get lonely.'

I cannot remember where I finished up but, with 'The White Cliffs of Dover' and *Mrs Miniver*, everyone seemed determined to take the curse off Mrs Kellogg Fairbank.

Meanwhile, Alexander Woollcott thought ahead. 'What I really have in mind is the long vacation next summer. It so happens that here in Vermont I live on a seven-acre island in a lake eleven miles long, which has the best swimming I know anywhere in the world. We keep open house here all summer long and there is a great coming and going of people your father thinks you would enjoy meeting.' As these people included Harpo Marx, Noël Coward and the Lunts, it promised to be interesting, with Woollcott himself as the leader of the sacred monsters. He offered me a job looking after his boat, ferrying such guests from the mainland, and I might have thought myself inadequate for I did not react with the enthusiasm which he expected. He phoned me constantly at school late in the evening, which I found unnerving as I have detested that instrument throughout my life, and he must have found my prevarication exasperating. 'Don't you realise who I am?' he demanded shrilly after one lack-lustre response. 'I'll send you a copy of *While Rome Burns* to give you some idea.'

This was a lost opportunity; I returned to England as I had yearned to do all along. I sailed on a banana boat from Halifax and, after an early alarm when we were attacked by a submarine which was sunk by an accompanying destroyer, the days became halcyon as I lay on the deck of the *Jamaica Producer* with a wind-up gramophone playing Sablon's *La Mer*, believing briefly that I was in love with a woman who had black curly hair and was twice my age. We arrived at Liverpool on 3 May 1942.

Haxton died in New York in November 1944 at the age of fifty-two from a collapsed lung. When he fell ill Maugham took him to a lake in the Adirondacks, a ghastly complex of nursing homes, and Haxton enjoyed a short-lived recovery. From then on, it was steady decline and Maugham stayed beside him during months of suffering on both their parts. Haxton's death was lingering and vile, with the additional hell that his hatred was released like the opening of sluice gates and Maugham had to listen to his ravings which he did impassively though he broke down at the funeral and sobbed uncontrollably. 'We had gone through a great deal together,' he wrote. 'He had grave faults. He was a heavy drinker and reckless gambler. He had great merits. He had immense vitality. He was fearless.' Then Maugham made the odd comment that Haxton could turn his hand to anything, 'persuading a stubborn car to behave reasonably or in the wilderness to cook a savoury meal'. One remembers the people one has loved for such accomplishments as a 'savoury' meal rather than for their virtue.

Tom Seyster wrote to me: 'I've had several letters from Willie Maugham. He was devastated at first but seems to have control of himself again.' Tom had written to me in 1943 of his father's death on his eighty-ninth birthday, adding, 'Bud is still in camp in Texas and trying to get overseas into the thick of it.' Bud? Was he the youth with the bowling alley? Seyster was 'busy all the time – ration board, Red Cross, air-raid warden – and Mike is as active as ever'. Mike? Was *he* the youth with the bowling alley? A clarification followed: a mention that Mike was missing his 'good raw steak'. This jolted me back in time. Mike! Of course – *a dog!* Another reason why I loved that house in Oregon, apart from that rose-pink porthole.

My resolve to be a journalist was strengthened with the publication of an article in 1943 which I sent to *Time & Tide*. It was called *Minor Ambassador*, about my time in America, and I received a fee of two guineas and a copy of the magazine. I was on my way. Leaving Wellington College early, I joined the ancient Central Press Agency in London as their Parliamentary and Lobby Correspondent at the age of seventeen, until I enlisted in the American Army and wrote to Somerset Maugham when he returned to the Villa Mauresque in 1947, offering to send him food from the well-stocked American PX stores in Wiesbaden. While admitting that he was not actually short of food, Maugham accepted the offer gracefully but only on condition that I told him how much the provisions cost, explaining that it would spoil the pleasure of receiving them if I were put to expense while he had 'plenty of money' in his pocket. As far as I can remember, I refused any payment because I could buy the rations so cheaply. Maugham's letter to me continued:

> You don't tell me much about what you are doing and what sort of life you are leading. I hope at all events you are getting a good deal of experience. If you want to become a writer it is very necessary to expose yourself to all the vicissitudes of life, and it isn't enough to wait for experience to come to you, you must go out after it. Even if you bark your shins every now and then, that again will be grist for your mill. I don't suppose you have much time for reading or many books at your disposal but, you know, the more highly cultured you can make yourself the richer your work will be. Few people know how much industry and how much patience are needed to achieve anything worth doing. I speak exactly like Polonius.

I was stationed in England and when Maugham came to London he invited me to dinner at the Dorchester where he was staying with his new secretary-companion, Alan Searle. If Haxton was the accident, Searle was the ambulance.

Maugham was fortunate to know them in the right order. First the ebullient catalyst, followed by the patience of a saint. Not only was the 'secretary-companion' an accurate label, they were lovers too. H. G. Wells remarked, surprisingly in view of the camouflage surrounding them, 'There is no difference between myself and my mistress and Willie Maugham and his American friend Gerald Haxton.' Apparently the same applied to Searle who confided to a friend that Maugham was 'the most marvellous lover I ever had', a startling disclosure considering Maugham's austerity. Yet Maugham saw the relationships in the same light. When Lord Linlithgow, the Viceroy in India, invited Maugham to lunch without Haxton, Maugham resented the snub and refused to go. Now Searle was to sit in attendance at the Villa Mauresque, lunching with Churchill and Lord Beaverbrook. He was a chaperone by nature, having been a prison visitor when he met Maugham for the first time back in 1928. Though he was commonplace compared to Haxton, I liked Searle at once. It was difficult to dislike him.

He greeted me warmly, with a slightly febrile look, in the Dorchester, and Maugham entered from the bedroom a few minutes later, promptly at seven-thirty. Instead of going downstairs, dinner was served in the main room of their suite. More fastidious than ever, Maugham was dapper in a white shirt, brown smoking-jacket, and black and white tie. A monocle dangled round his waist and his expression was tinged with the slight disgust which Graham Sutherland was to catch in his portrait, yet he was scrupulous towards me, treating me on equal terms without condescension. By now I was aware of the massive reputation surrounding him and made notes afterwards. He relieved his boredom by resorting to malice, saying that Emlyn Williams was giving the worst performance he had seen on the London stage in *The Winslow Boy*, while deploring Angela Baddeley's figure and the enormity of her breasts. When I dared to suggest that the new production of his play *Our Betters* was disappointing, he explained that Ivor Novello had produced it because his friend Dorothy Dickson needed the work. 'He's very nice, but I don't think he has much discrimination. The part calls for an exceptional actress, and she's incapable of that. Cecil Beaton's sets succeed in obscuring all their faces . . .' he paused for effect, 'p-perhaps that's just as well.' I suspected that Maugham calculated his stammer, also that he gained perverse pleasure from his self-deprecation which seemed modest but was really the vault of vanity. He quoted the wife of Ernest Bevin, with whom he had dined recently, who exclaimed, 'You write books, don't you? You must be a clever man!', and King George VI who told him, 'I've seen all your books though I've never actually read one.' He described the Nuremberg Trials as a dangerous precedent: 'The Russians wouldn't hesitate to try all our statesmen, our generals, even the King himself if we are defeated in a future war.' As for his return to London, he found it deeply depressing and felt like a stranger in a foreign city: 'I miss the friendliness and hospitality of the Americans.' He yawned and said he was feeling tired but before he retired to his bedroom he signed the books I had brought with me, as if this was a genuine pleasure rather than an imposition, inscribing *Cakes and Ale* with the words 'The author's favourite book, from his friend W. S. Maugham'. This was lost in a subsequent burglary; if anyone has it now, I would gladly buy it back.

Somerset Maugham

When I was transferred to Germany, and Maugham and Searle were back in France, I sent them a tin of particularly succulent chocolates, bought in the American PX. In his letter of thanks, 'You should not spend your money like this, when I have so much,' Maugham invited me to spend Christmas at the Villa Mauresque, with the warning that all he provided for his guests was 'board and lodging and they must amuse themselves as best they can'. I should have taken this more literally.

I hitched a flight on an Army plane, leaving Frankfurt in a snowstorm, arriving at Nice in crisp winter sunlight. I made my way to the Villa Mauresque where Alan Searle was asleep on the drawing-room sofa and was so startled when the butler announced me that he fell off and broke one of his fingernails. Not the whole nail, just the top of it. This was such a calamity for Searle that I felt unwelcome and guilty. When Maugham appeared, he was shown the jagged nail and cackled his sympathy but did not seem to hold me responsible. He was at his most benign.

That first evening in the dining-room, surrounded by the unexpected sweetness of paintings by Marie Laurencin, Maugham was positively jolly as he outlined the plans for the next few days. Had I been to the south of France before? Never! Capital. They would show me Nice, introduce me to so-and-so further along the coast, there was this nightclub in Cannes which I would enjoy, and of course the Casino at Monte Carlo. A cornucopia of treats was promised. The meal was delicious, prepared by Anette who had worked for Maugham before the war, starting with her speciality of mashed avocado and crisp fried bacon. I had been shown the garden by Searle after he recovered from the accident with the fingernail, and had marvelled at the orange trees with oranges upon them though this was just before Christmas. Haxton had smuggled some avocado stones in the bottom of a golf-bag when they returned from California before the war, and the trees were now profuse, yielding hundreds of the fruit each year. Cyril Connolly hid several in his luggage at the end of a visit and was caught. That was mortifying enough; it was worse that he had to hand them back.

The garden was enchanted, a tribute to the thirteen gardeners employed before the war though there were fewer now. There were steps and urns and statuary, trees in abundance, pines and cypress lining the pool where the water gushed from the mouth of the head of a Cardinal – at least that's what it looked like though it proved to be a faun by Bernini. Everything about the Villa Mauresque was enchanting, to start with. The name had nothing to do with Maugham himself but was built by Leopold II in 1906 as a villa for his father confessor who asked for a house in Moorish style. This explained the Moorish sign above the front entrance, to ward off the evil eye, which Maugham adopted for the covers of his books, and the courtyard in the middle of the house.

There was only one thing wrong with the food, there was never enough. I was proffered a second helping and took this eagerly but I sensed that it would have been tactful to decline. At the end of that exquisite dinner, realising that this was all I would get until breakfast, which turned out to be 'continental' with a vengeance, I helped myself voraciously to the nuts and glacé fruits which accompanied the coffee. Again, I sensed that a greater moderation would have been appreciated. But it was neither my appetite which offended, nor my thirst, for I drank little in those days, but my clothes. That was the only explanation I could find for the change in the atmosphere the following day, and the unnerving silence regarding those promised treats which were never referred to again. I had arrived in the only clothes I possessed, my GI uniform, and assume it was forbidden to wear 'civvies' in the American Army for I cannot remember any soldier doing so. Maugham and Searle might have expected me to reappear in the immaculate clothes of a young Guards officer – tweed suit, Lobb brogues and Locke trilby. Beverley Nichols described the care with which he packed for the Villa: 'Dinner at eight with the Master *meant* dinner at eight, and a black tie *meant* a black tie. Willie liked his young friends to be smartly dressed, and I was happy to oblige. There were new shirts from Charvet . . .' But I was unworldly in spite of my travels.

Perhaps Haxton, had he been there, would have coped as he did when Godfrey Winn arrived in 1928 wearing a grey flannel suit. 'This is the South of France in August,' said Maugham scathingly, 'not Finals Day at Wimbledon.' He had the grace to tell Haxton, for Winn was young and poor, 'Get him some linen slacks, shirts and espadrilles at the Bon Marche, like yours.' Winn recorded ungratefully that he did not wish to resemble Haxton in any way whatever, but at least he was bought the clothes, which was more than Searle did for me. If Graham and Kathy Sutherland had been there, for they were invited that Christmas but had to cancel at the last moment due to illness, I am sure it would have been different. They were sophisticated enough to cope with such a situation; I could have been introduced as *their* friend. But Maugham and Searle were landed with a young, uniformed GI who could have been interpreted as a 'pick-up'. This is what I imagine, for appearances were all important to Maugham. So I was virtually confined to the Villa Mauresque as if I was contagious. Of course the answer could be even simpler, that they found me a disappointment, and as Ted Morgan remarked in his biography: 'Those who disappointed him were summarily dismissed.'

As I have written elsewhere, my naïvety was almost obscene until I lost it suddenly in Soho a few years later, and it must have been vexing to Maugham and Searle. I remember a state of anticipation never realised. The days passed pleasantly enough with their strict routine: a breakfast tray and no sound of activity until Maugham descended from his study on the roof for his pre-lunch cocktail – a very dry martini or bacardi. I was allowed to go for short walks in my Army overcoat but they dissuaded me from wearing my GI's cap. Accompanying me, Searle used me as his confidant, revealing that the great love in Maugham's life had been an English actress who turned him down when he asked her to marry him, immortalised later as Rosie in *Cakes and Ale*, a story which I accepted implicitly. Also, that Maugham had just received a tiresome letter from a woman who was distraught because she was afraid of losing her husband. What should she do? '(a) You must be sexually attractive. (b) You must be sexually satisfactory. Yours sincerely, W. S. Maugham,' was the Master's crisp reply, or so Searle said. Maugham was patient to the point of martyrdom. When I took his photograph in the garden with my cheap camera, the release went off like a revolver. Maugham winced every time I pressed it, and warned me: 'I am sinister in appearance and nothing can be done about it.' When I enthused wildly about the novel *If Winter Comes*, Maugham winced again and said it was 'interesting', or some such word, without putting me down. Encouraging my ambition to become a writer, his advice was significant for he might have had himself in mind as well: 'If you have only a small streak of talent and are prepared to develop it by sheer hard work, you can achieve a good deal, perhaps a great deal.'

The nights were so warm that I remember wandering through the magical garden, full of rustling trees and fragrant smells even in winter, in a state of self-indulgent ennui rather than dejection. This must have been tiresome too, but what was I doing there in the first place, why had I been invited, how had I offended? Like one of those top Soviet officials, seen grinning next to Stalin yet mysteriously absent in later photographs, I felt erased. Re-reading Ted Morgan's biography of Maugham, I found a reference and the episode suddenly made sense. According to Morgan, 'Alan wrote to Jerry Zipkin that he had scattered his heart all over Europe, and there was hardly anything left for England. In December they went back to the Mauresque and spent Christmas with a lonely American soldier, recruited by Alan as their only guest.' The dates were wrong, not 1953 as suggested but 1947 (presumably a misreading of the date in the original letter, sent by Maugham to his old friend Bert Alanson which provided Morgan with his material), unless Searle made a point of recruiting American GIs as their only Christmas guest. *Recruited!* So that was it.

Christmas Day at the Villa Mauresque was not a merry occasion. Maugham suffered no sea-like change or Scroogeish transformation, appearing more crusty than usual. Idiotically, I had given all my presents – tins of chocolates and other foods from the PX – on my arrival, which deprived me of any semblance of generosity on the day itself, and as we had never driven into Cannes or Nice there had been no chance to buy anything there as I had hoped. In my turn I received no presents whatever from either of them, possibly as a punishment for failing to be the glittering guest of their expectation. As we went into lunch, Maugham stammered: 'I'm afraid the price of meat is so s-scandalous in France these days that I couldn't afford turkey. We're having f-fish instead. At least we're not reduced to eating d-dog.' This surprising allusion echoed his constant fear during the war that the local French would be forced to kill and eat his two dachshunds.

To compensate for the lack of presents, Maugham delivered his verdict on every person mentioned: Alexander Woollcott was 'a very stupid man'; James Agate, whom I had met at my father's club in London, was 'vain and pretentious. A sensualist and a drunk.' As for Mrs Kellogg Fairbank, I had to break the news that she was in a 'home' – 'I'm afraid to say that it seems she's gone out of her mind.'

'You do surprise me,' said Maugham, looking happier. 'I never thought she had a m-m-mind to go out of.'

Now it was his turn to break some news to me: 'You will be sorry to hear,' he told me with relish, 'that your godfather Tom Seyster has adopted an American marine. A pity, he'd always intended to leave you the lot when he died.'

Was Maugham obsessively mean? Undeniably. He gained a pleasure from it as really rich people do. When Sutherland painted him, Maugham haggled over the price and as this was Sutherland's first portrait he was uncertain what to ask for it. Finally, Maugham arrived in his chauffeur-driven car at the Voile d'Or where the Sutherlands were staying, and counted out the notes punctiliously: 'Please don't think me m-mean, Graham,' he explained, 'but I've got some very expensive guests staying with me at the moment and they've all sent their clothes to the c-c-cleaners, so I can't afford to pay you more.' Graham Sutherland told me that the money amounted to £200, a vast difference from the $35,000 claimed by Ted Morgan, and more believable.

Alan Searle in the gardens of the Villa Mauresque

Maugham wielded his meanness like a weapon, torturing Searle sadistically. 'I like those trousers,' he told Searle one morning, 'I wish I could afford a pair like that.' And Searle confided to me privately his fear that he might be left penniless. 'Willie tells me that he lived comfortably on £5 a week in London when he was a young man, and has made sure that I won't have less than that. He can't mean it, can he?' Searle's alarm was due to Maugham's implicit assumption that he, like Haxton, was damned lucky to have his keep and live in luxury with a modest wage as well.

Maugham acknowledged his debt to Haxton for his help in turning 'Rain' into a play when he sent a cheque for $10,000 to Bert Alanson asking him to invest half in Haxton's name: 'He has been very faithful and devoted to me for many years. Of course he has not been able to save anything and I should like to be the nucleus of some provision for him in case I die.' That was kind and thoughtful of Maugham but, when you consider that the royalties from *Rain* amounted to more than a million dollars, the investment of $5,000 was not excessive. Syrie did better: a house, a Rolls-Royce, £2,400 a year for her, and £600 for Liza. But Syrie had lawyers.

Maugham's frugality can be seen as an entertaining diversion, almost a cat-and-mouse (or crocodile-and-cat) game where Searle was concerned, but it had the unfortunate effect of dividing his family towards the end of his life, when Alan in his insecurity encouraged him to turn against them. Maugham's attempt to 'adopt' Searle, as Seyster had adopted his marine, was foiled in the French court but Searle had no cause for worry, except in the event of Maugham's sudden death before everything was settled. Instead, Maugham lingered interminably and miserably, half-in and half-out of the world he viewed so cynically. Due to the Niehans injections, which Searle shared as a sort of guinea pig, his aged body responded resiliently but his mind deteriorated until there was little there. He was over ninety when he died.

Searle received the contents of the Villa Mauresque which was sold for apartment blocks, and all the royalties which came to more than $50,000 a year, plus a legacy of £50,000. In the event, Maugham's will was impeccable, with his royalties going to the Royal Literary Fund on Alan's death, a trust from which I have benefited myself at a bad period in my life, for which I am eternally grateful.

In the end, it hardly mattered to Searle. The money allowed him to live in luxury in Monte Carlo but, suffering from Parkinson's Disease, he was unable to frolic as he had hoped. By chance, we met on his last visit to England when he travelled to the West Country to stay with a mutual friend. He told me of the day when he heard a bang upstairs and hurried into the room to find that Maugham had fallen, hitting his head on the fireplace. Maugham looked up and recognised him again: 'Is that you, Alan?' he asked. 'I've wondered where you've been. I wanted to thank you for everything you've done for me.' These were his final words.

And that's the point. Maugham might have been a monster, but a sacred monster with greater merit than people grant him today. And, though he is currently out of fashion with the critics, there is no denying the happiness he offers his readers as one of the great pleasure-givers of this century. In this respect, Maugham has the last laugh – or, in his case, a dry chuckle.

He saw life as an arid affair, alleviated by his wit. A couple of days after Christmas we drove into Nice for the first time – I was in a borrowed overcoat – to a massive warehouse crammed with furniture and bric-à-brac which had been seized by the Germans during the Occupation, waiting to be claimed by the original owners. As we wandered through the debris, like the auctioneers in the final scene of *Citizen Kane*, Maugham's expression grew increasingly taut. 'My God!' he exclaimed at last. 'They were damned lucky to have such stuff l-looted.'

The next day I flew to London for the rest of my leave and my twenty-first birthday, though it took several more years before I really came of age. As I said goodbye, my youthful enthusiasm might have pierced Maugham's façade but he remained impassive.

Halfway to the airport I realised I had left my passport behind, so the taciturn chauffeur turned round impatiently and we raced back. Searle hurried down the staircase waving the passport which had been discovered by a servant. 'Do go and see Willie,' he implored. 'He wants to see you so much. It won't take a moment.'

I raced up the staircase to the top of the house, through the famous Gauguin door brought back from Tahiti, into the forbidden study where Maugham sat at his desk looking forlorn. 'Please forgive me,' he said pathetically, 'I'm so s-sorry.' I wish I had put my arms around him but I stood there smiling brightly, thinking of my flight. Anyhow, I did not understand.

'That's all right,' I exclaimed, and ran down the staircase, through the front door with the Moorish sign above, leaving the Villa Mauresque for the last time.

A Wit in Hyde Park

BONAR THOMPSON

Every adolescent needs an idol. Disconcertingly, the object of idolatry is frequently someone disreputable. In my case, in the lull between school and my job with the Central Press, I walked to Hyde Park Corner every Sunday afternoon to listen to an orator called Bonar Thompson.

His appearance was impressive from a distance, dilapidated in close-up. The black hat which he wore as a trademark was stained with sweat; his thick lips were wet; his eyes wet also, and bloodshot; his false teeth clattered and his hands trembled. When he removed the black hat the effect was startling, for his grey wire-wool hair was curled in locks, like a bad wig supplied for a melodrama. Worst of all he tried to conceal his pallor by covering his stubble with theatrical pink powder. I found him irresistible. To me he symbolised rebellion at a dreary moment in post-war Britain when wit was rationed and there were no pop-stars to worship. Nor did I feel the urge to decorate my room with photographs of footballers or Joan Crawford.

Instead I made my weekly pilgrimage to listen to Bonar Thompson. Described by the *Socialist Leader* as 'the most brilliant intellectual vagabond of the century', Bonar could be pertinent and funny, devastatingly so to a seventeen year old:

> 'When a national leader announces that he will fight to the death, he is generally in dead earnest. He is referring, of course, not to his own death but yours.'

> 'The vilest acts of which a man is capable have been done by good men for the loftiest reasons and on principle.'

> 'To succeed in life it is not enough to be stupid, one must have good manners as well.'

> 'On the London buses a notice says *Spitting Prohibited: Penalty Twenty Shillings*. In the British Museum a notice says *Spitting Prohibited: Penalty Ten Shillings*. What's the moral? If you must spit, spit in the British Museum.'

He shouted aloud what others dared not admit in public and I listened at that wind-swept corner as spellbound as the acolytes must have been by Oscar Wilde in the greater comfort of the Café Royal. Bonar Thompson stood alone among the fanatics on their platforms around him whom he ridiculed mercilessly.

At the end of his speech – or performance – he delivered the same peroration: 'I should be guilty of ingratitude, worse, of discourtesy, if I allowed the meeting to disperse without moving a hearty vote of thanks to myself for what has been an artistic and intellectual experience of the greatest value. I only wish I could show my appreciation of myself in some substantial way, as an obligation and a duty towards one who has rendered me so many years of faithful service. A quaint sort of public entertainment, not above making a motley to the view. Until my next meeting at five o'clock – *forward to the Gates!*'

'When I think of people in Mayfair, feeding on caviare . . .

. . . I say it's a disgrace, a scandal – I wish I could join 'em!'

This was the rallying cry to follow him outside the Gates at Marble Arch where he stood uncomfortably, head slightly bent in the servility of having to accept the coins pressed into his hand by the few faithful admirers who bothered to follow him. This humiliation was due to a petty act of officialdom forbidding collections inside the Park itself. Michael Foot was one of those admirers and described it as 'a piece of gratuitous tyranny if ever there was one', praising Bonar as a 'one-man satirist of the universe – the best one-man act in London in his own time at least – a priceless piece of England's endless loot from across the Irish Sea.'

So I was not alone in my admiration. Unfortunately, such admiration comes cheap. A rainy afternoon wiped out his pathetic earnings, and it rained constantly. I failed to realise that, from every practical viewpoint, Bonar was a failure.

He was born in 1888 near Antrim in Ulster, the illegitimate son of a farm labourer: 'The fact that I was born out of wedlock was not nearly so important as my being born out of pocket.' And he was brought up by his Aunt Eliza, a good, God-fearing woman whom he detested. 'What my aunt told me about Calvin's grim God was not calculated to inspire confidence. Her ignorance of this world was balanced by an incredible certitude about the next. Every spare moment was given over to the study of celestial geography, topography, climate and general flora and fauna. "There will be no winter there," she often told me of heaven. "No cold, no rain. It will be perpetual summer there. And there will be no steep hills to climb."' From her, Bonar inherited a loathing of Puritanism which lasted a lifetime.

During his childhood, Bonar never earned more than twopence a year. When he worked on the farms he earned more but developed a lasting aversion to work. At the age of thirteen he was summoned to Manchester by his mother and listened to the public speakers in Stevenson Square, a welcome and cheap entertainment in a time before radio or television. 'I had never seen anything of the kind before . . . It seemed a wonderful thing to me that these men should be able to hold the attention of the crowds . . . Socialism, however, became too tame for me. I found anarchism more to my taste.'

Several of the public speakers were 'stars', one example being F. G. Jones whose manner was astringent. When a young admirer gasped, 'Am I really speaking to the famous F. G. Jones?' he received the terse reply, 'You are, but not for long.' An eccentric called MacCutcheon never used transport of any sort, walked everywhere dressed in homespun grey, and preached the simple life: 'Grow your own dinners, milk your own cows, weave and spin, hoe and plough, and let each man be his master.' With his hatred of machinery, he urged the Manchester unemployed: 'Blow up all the big cities with dynamite. Put the people on the land. Make England a garden.' Inevitably, his meetings ended in uproar when he attacked the police: 'Look at the Chief Constable over there, the big, hulking clodhopper, standing there gaping like a booby.'

Bonar's ideal was Tom Mann. 'Fire, vehemence, passion, humour, crashing excitement – there has never been anyone to equal him. His personality in those days was like a human dynamo, and he was unique among all the speakers of the revolutionary school – he was entirely free from any kind of spite or spleen against anyone whatsoever.'

Bonar was hooked. 'I resolved to become a speaker myself. To sway masses, to dominate crowds, to hear the applause – here was an easy road to fame. More than that, it was a chance to escape from poverty and hard, irksome, badly paid labour. Had I been able to get on the stage I should never have bothered my head about socialism, but I was too shabbily dressed, too lacking in self-confidence.' Far from being an 'easy road to fame', he had chosen the hardest, but he had his speech ready and, when a speaker failed to turn up at a meeting for the unemployed, he ascended the rostrum instead. 'As soon as I had uttered the first couple of sentences all nervousness left me. I became saturated with a glow of elation . . . The effect on the crowd was gratifying . . . Soon I became known as the Boy Orator. Unfortunately, within a few weeks my stock of resounding phrases had worn out and all my golden words were spent.'

Consistently opposed to work – 'the great problem of our time is not the solution of unemployment, it is the solution of *employment*' – he was forced into accepting a job with the railways in order to survive, but hated it so much that he preferred the alternative of prison: 'My determination never to seek employment again unless I got a wage sufficient for human dignity became so strong it was almost an obsession.'

Though he admitted that prison held the usual terrors, he saw no disgrace in being sent there for a political offence. As he pointed out, 'The Pankhursts never looked back after they had been to gaol in a blaze of publicity. It was a good racket.' So he joined a group of active insurgents and at nine in the morning threw a stone ginger-beer bottle through the window of Lewis's and was led away as he cried out defiantly: 'It may be the match to the gunpowder. Our action may lead to a working-class uprising.'

Held in Strangeways for three weeks, he was sentenced to a year's imprisonment after defending himself in the dock with his usual melodrama: 'No man with a human heart can stand by and hear little children crying for bread without doing something, however desperate and unconstitutional it may be, to remove the cursed system which allows such things to exist.' He had the wit to add privately that as he was the only child he had heard crying for bread, and that because his aunt gave him brown bread instead of white, 'one can see what treacly clap-trap it was though quoted afterwards as a cry wrung from a soul seared by the sight of human suffering. What bunk!' Self-mockery was Bonar's saving grace. When he was released in 1909 he received an ovation from a crowd of unemployed admirers, and drifted south to London where he found his niche at Hyde Park Corner and Tower Hill.

'I had the arrogance of ignorance and a staggering belief in my own infallibility.' Yet even on a good Sunday, with three meetings, he made less than ten shillings: 'Had collections been allowed on the spot, I should have taken a great deal more, but Londoners are not in the habit of running after people to give them money.'

This was his life in 1911. When I knew him in 1945 it was much the same, though two wars had intervened with numerous arrests. Before the First War he was fined forty shillings for calling the Kaiser 'a criminal lunatic', and the money was donated by admirers outside the court, but after war was declared people were less sympathetic when they saw him still in mufti.

'Young man, why aren't you in khaki?' a lady demanded in the street.

'Because there's a war on, Madam.'

The subject of war became an obsession. 'No idea is worth dying for. It is even more important to realise that no idea is worth living for. Many of you are too young to have been in the Boer War, one of the best and cheapest we have ever had, and well worth reviving. I was one of the first, if not *the* first, to forget to volunteer for that struggle in South Africa. I have never regretted it, and attribute my present existence and lack of solvency to that first step I neglected to take.'

Though George Lansbury spoke on his behalf at the tribunal, he was sentenced to fifty-six days' hard labour at Wormwood Scrubs. After this he sold tooth powder in the markets but the Hyde Park platform lured him back. His bitterness increased, partly because he was a loner, not allied to any movement, detesting the usual jargon. Though he preached revolution, the 'comrades' of the working-class movement regarded his humour with suspicion. Communists were a constant butt: 'In their bleached and stringy little souls they hated and feared all that was noble in life. Karl Marx, the world's champion bore, with his mean, selfish, peevish disposition and his inability to say a good word about any living creature, is their hero and their god. It is to the eternal glory of William Morris that he refused to have anything to do with the dreary old misery-monger. Like many others of a generous nature, he could not stomach the man.'

Like several of the sacred monsters in this book, Bonar could be described as 'his own worst enemy', that tiresome phrase directed so glibly at those who are true to themselves: 'I am neither right wing, left wing, nor any part of the political chicken. In 1926 I gave up socialism to become a confirmed sceptic. I have no party, no policy, no remedy, no message and no hope.'

His curious choice of life forfeited the pleasures he would otherwise have enjoyed. He was forced to sleep out, washing himself in the Serpentine which was illegal; he was denied good food and drink – sometimes any food at all; and the luxury of a seat in the stalls. He relished the theatre and scraped enough together for the Old Vic gallery as part of the first-night group which shouted abuse or admiration to the annoyance of 'the unresponsive blocks of wood' in the expensive seats below. 'I look upon such persons with feelings of intense hatred. Another thing I object to is the presence of too many "nancy-boys" among the small-part players on stage. I have no prejudice about a man because he is homosexual, but I resent the squeaking and twittering of these young men while there are good men unemployed. Let these young perverts take up dressmaking or needlework instead of plaguing theatre audiences with their ninnying.'

Conversely, Bonar could plague an audience himself. As a special 'treat', I took him to the theatre whenever possible, in spite of the embarrassment as he rose to his feet before the curtain had fallen to express his enthusiasm. Yet I was delighted that he should enjoy the outing so hugely. We must have appeared an odd couple: the ravaged old man, plainly paid for by the pristine public schoolboy. My grandmother was startled when I brought him home for tea and he removed the stained black hat to reveal that extra-ordinary ill-fitting hair (though all his own) but her good manners did not falter and they were able to talk about Sir Henry Irving, whom she had known and to whom Bonar bore a slight resemblance, while I watched them with pride and relief.

I should explain that our relationship was impeccable. He wrote to me constantly, signing his letters, which sometimes ran to eighteen pages, with a formal 'Yours cordially, Bonar Thompson'. We did not drink together because I had not yet started and he had stopped, on doctor's orders, while retaining his detestation of teetotallers. I did not smoke, while he did incessantly, with a lot of fuss and spittle as he rolled his own. We never had an intimate conversation. I assume he was flattered by my idolatry but the sympathy between us was bonded by words and we collaborated on a play about a Hyde Park orator who stood for Parliament, elected by grateful voters who were sick of the deceits of the rival Tory and Socialist candidates. The orator, needless to add, was based on Bonar who would play the part himself at one of the small fringe theatres scattered around Bayswater where he gave his one-man shows when his health allowed him to. We called the play *Paradise Postponed* (a title later used by John Mortimer, though he could not have known of our endeavour) and it lived up to this for we failed to finish it though it gave us pleasure and much wishful fantasy at the time.

I kept his letters. One refers to a small gift, after I had enlisted in the American Air Corps:

> the enclosure of a pound, a thousand thanks. You are number one friend of the genuine calibre whose goodwill I value very sincerely. I'm living for the day when loud calls for the author will resound through the crowded theatre. It will be my cue to make the familiar gesture towards the wings while a smart soldierly figure in uniform comes forward to greet the rising storm of delirious applause: 'This is the happiest moment of my life,' declared the gallant co-author of the most brilliant, original, iconoclastic, witty, profound, tragic and heartrending drama it has ever been my lot to see upon the stage of an English theatre. Bonar Thompson was his usual distinguished and brilliant self with this difference: he revealed a genius for acting that has never been surpassed.

And so on for pages. As so often, we put more effort into the anticipation than the play itself.

That letter came from the health resort of Champneys after a physical collapse, his treatment paid for by loyal supporters like Michael Foot. His wife, who suffered from arthritis, went with him. She was a large woman who remained defiantly cheerful against the odds and worked as a cashier at a cinema's box office by day. Sometimes she played Lady Macbeth to Bonar's Macbeth in his dramatic recitals, but even I, in all my idolatry, had my doubts about that.

Indeed, it was hard to imagine him married at all, but they were devoted in spite of one unfortunate tendency. Like many people who can scarcely support themselves, Mrs Thompson needed to look after something else. Any cat she encountered on the street was presumed homeless and had to be cared for. Consequently, the sour stink of cats'

Bonar Thompson at home, a deceptively distinguished setting

piss and the smell of boiling fish were so overpowering that I gagged every time I descended into their dank basement in Notting Hill where the walls glistened with moisture. Finally their neighbours in Arundel Gardens could endure it no longer and summoned the sanitary inspector who reeled in dismay at the sight of so many cats hanging in sinister attitudes around the appalling room.

As tactfully as he could, he suggested that some should be 'put away'. Bonar had frequently confessed to the same urge himself, but studied the man scornfully as he sprang surprisingly to their defence. 'There seems to be some misapprehension here. Cats are beautiful animals. Who has ever heard of a beautiful sanitary inspector? No sir, it is *you* who should be put away!'

I am pleased, now, to realise the difference I must have made to their lives. This was due simply to the American Army's PX stores which I could use in London at a time when food was scarce. When I arrived at that ghastly room clutching gifts of chickens, chocolates and other luxuries, I must have appeared like Father Christmas.

After that I was transferred to Germany but continued to visit Arundel Gardens and Hyde Park Corner when I was demobbed and went to Cambridge University. Imperceptibly and inevitably, our lives drew apart. Never having heard him in his prime, I had not realised he was past it. Now I began to sense how ill he was, shivering outside the gates as he waited for the faithful few to give to his 'collection'. He had enjoyed his day, publishing a magazine called *The Black Hat* with forged letters of support from Bernard Shaw and Mussolini, and revived this in 1947 with the subtitle 'Not to echo but to speak'. Sadly it spoke for only one issue and the rest was silence. He had published his autobiography, *Hyde Park Orator*, in 1935, with a preface by Sean O'Casey attacking it: 'Bonar Thompson has his knife in what he calls the Labour Movement.' Yet he retained the respect of Michael Foot who referred to him as 'a triumph of the human spirit. Bonar Thompson knew, in his aching bones and bleeding feet, a physical pain for multitudes of our people which by comparison even the thirties never experienced.'

More surprising was the praise from the Conservative MP, Beverly Baxter, also the dramatic critic for the *Evening Standard*, who described him effusively as 'a world figure. Poverty could not rob him of a rich inheritance of wit, melancholy, an artist's hands and hair, ironic humour, a love of language and a genius for making nothing pay. When the flying bombs came along, this was the moment to take a theatre and he gave us Wilde's *Ballad of Reading Gaol* and caught the horror and the pity of it with a sensitive appreciation of his fellow Irishman's genius and personal tragedy.'

I took friends to see his performance and remember a letter of protest from the woman who had sailed on the *Jamaica Producer* from Canada, with whom I kept in touch, 'Not that bloody Ballad again!'

My disillusionment came at last when I took a friend to one of the solo shows. He was more sophisticated than me and saw through the façade which I had glamorised. 'Let's go after the interval,' he whispered. 'He's just an old has-been. He's *dreadful!*' As the scales fell, I saw Bonar as *pathetic*. It was a queasy moment to feel ashamed of the man I had admired so much.

I saw him once more when I interviewed him for a television programme on Notting Hill Gate, several years later. The ghastly room looked and smelled much the same, and the arc lights revealed his dilapidation cruelly, as did my own, now-opened eyes. He performed his tricks for the camera and repeated his heresies but their impact had gone and he knew it. The camera crew were unimpressed, recoiling from the surrounding mess and stink, and as we waited for them to change the film Bonar and I made small talk and dared not catch each other's eyes. Considering his illness (by now he survived on cornflour mixed with water), I was astounded to learn from Michael Foot that Bonar lived to the age of seventy-five.

I am ashamed that I did not keep in touch but smile as I remember Bonar's suggestion for his epitaph. 'I have never failed to keep my audiences,' he told me sadly. 'Unfortunately they have failed to keep me. *The Collection Was Not Enough.*'

A Shouting Match in the South of France

KENNETH TYNAN

'Perhaps I should have warned you,' said Ken Tynan on the plane, with a quick, uneasy look. 'Gordon Craig is deaf.'

I was due to interview Craig for television the next morning, on the eve of his ninetieth birthday. In mid-air on the way to Nice, it was a curious moment for such an admission.

'How deaf?' I asked, for there is deafness and deafness and it is usually possible to make oneself understood.

'He's t-totally deaf,' Ken stammered without the hint of an apology.

'That could present a problem,' I remarked calmly. It did not occur to me that Ken was speaking the literal truth.

When we drove up the hills of Provence that evening, there was a crisp winter sunlight and fears were forgotten. Craig's devoted housekeeper regarded us apprehensively, but we were shown into the old man's study and the shouting-match began.

In spite of Ken's experience as an actor, which meant that he was accustomed to projecting his voice to the gallery, his voice did not penetrate Craig's wall of silence. Furthermore, Ken's stammer made lip-reading difficult. Fortunately, I managed to volley a few words across the dividing line as I yelled my introduction, with the advantage that my great-uncle Bram Stoker had managed the Lyceum for Henry Irving and Ellen Terry who was Craig's mother. This established a bond, while Ken looked on admiringly, and I relaxed as I began to feel I might achieve a worthwhile interview with the grand old English stage-designer after all. Then I sneezed, probably due to the nervous tension. If I had sneezed once, that might have passed without attention, but it became a sneezing fit. I have had these since childhood and to say I *suffer* from them would exaggerate their importance. Nerves or excitement and nothing to do with impending flu, but once I start there is no stopping me.

Gordon Craig might not have heard a single 'tishoo' but now he saw me disintegrating before him in a series of spasms, trying to avert each explosion with massive gulps only to be followed by the hideous, inevitable grimace as I suffered the next seizure. Ken thrust his handkerchief into my face in the hope of cushioning the next attack, but I judged it wiser to withdraw with a wave, interrupted by yet another convulsion as I staggered out of doors.

This was forgotten in the morning when we assembled with the camera crew at Craig's cottage and Ken rang the bell. It took some time before the protective housekeeper allowed him inside, and when Ken came out again he looked ashen, waving a piece of scribbled paper like Chamberlain returning from Munich, though far from triumphant as he broke the news. 'Something terrible has happened. You remember you sneezed last night, well he's decided that you're the harbinger of death, that you're riddled with germs and have come to f-finish him off if you go near him.'

'Oh God,' I interrupted. 'You mean he won't do it?'

'Not exactly.' Ken gave an agonised smile. 'He's made a suggestion – that you stand in the garden outside and shout your questions through the window while he's safely tucked up inside.'

The cynical camera crew tumbled about with laughter yet the mad idea had a certain logic: as Craig would hardly be able to hear me inside the house, it would not make much difference if I was placed outside it.

Ken found the solution: he would sit opposite Craig during the filming while I stayed outside at the front door where I could shout my questions to Ken's assistant who would write them out in large letters on the placards we had brought with us that morning. Ken would hold these up in front of Craig's face for him to squint at and, with any luck, he might volunteer some sort of answer.

And this is exactly what took place. Afterwards, Craig was carried into his bedroom in a state of exhaustion, and I was smuggled inside to sit in Ken's chair while Ken sat in Craig's. Pitching my voice a fraction more loudly than usual, to indicate that the grand old man was slightly deaf, I filmed the questions which had been relayed to Ken. When *Tempo* was transmitted a few weeks later, the deception was so unnoticeable that a stranger stopped me in the street to say how lucky I was to have enjoyed such an interesting conversation with such a sweet old man. I did not have the heart to say we had never set eyes on each other after my sneezes, that I had not been in the same room when the interview took place, and I did not find him a sweet old man at all but a disagreeable, cantankerous old fool. This was the first and only time that I 'faked' an interview on television and I realised how alarmingly easy the lie can be though I doubt if there was any harm in this particular case. As we parted at the airport, Ken shook with the laughter of relief. 'That's one for the memoirs,' he cried. 'I wonder who'll be first.' Sadly, it fell to me.

Ken Tynan's life and mine clashed at several crucial points; in fact I was partly responsible for launching Ken on his career as dramatic critic.

After leaving the American Army, I had arrived at Pembroke College, Cambridge armed with two letters of reference, from the Dean of Westminster and Somerset Maugham, the one to take the curse off the other. It was 1948. The undergraduates were serious 'old' men in their late twenties, back from the war, or wide-eyed boys straight from school or National Service. It seems odd but we were remarkably sober and innocent, with two subjects virtually lacking in our conversation: sex and politics. Like the rest of England we suffered from the post-war anticlimax, but Oxford, as always, was more sybaritic and one figure in particular had risen from the ashes like a phoenix, flashed like a kingfisher, and preened with delight at finding himself so brilliant in such a lack-lustre world. Seldom can a second name have proved so prophetic as that of Kenneth Peacock Tynan.

Unlike most of us, he was obsessed by sex and devoid of inhibition. When he arrived at Magdalen, followed by a cortège, he warned one of the porters: 'Take a care with that trunk, my man, it is freighted with golden shirts.' Inevitably, with such gaudy behaviour, he was accused of being 'queer' – a misunderstanding which echoed through his life – but he was a seducer in the broader sense. 'I watched him seduce people to give them confidence,' said Peter Parker, his contemporary at Oxford. 'He was very assured and he'd wind you in on his reel.'

Ken was a legend when I arrived at the rival university and, though he was on the point of leaving Oxford, I tracked him down asking if he would write for *Panorama*, the magazine I had started with my old schoolfriend Anthony West.

From the outset we aimed high with the conceit of youth which brooks no opposition, featuring photographs, fiction and cartoons, though scant mention of college activities which were so ponderous at the time. I took the photographs and wrote features and stories under different names; the Shaffer twins wrote about their favourite subject, themselves; Alan Brien wrote on John Schlesinger's first film at Oxford; and contributions were bludgeoned from an odd assortment of family friends: Harold Laski; Henry Williamson; Cecil Beaton; Feliks Topolski; and my father who wrote on lion hunting in Africa.

For an undergraduate magazine it was startling, but *Panorama* excelled when Gavin Lambert became our film critic, and Ken Tynan our dramatic critic. Both were formidable. Gavin edited the film magazine *Sequence*, with Lindsay Anderson who wrote for us as well, and they held court attended by such admirers as Jill Bennett and Karel Reisz. With Lindsay, certain idols like John Ford were sacrosanct. Gavin was more feline with a waspish wit and sly smile. He gave his verdict with such authority that he was accepted implicitly as the young guru of British cinema. While Lindsay ached to make films and was starting to do so, Gavin maintained his strength by criticising everyone, with the occasional bemused concession to Judy Garland. Ken felt uncomfortable in this coterie, preferring to dominate a court of his own where he could direct the wit towards himself. By saying little, I managed to straddle both.

At the age of twenty-three, Ken had a vaulting talent and in many ways had reached his peak. His ambition was outrageous, but so was his enthusiasm and this I admired most of all. It is part of the virtue of a sacred monster to be an enthusiast, but you need an obsession and Tynan had that too – a passion for the theatre. At times his stammer created a distance from the person he was talking to, leaving him agonised and speechless, but when the words escaped on paper they revealed his astonishing ability to bring

an actor to life. *Panorama* provided a perfect outlet. When he described Ralph Richardson bluffing his way through a mediocre play 'as bewildered as a glass eye', it was possible to envisage the performance. His perception could be lethal (of Ustinov, 'He does too much too soon') and prophetic: 'Richard Burton, the best of our youth . . . is a still pool, running fathoms deep; at twenty-five he can make silence garrulous . . . He smiles where lesser men guffaw; relaxes where they have strained; and ruefully but relentlessly prepares Falstaff for the key-cold rejection.' Then, with a twist of the dagger, he added, 'He is always likeable, and always *inaccessible*' (my italics, because I find the word so apt). Peter Brook was 'little and dapper – like something out of Kenneth Grahame, a quiet, miniature thug, not pretty but glittering'.

Attracted irresistibly by stardom, he resisted idolatry and indulged in a bravura profile of Noël Coward which few would have attempted at the time and few magazines would have published:

> Benign, yet flustered as a Cardinal might be at some particularly dismaying tribal rite . . . Taut facially, as an appalled monolith; gracious, socially, as a royal bastard; tart vocally, as a hollowed lemon – so he appeared for us at the Café de Paris . . . Coward's fastidiousness, outrageously enough, is that of a first-rate male impersonator . . . I do not know if he has false teeth but, if pressed, I would plump for the affirmative.

When they met afterwards in the Ivy, Coward wagged a reproving finger and said, 'I thought *you* came out of it terribly well.' But they became friends. That was another point in Ken's favour, though there could be a naïvety unexpected in such a sophisticated man. He was genuinely startled when Orson Welles took offence when he described his Othello as *Citizen Coon* in a rare lapse of glibness. On another occasion, Ken abandoned his usual discretion by going backstage after a first night to praise a mutual friend so warmly that she told all her friends to read his notice, assuming that it must be good. 'There is nothing wrong with her performance,' he remarked in his column, 'that six months' fasting would not improve.' (I quote from memory.) Such flip cruelty was beneath him, but when he had a serious criticism to make he was not deterred by the thought of losing the friendship of someone he admired, though surprised by their reaction. A few years later, I accompanied him to the Edinburgh Festival to photograph Richard Burton and Claire Bloom in *Hamlet*, for American *Harper's Bazaar*. 'Why is Burton so cold to us?' I asked afterwards. 'I think it might be something I've written,' said Ken, puzzled.

Once he double-crossed me. I mentioned that I was writing a profile of the London Palladium, from the stars down to the cleaners, a novel idea at the time which I described in some detail though he seemed disinterested. I wrote out my suggestions and sent them to the Palladium's press officer who phoned me back with curious hesitancy. Finally he came clean. 'This is very odd,' he explained. 'It really can't be coincidence, but you do realise that someone has been here for the last few days doing *exactly* what you've outlined?' For a moment I was mystified. 'Who is it?' I asked. 'I'm afraid I can't tell you that,' he replied nervously. Then I understood. 'Are his initials K.T.?' 'Yes.'

I was shocked and so bewildered that I phoned Ken in the hope of discovering some mistake. Instead he answered brightly: 'Dan, if Freud hadn't lived you could challenge me to a duel, but he has so I plead my subconscious.' I had the last laugh: the magazine for which he was writing turned the feature down, and so did I.

It was easy to forgive Ken such excesses because of his dedication to the theatre and all it embraced. At Oxford he gained a reputation as a producer as well as an actor. Sandy Wilson, who worked with him and went on to write *The Boyfriend*, told me that Ken's range was not properly exploited, especially his talent as a director. This was dented after Ken's dismissal from Cocteau's *Intimate Relations (Les Parents Terribles)* when the formidable actress, Fay Compton, complained about his interpretation. This shattered his confidence, though he had the courage – in spite of his stammer – to test himself in the production of *Hamlet* starring Alex Guinness. Though born to play the skull in the graveyard scene, Ken took the part of the Player King and Sandy Wilson believes that he could have been impressive. Unfortunately, the first night proved a theatrical disaster, largely due to the lighting. The ghost scene was played in the glare of sunlight, the court scene in near darkness, and Ken was scarcely visible under a huge hat and a plastic left ear. The point of the plastic left ear indicates the aberrational nature of the show, though I believe the ear was dropped for the rest of the short, ill-fated run.

Writing as the critic of the *Evening Standard*, Beverly Baxter affected a generosity: 'I am a man of kindly nature who takes no joy in hurting those who are without defence, but Mr Kenneth Tynan . . . would not get a chance in a village hall unless he were related to the vicar. His performance was quite dreadful.'

This coincided with the latest issue of *Panorama* which had included an anonymous and scurrilous diatribe 'The Monstrous Regiment of Critics' which singled out Baxter in particular as one of 'the awful people one overhears in the interval, additionally sinister because one knows the commonplaces they utter will appear in print'.

With incestuous relish, the *Standard* published Ken's defence on 22 May 1951 under the heading BAXTER'S DREADFUL MAN HITS BACK: 'I am quite a good enough critic to know that my performance is not "quite dreadful"; it is, in fact, only slightly less than mediocre. I do not actually exit through the scenery or wave at my friends in the audience.'

Then he suggested the explanation for Baxter's bile: 'Mr Baxter had every excuse for feeling quarrelsome. That very morning he had received a new magazine called *Panorama* more than half of which was taken up by a gigantic pseudonymous attack on almost every practising dramatic critic. Naturally he felt gloomy after all this,' wrote Ken after quoting a reference to Baxter's 'prejudice, mood and fogged generalisations'. He continued, 'Spotting that I am *Panorama*'s critic, he might have leapt to the conclusion that I wrote it.'

In fact, 'John Knox' was Gavin Lambert who remained curiously silent throughout, and so did I though *Panorama* could have gained from the publicity. Lindsay Anderson recently confirmed that Lambert wrote it alone: 'Better than anything Ken could have written. It did make an impact at the time, didn't it!'

Baxter denied Ken's allegation arrogantly: 'Perhaps it is my fault and misfortune that previous to his performance I had never heard of him – and after that performance I doubt whether as an actor I shall ever hear of him again.'

Baxter was unaware that he was currently out of favour with Lord Beaverbrook, his friend and fellow-Canadian as well as his employer. However, the *Standard*'s editor was fully aware of this and, believing that Tynan had written the attack on Baxter, he seized the chance to commission Ken to write some devastating profiles on the idols of the day – 'IS VIVIEN LEIGH GREAT? I say "No!"' 'Overpraise in the end is the most damaging kind of praise, especially if you are an actress approaching forty.' To paraphrase Lonsdale, it was not unkind to say that Vivien Leigh was forty, it was unkind because she *was* forty. The series created the intended stir and Tynan replaced Baxter as dramatic critic of the *Standard* in April for the next fifteen months, until he was fired in his turn when he threatened to sue the *Standard* for libel if they continued to publish readers' letters against him, an ironic reversal of the earlier events. Beaverbrook told Milton Shulman that he couldn't employ 'a fellow who threatens to sue his own paper' but by then Tynan's reputation was established.

Lambert's attack on the critics spared no one apart from Tynan – another reason why people assumed that *he* had written it – condemning Ivor Brown of the *Observer* as 'the sergeant-major who got his stripes many years ago, and since that time has seen long and dishonourable service. Brown's style (this is not quite the right word for it) is famous for its puns. He has brought this entertaining pastime to a very low ebb . . . The kindest thing would be to assume that he is, in fact, just tired and due for a pension, but he seems determined to die with his boots on.'

Ah, the careless brutality of youth! I had joined the Savile Club under some arrangement advantageous to undergraduates, where Ivor Brown was a member and took a kindly interest in me. When I invited Tynan there as my first guest for lunch, I was unaware of the stir he created in his vivid lavender suit with matching shoes, nor that I had broken the rules by photographing him on the Club's ancient staircase. Afterwards, Brown took me aside and advised me that Ken was not the type of person who was welcome at the Savile. If he believed that Ken had written 'A Monstrous Regiment of Critics', there might have been justification, but I assume he made the common mistake of thinking that Ken was homosexual. This angered me so greatly that I resigned from the Savile. In 1954, Ken signed a contract for the *Observer* to become their dramatic critic as the replacement for Ivor Brown, a choice which Brown endorsed at first and then tried to discourage, but David Astor had recognised Ken's potential.

While he was still at school, James Agate – a sacred monster personified, though kind to me at my father's Savage Club – had the wit to prophesy: 'Here is a great dramatic critic in the making.' Now the prophecy was fulfilled. Ken might have replaced Baxter and Brown but he was truly Agate's successor.

The period I have described was Tynan's heyday. We continued to see each other constantly; I worked for him as photographer for American *Harper's* and interviewer for *Tempo*. Perhaps his ambition alarmed me, for I was always slightly in awe. When I said something which entertained, his face would light up and his body shiver with pleasure, but I remember also how cursory he was towards my parents when I introduced them at a drama festival in North Devon, no more than a flashed smile and waved retreat yet, if he had bothered to talk to them, he would have discovered that my father watched Moskvin and Knipper-Chekhova (Chekhov's wife) play their original parts in *The Cherry Orchard* in the winter of 1928, and even Stanislavsky in one act of *The Three Sisters*. Ken was always in a hurry. 'People think I am enjoying myself too much,' he complained to me years later. 'It was never my aim to run a National Theatre and I think I paid my debt to society by assisting Sir Laurence for ten years, but that gets forgotten because I did one revue, *Oh, Calcutta!*, which had an erotic purpose and used a sentence on television which included the word "fuck" – an episode which must have lasted all of ten seconds of my lifetime.'

Yet this was held against him and, after his Memorial Service at St Paul's, the actors' church in Covent Garden, a few of us gathered in the pub opposite where Peter Parker expressed a regret that Ken had not fulfilled his promise. While resisting the temptation to point out that Sir Peter was currently the head of British Rail, I argued that, while the direction of Ken's ambitions might be queried, he had achieved what he wanted: the association with the National, the erotic frolics of *Oh, Calcutta!* even though it failed to earn him the fortune it should have done. A collector of sacred monsters himself, he became their confidant: Orson Welles, Marlene Dietrich, Hemingway and Noël Coward.

The same age as me, he died too young because he was unable to control his smoking, and I am glad to remember him at his happiest when we met for the last time shortly before he left for America. Both of us had mellowed. He was sunnily content in his second marriage to Kathleen and, when he fetched his daughter from school, I was amazed that someone so impatient could drive so calmly.

Over lunch, we laughed like conspirators as we recalled the launching-pad which *Panorama* gave us. I cannot grieve for someone who had so much fun.

Moby Dick in Paris

ORSON WELLES

Even at school, Ken Tynan hero-worshipped Orson Welles, writing in the school mag: 'Orson is a self-made man, and how he loves his Maker.' Before he was twenty-three, he had caught the idol's attention: 'Whatever you are, Mr Tynan, there is no doubt that you are some sort of magician. You materialised out of a puff of Paris fog, handed me the manuscript of this book and before vanishing somehow bamboozled me into reading it and writing this.' The book was *He That Plays the King*, published with Orson's introduction in 1950, inscribed for me that Christmas:

> Mene, mene, tekel upharsin
> Is my Chrissmuss wish for Daniel Farson:
> Better to write upon a wall
> Than never to have writ at all.

Ken signed this with a flourish in a couple of seconds, as if he had been waiting for such a moment. I doubt if he had; spontaneity was one of his gifts.

I shared his hero-worship of Welles. My first impression of *Citizen Kane* in Ottawa was unforgettable. I haven't the faintest idea where I was when Kennedy was assassinated, but I remember that Canadian cinema so clearly I can almost smell it. I was sorry that I had not gone to the school in Illinois where Welles had shone before, learning his craft with the film equipment it provided. Even now I can quote much of *Kane* by heart, yet every time I see it I discover something new.

Consequently, I was eager to go to Paris in my turn, to interview Welles for *Panorama*. He possessed the qualities of a sacred monster in abundance: gusto, a strange retention of innocence, and a grand irreverence. And, of course, the brilliance. At the time he was appearing in his own play *The Unthinking Lobster*, a double-bill with his version of *Helen of Troy* starring his discovery, Eartha Kitt, who was twenty-two years old.

I cannot comprehend this now, but I failed to attend the performance which was hardly a polite introduction, and when I stressed that I had just seen his film of *Macbeth*

Orson Welles

he roared with an anger which was not entirely mock: 'That's no use to us. Go and see the play, we need the money.'

'Are you handling all your finances, Mr Welles?' I asked, a question which must have been due to nerves. He peered at me with new interest and shook with silent, tragic laughter, turning to Eartha Kitt as she came into his dressing-room to kiss him goodnight. 'Do I handle my finances!' he boomed. 'What a question.' Hilton Edwards of Dublin's Gate Theatre, and a member of the cast, was consulted too: 'Did you hear that, Hilton?' Turning back to me, he continued: 'Yes, I am. Since the backers withdrew from *Othello*, the film I've just been making, I've carried on by myself, hocking and borrowing everything I could lay my hands on. I'm the first man since D. W. Griffith who has financed a film on his own. Everything I've got is in that film.' As for *Macbeth* and the poor reviews, he had this to say: 'I don't know if a film I've made is good or bad. I just experiment while making it. I open the paper and see that *Macbeth* is the greatest film ever made; others say I've murdered Shakespeare. If I believed all the successes I've apparently had, I would be unbearably conceited; if I believed all the failures, I'd have killed myself.'

He broke off with a roar. 'Look here, I've had enough. It's ridiculous. I can't have people coming in like this, why don't they stop them at the door?' I winced but he referred to a flashlight photographer who was hovering outside. 'Has your paper made an appointment?' The man said he was from Italy. 'Look here, I can't do it,' said Welles impatiently. Even so, the room was filling up. People drifted in and out. One man announced, 'I'm the only person I've met who likes the first play better than the second.'

'That's the way it is,' said Welles in the sing-song voice of Kane. 'Some people enjoy the first play, some the second. No one enjoys them both.' The man and the two women with him laughed sycophantically, but the mood changed when the man asked how the play was doing.

'Since Korea, you know, the theatres are half-empty.' Welles disappeared behind a screen, emerging in his underclothes with a glass of champagne. Another young man came in, examined the bowl of roses and the empty magnum. 'A pity they're so faded,' he said of the first, and, 'A greater pity that the champagne has faded too.' He flashed a smile and walked out.

Welles finished scraping his soapless beard with a razor and was now sprinkling himself with toilet water which he handed to Hilton Edwards who handed it to me. Soon he was dressed, the dressing-room entourage vanished, and we walked through the Edouard VII theatre impressive in its emptiness to the Rue Madelaine. 'This,' said Welles, 'is the moment I like best of the whole day.' Speaking to his waiting chauffeur in the tone reserved for the very young or feeble-minded, Welles handed him the invitation card to a ball given by Jacques Fath which he was due to attend that night. 'This is the name of the château,' Welles explained. 'Find out where it is, and then find us.'

We sat down at a café nearby and Welles relaxed, ordering a lager and pointing to a poster for *The Naughty Revue* across the street. 'Now that's where we ought to be. Come on then, what do you want to ask me?'

For someone so pursued, he was considerate. Apparently penniless, with the prospect of arrest for tax evasion if he returned to America, he seemed like a stranded Moby Dick on a foreign shore.

'Film production is too complicated, too many political and financial snags. If *Othello*, dealing with adultery, miscegenation and suicide, were written for the cinema today it would almost certainly be turned down. That's why I have no wish to produce in England, though it would be nice to work under Carol Reed again.'

'Do you ever wish to return to the States?' After an embarrassing silence, he said, 'It seems so blunt to say just "no". Anyhow, not for the moment.'

Already he was cursed by *Kane*, the great success which came too soon, and almost seemed to resent it. 'There's nothing I've done that D. W. Griffith didn't do. I am guilty of every sin except talk about the *art* of the cinema.' He laughed hugely.

Now that we were alone, I was able to relax and confided my ideas for films – never fulfilled – including one in which a murdered man is remembered by various people and appears physically different, depending on who remembers him, lover, mother or wife. Welles had considered a similar idea himself. 'What I really hope to do next is a film about *sex*. When you come to think of it, there are few films actually on sex, they're usually about sexy people. This will be on obsessive love.'

When he added that he hoped to make a film on vampires, I mentioned that my great-uncle was Bram Stoker who wrote *Dracula*. With a roar, Welles sprang to his feet in homage. 'Let me shake your hand. I *knew* Stoker, when I came to Dublin, and he told me that he had written this play especially for his friend Henry Irving who tossed it aside impatiently, with the single word "*Dreadful!*" But, did you know,' Welles's voice, already resonant, deepened as he leant forward, 'Stoker had his revenge! He turned his vampire play into a novel and if you read the description of Count Dracula you'll find it identical to Irving.' He bellowed with laughter and I smiled, for though I relished the story I knew that Dracula has a big white moustache in the novel, and that Stoker died three years before Orson Welles was born.

Welles's sing-song lilt and raucous laughter were attracting attention. Several people came up to our table: a Frenchman wanted the honour of shaking hands, two American women asked for his autograph.

'My! I wish I could write my name as quickly as you do,' one of them gushed girlishly, and when they had left Welles grinned and began to mimic in a Southern accent: 'My! Oh my, if I could push my poor little old pen . . . ' He broke off as the chauffeur returned with the announcement, 'I can get us to where I'm going if I know where I've got to go.'

Welles turned to me sadly: 'That's French logic.' He shouted at the chauffeur: 'Try again.'

We had more drinks. I've forgotten the actor whom Welles described 'as about as cute as an unopened pimple', though I remember him claiming that *The Man Who Came to Dinner* was not entirely based on Alexander Woollcott. 'That part where he's so rude to his nurse, that wasn't Alex, that was *me*, when I had jaundice,' he announced proudly. 'And that scene where he tries to wreck his secretary's life, that was *me* too.'

It was one o'clock when the chauffeur drew up again with the assurance that he knew the way. With a farewell wave, worthy of *The Third Man*, Welles slumped in the back of his Citroën as it shot into the night.

I was left with the bill. I had begun to suspect that Welles, like royalty, did not carry money on him, with the difference that he didn't have any. By luck, I had taken some photographs of a French girl at Cambridge to the offices of *Elle* that afternoon, where the editor, Helene Lazareff, not only bought them but had the consideration to pay me in French francs on the spot. This enhanced the rest of my visit to Paris and allowed me the honour of paying for Orson Welles. When I read of her death in 1988, I remembered her with gratitude.

The next evening I met Welles outside the theatre to take his photograph. The carefree rapport was gone, the responsibilities of the actor-manager had reasserted themselves as he was besieged by anxious members of the cast with trivial questions about the evening's performance. Also, by those whom he paid to deal with such problems. Also, by someone to whom he owed money.

His temper was not improved by the fact that his chauffeur had failed to find the château, yet persisted in trying to do so despite Welles's pleas to return home. He had spent the small hours touring the French countryside, losing part of the small amount of sleep he allowed himself. Still friendly, he endured my photography courteously.

'Thank you,' he cried when it was over, and disappeared into the theatre, a lonely man pursued by his hangers-on.

AN ASSIGNMENT ON A FILM-SET

In spite of his reservations, Welles came to England. He produced *Othello* and a turbulent *Moby Dick* on stage, and we met again when I presented him in the first midnight show on British television, a studio discussion on the Method School of Acting. This was Ken's idea. Rex Harrison was the other distinguished 'guest'.

However, Welles had sneaked into England several years earlier, virtually unnoticed, to appear in *Trent's Last Case*, one of the curious British films made by Herbert Wilcox with major stars, which ended in his bankruptcy. Welles was lured by a huge fee which he invested in one of his own, disaster-ridden film productions, allowing him a few more days of footage. Always prone to heavy make-up, like Olivier who appeared in another Wilcox film which vanished without trace, Welles resorted to swollen cheeks, a false nose, and general camouflage to hide his shame.

The British 'stars' included Margaret Lockwood who told me that she offered to 'stand in' when they filmed one of Welles's reverses. 'And you know what he told me,' she related excitedly, 'he said he'd rather talk to a chalk-mark! That's what I call a great actor!'

The male lead was Michael Wilding who had appeared with Anna Neagle (Mrs Wilcox) in such frothy affairs as *Maytime in Mayfair* and *Spring in Park Lane* which had been a huge success at the British box office and made a fortune for Wilcox. *Trent's Last Case* was less promising. I was sent down to cover it as a photographer and during one of those interminable delays in the studio I joined Wilding in a far corner of the cavernous set where he sat beside a piano. As we talked, I noticed a curious disturbance at the other end as the technicians gathered gradually around a young girl until they encircled her with watchful, silent lust.

'What's that?' I asked.

'*That* – is my wife. She's called Elizabeth Taylor.' With a sort of smile, he raised his eyebrows and played a few bars of a currently popular tune, 'They tried to tell us we're too young . . . ' He closed the piano and grimaced. 'Now I know I'm too old after all!'

I photographed her a few moments later and understood the devastating effect she

Elizabeth Taylor

was having on the camera crew, hardly a sacred monster then, though she became one. We met several years later when I interviewed her and Mike Todd on television before the London première of *Around the World in Eighty Days*. As so often in her life, Elizabeth Taylor's appearance had changed dramatically. Now she seemed bloated and greasy by comparison. Certainly she was ruder. Dressed unfortunately in a split Chinese gown (I wondered if she had split it), she called her husband Super-Mouse while he used the endearment of Sugar-Piggy which was at least appropriate.

If I seem uncharitable, this is because neither of them looked me in the face throughout our short *This Week* interview but giggled and blew kisses to each other. When I tried to ask a question, Todd did not even swivel in his chair towards me but replied, 'Bite your lip!' As the interview was 'live', I should have walked out of the studio and left them to it.

A Meeting
in a Cavendish Bedroom

TENNESSEE WILLIAMS

Obsessed with *Panorama*, I haunted the London advertising agencies with Tony West during our vacations, gaining enough orders to keep the magazine going. We were entirely self-supporting and when I read of the huge losses made by magazines today I find them inexplicable. However, we did not pay ourselves any salary.

Acting on impulse one morning, I photographed Rosa Lewis on the doorstep of her Cavendish Hotel, when she must have been in her eighties, and asked to see Tennessee Williams who was staying there. Though I should not dare attempt it today, the nerve of such an approach is frequently rewarded. I sat in the foyer of the Ritz years later and asked to see Paul Getty who told me to come up to his suite immediately. After our interview – 'Why are millionaires so mean, Mr Getty?' 'They're not mean, they simply have a healthy respect for money' – I asked him why he had agreed to see me. 'Because you have your job to do, just like mine.' His Buster Keaton expression was replaced by a kindly smile. On another occasion, seeing an American with an interesting face, during the interval of a play, I went up to him, explained that I was a photographer, and asked if I could see him the next day. 'Sure,' he said, 'why not? That'd be just fine.' He told me to call at Claridge's at ten. 'Thank you, sir,' I said. 'Could you tell me your name?'

He looked at me with surprise. 'Sure,' he chuckled. 'John Huston.'

When I entered Tennessee Williams's bedroom in the old Cavendish, I told him about *Panorama* and thought it might be nice if we could publish one of his short stories. He looked out of the window for a moment, apparently sniffing the air. When he turned round he smiled and offered to give me two which might be suitable. He sorted through his papers and handed me two yellow typescripts. When I presented him with ten one-pound notes, he accepted them graciously. 'It is so well-comm,' he drawled, 'to have the money in cash.' I had no idea of my presumption.

Later he took me to the rehearsal of a play that was due to open in London. I think it was *Summer and Smoke* and, when we left in the taxi afterwards, he asked me what I thought of it. 'I think the actress is wrong,' I told him, with the candour of youth. 'Oh God,' he moaned, 'so do I.'

The stories proved far from 'suitable'. One concerned an old share-cropper in the Deep South who bought himself a bride but suffered from a seizure of anticipation as he drove her home, writhing in his bed upstairs as he heard the girl and his strapping son hard at it in the room below. Today this story would seem mild, but in the climate of the time it was so shocking that I hid the yellow pages so successfully that I never found them again.

The other story, 'Two on a Party', struck me as fairly innocuous until we published it. In my delayed adolescence I had failed to realise the implications of Cora, an ageing 'lush', and Billy, a balding 'queen', who cruised the New York waterfront together. Why Billy should worry over his thinning hair, when he knelt (?) before the nice sailors they

Tennessee Williams

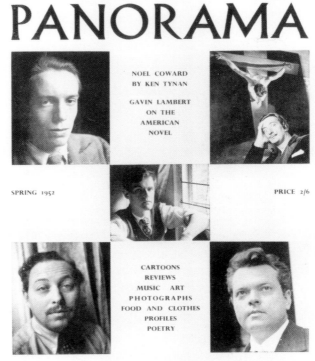

THE SIXTH

PANORAMA

NOEL COWARD
BY KEN TYNAN

GAVIN LAMBERT
ON THE
AMERICAN
NOVEL

SPRING 1952

PRICE 2/6

CARTOONS
REVIEWS
MUSIC ART
PHOTOGRAPHS
FOOD AND CLOTHES
PROFILES
POETRY

'TWO ON A PARTY' BY TENNESSEE WILLIAMS

The sixth edition of *Panorama* which contained the controversial story by Tennessee Williams

brought back to the hotel, puzzled me, and I was totally unprepared for the horrified reaction in the *Bookseller*:

> To an unsympathetic reader it might very well appear to be a coldly deliberate exercise in pornography. Presumably the publishers and printers measured their responsibility before publishing such a piece in a paper specially designed for young people, and are prepared to meet any consequences of that decision. A possible charge of corrupting the young is no laughing matter.

Corrupting the young! I almost squealed as I read the phrase. I was scarcely twenty-three myself. Failing to realise that *Panorama* had come of age, and might have continued in its own right as a successful national magazine, the subsequent scandal confirmed my suspicion that this should be the last issue. Several times in my life, I have veered away at the moment I have neared success.

When I met Tennessee Williams again it was many years later. He had changed. The southern graciousness had been replaced by alcoholic cruelty. He did not remember me or *Panorama*. Towards the end of his life, he qualified as a sacred monster. Yet, ironically, 'Two on a Party' was one of his finest stories, far stronger in the first version which we published than the protracted re-write included in later anthologies.

An Insult in the Kasbah

JOHN DEAKIN

Another reason for the closure of *Panorama* was simply that Tony West and I had left Cambridge and were heading in separate directions. Also, as I shall explain, a feature in *Panorama* had lifted me on to the first rung of a new ladder, just as it had Ken Tynan. I was to join the staff of *Picture Post* in the near future. Meanwhile, there was a period of abeyance and I drifted into Soho where I found a sacred monster of my own. Soho, after all, was a stamping ground, if not a breeding ground, for the species.

Anyone who has read my book on Soho will recognise John Deakin, described by George Melly in his introduction as: 'Dan's evil genius, a vicious little drunk of such inventive malice and implacable bitchiness that it's surprising he didn't choke on his own venom.'

Barbara Woolworth Hutton would have concurred.

We flew with Lady Rose MacLaren to Tangier where she was staying with her cousin, David Herbert. He met us at the airport and within ten minutes I was charging into the Atlantic surf at Robinson's Beach, followed by lunch in the simple open-air restaurant nearby, swilled down with quantities of chilled white wine. It was the perfect arrival, and I said so.

'No,' Deakin exclaimed, 'this really *is* perfect.' He sounded as if he was correcting me and leant back shutting his eyes in a Maughamish grimace which resembled pain but surely was that of blissful relief as the trellis of bamboo sticks above us cast criss-cross patterns on his wizened shoulders. 'This is my sort of life. *I* can understand it.' As I revived in the sun, with bowls of tomato salad drenched in olive oil, I thought it was my kind of life as well and wished that Deakin's tone of voice had not implied that he alone could show appreciation.

Yet Deakin had a point. This was the kind of life he wanted to lead and had tasted when he lived with the American millionaire Arthur Jeffress. Though Deakin billed himself as a 'slum child from Liverpool', he was a born sophisticate though he tried to conceal it with a calculated veneer of naïvety. After he met Jeffress, Deakin became his travelling companion – to Hollywood and the South Seas. In Italy they rented the famous Palladian Villa

Rotonda; later, Jeffress bought a palace in Venice with his own gondoliers. In the war Deakin was assigned as a photographer to the 8th Army in North Africa and attended one of Monty's briefings when the Field Marshal warned the assembly that they were outnumbered, that 'Wommel' had superior tanks, and the British were wholly vulnerable. In the uneasy silence which followed, Deakin's anxious whisper could be heard as he turned to the War Correspondent, Warwick Charlton: 'Do you think we're on the right side?'

Deakin enjoyed his war, especially the paying of compliments to fellow officers: 'You're looking absolutely gorgeous today, Geoffrey!' but when it was over Jeffress stopped his allowance and they separated.

'I really loved that bastard,' Deakin told me once. Yet, when I met Jeffress, they might scarcely have been friends. 'Poor little mite,' he said, surprisingly. 'After he left, we found so many empty bottles. Everywhere.'

Ever resilient, Deakin became a distinguished photographer and had just been given the sack by *Vogue* when we flew to North Africa. Lady Rose paid for his holiday, as a treat to cheer him up.

Our sleeping arrangements were odd. Rose stayed with her cousin, Deakin was booked into a hotel in the centre of town, while I, in my folly, had rented a villa on the hillside which proved difficult to find when I returned by taxi at night. As I was alone, the luxury was ludicrous. I slept each night in a different room and, when I invited Deakin to stay with me, he gave me a pitying smile: 'You've made your bed, so lie in it! I like to be in the thick of things, kiddo.'

David Herbert proved an impeccable host and planned Rose's visit meticulously. The acknowledged 'King' of Tangier, he knew everyone and as we were Rose's friends we were invited to dinner on our first evening, Deakin was late and slightly unsteady. As a casual afterthought, Herbert handed us each an envelope with a printed invitation card inside: *Mrs Barbara Woolworth Hutton requests the pleasure of your company for a ball on the roof of her house in the Kasbah.* This was followed by the date and a warning: 'In case of wind, your hostess requests you to indulge her by coming another night.'

'I see the poor thing suffers from flatulence,' said Deakin.

Rose gave a nervous smile and Herbert explained: 'The mistral can last for days.'

'Do you know Barbara Hutton?' I asked, impressed.

'Very well indeed. In fact we're having drinks with her tonight.'

'Barbara Woolworth Hutton,' mused Deakin. 'It's a name to conjure with.'

Barbara Hutton and Deakin. I pondered on the combination – Godzilla Meets the Monster – as Herbert drove us up the hill, through the main gate of the Kasbah. From the distance came the noise of drums and trumpets as soldiers practised for a visit from the Sultan. We drove round various twisting alleys and stopped outside a nondescript exterior. Mrs Hutton's palace was revealed in its full grandeur as we were led through courtyards to the Throne Room where the richest woman in the world was waiting to greet us.

My first impression was that of a beautiful woman. She wore a bright red sari, bought in San Francisco; her hair was soft and brightly yellow, swept upwards, neatly; her figure, from what I could see of it, was lithe, almost fragile; and her dark eyes moved restlessly as she spoke like an actress listening to a distant prompt which none of us could hear.

My second impression confirmed that she was rather common, and sexy. Perhaps the latter was due to her legendary wealth.

There were several fawning guests smiling too brightly as people do at the start of a party, expressing murmurs of delight when Barbara Hutton announced that she would take us on a guided tour of the palace.

'Do we have to?' Deakin asked me. 'I'd much rather stay here.'

'Of course we do,' I replied crossly.

Barbara Hutton addressed us merrily. 'Ever since I was a little girl I wanted a Moorish palace. This was built by the correspondent of the London *Times* in the early 1930s, and it was taken over by our Consul, Maxwell Blake, who added to it considerably. When Blake retired, he was going to sell to Franco but I topped Franco's bid.' With odious sycophancy, I remarked that it must have been satisfying to beat him.

'Not at all,' she corrected me, 'I consider General Franco a truly great man.' After that I kept silent, but Deakin did not.

'Venetian,' Barbara Hutton explained as we entered a room lined with mirrors.

'I am perfectly aware of that,' he interrupted her, a finger to his lips as he scrutinised the scene. 'Unfortunately of the *wrong* period. Now if this room had been mine . . . ' As he proceeded to tell her what she should have done, the Americans looked at him in alarm, Herbert glared, and Rose said, 'Shush.' Barbara Hutton shot him a cool look and continued her tour with Deakin gradually taking charge. 'No one likes chinoiserie more than I,' he told us, 'but it's a shame that . . . ' The Americans backed away. We entered another room where Barbara Hutton paused with a knowing smile. 'And this,' she revealed, 'is my bedroom.' It was surprisingly bare with little furniture except for a large bed draped by a delicate tent of netting. 'I was once bitten by a mosquito,' she explained. There was not much to say, but Deakin said it: 'The sort of bed movie actresses are strangled in.' This was a fatuous remark but he gave it a wealth of sinister meaning, as he did in the next room which contained nothing apart from a pile of mattresses on a bed.

'Ah,' Deakin exclaimed with significance, 'now I understand. The Princess and the Pea.' Plainly unaware of the fairy-tale, the Americans stared guiltily at the mattresses as they thought of another kind of pea. Barbara Hutton had been the Princess Midvani, but surely this strange little man was not implying . . .

By now there was no stopping Deakin. When we returned to the Throne Room and she sat on the dais, pointing out the jewels which encrusted the scarlet tapestry, he declared that they would provide him with 40,000 cufflinks. She ignored him and continued her inventory, explaining that the tapestry had been given to her as a child but this was the first home with enough space to hang it. To everyone's relief, Deakin disappeared and conversation started to flow though the drinks did not.

Mesmerised, I nodded approvingly when she confided to me, 'If I love, I love, but I've

Far right: On the roof of Barbara Hutton's palace, attending the ball

never flirted,' and wondered about the dark young man of twenty-three who watched her with a stillness which suggested he was Spanish. In fact Lloyd Franklin was a former trumpeter in the Life Guards who had wandered south with his guitar after finishing his National Service, ending in Dean's Bar in Tangier where he played for his keep. Dean's Bar was as famous as Harry's in Venice, Bricktops in Rome, and Muriel's in London.

A few weeks earlier, Lloyd Franklin had played at a party where he was noticed by Barbara Hutton who asked him back for a drink in the Kasbah, and he had not been seen in the outside world again. Already the newspapers were gossiping about Barbara Hutton's latest love. With his youth and her wealth, the gossip was snide but, in spite of some caustic comments from Deakin earlier, I found it a romantic story and thought the young man behaved with exemplary composure. Unfortunately he sang. He produced his guitar and began to perform, not the flamenco which would have been bearable in such circumstances, but a song called 'The Hole in the Elephant's Bottom' which was greeted with squeals of delight from the Americans.

When he finished there was vigorous applause, as much to please her as him, followed by one of those unnerving silences which can fall on any party inexplicably. It was shattered by a deafening cry from behind the arras which ran down the side of the room. 'When that second-rate strummer has finished,' Deakin shouted at the Moroccan servant he had found at last, *'I'd like a drink!'*

'David's taking it awfully well,' said Rose the next morning when she broke the news that Barbara Hutton was cancelling the ball.

'Cancelling the ball?' I exclaimed. 'But it's the social event of the Tangier year.'

'Yes, I know,' said Rose with a very sad sigh, and looked towards Deakin tragically. 'You see, she refuses to hold it while you're still in Tangier.'

'I have my invitation card,' he replied defiantly in spite of his hangover. 'No one is going to stop me.'

'That's the trouble. She won't be so discourteous as to ask for it back, so she's cancelling the whole thing – unless you leave. Oh, dear, I am so sorry.'

I suspected that Cousin David had told her where her duty lay. 'If it will make it any better, I'll fly back with you. David's booked us plane seats on the day of the ball.' I felt that I should make the sacrifice, but kept quiet, wanting to go to the ball myself. When the news of Deakin's decantation was brought to her, Barbara Hutton announced that the ball would continue as planned and the Tangerines sighed with relief.

'I'll pray for wind as I have never prayed before,' said Deakin bitterly.

As David Herbert was in charge of the guest list, the residents who had not already received their invitations held sudden cocktail parties in an effort to gain them, and we were cast into a social whirlpool. Disgrace made Deakin abandoned and, though he was included in the parochial routine of dinner parties given by the expatriates, his presence became unwelcome and he drank at Dean's or the sleazier bars in town where I joined him, thankful to escape the snobbery. I was supposed to meet him in Dean's on the last night of his holiday, but we misjudged the time. Rose and David Herbert were there instead, looking severe.

'What's happened?' I asked.

Rose explained that she had gone to Deakin's hotel to pay his bill, where she had been greeted by the manager with some embarrassment. Apparently there was the matter of the telephone which 'Mr Dickens' had broken.

'How could he break a telephone?' I interrupted.

'God knows. It was in some alcove beside the stairs and he knocked it over as he staggered up to his room, smashing it to pieces on the stone floor. That's not all. Deakin must have fallen asleep last night with a lighted cigarette which smouldered right through the sheets and the mattress. I suppose it's lucky he didn't burn himself to death. To make it worse, the poor lamb made his bed concealing the damage, but this is the day for fresh sheets and the maid discovered the burns. The bill is unbelievable. They've charged for the mattress, the sheets, the telephone, and quite apart from the room he ran up an enormous bar bill as well. It's really too bad.'

'Poor Mr Dickens,' I said.

'Poor Tangier,' said David Herbert.

Meanwhile, unaware of Rose's confrontation with the manager, Deakin happened to meet an old friend from Paris who insisted on taking him to the home of a Moroccan painter for a drink. After several of these, Deakin remembered our meeting at Dean's and thought he would surprise me by borrowing the Moroccan's robes. He hurried gleefully to Dean's where he made a startling entrance dressed in turquoise from head to foot with a small wicker hat like a pill-box on his head.

'To my horror,' he wrote from London afterwards, 'there was no you, only David H. and Rose, and their mouths fell open. Far from the gales of laughter I expected, I just looked and felt plain silly. You'll have heard about the hotel. Rose's disapproval on the way back was really something. I must say the hardest bread and butter letters I have ever had to write were to Rose and David H. What could I say? Thank you for letting me behave so badly. The reason I drank so much was from fear. I hated having to return to England and face all my debts – I was good and scared and with reason.'

I had gone to the ball where I was photographed crouching subserviently beside Barbara Hutton on the roof of her Kasbah, but it was not the same without Deakin's irreverence. When I returned to London I found him restored to his old ebullience. 'The news had reached Soho,' he explained, 'and far from being shunned for my bad behaviour, I have been wined and dined for my blow-by-blow report.'

I shared his new notoriety at a crowded lunch in Wheeler's. At one point he looked forlorn. 'Did Barbara really dislike me that much?'

'Do you want to know what she said?' I asked him cruelly. '*Really* want to know.'

'Oh, come on,' said the others impatiently, 'tell us.'

'She told David Herbert that you were the second nastiest little man she has met in forty years.'

Everyone cried out: 'But who was the *first*?'

And who the sacred monster?

PICTURE POST

Panorama helped my career as it did Ken Tynan's. I had taken a series of photographs of a young actor as he might be seen by various magazines. One parody was aimed at the dreary socialist policy of *Picture Post* at that particular moment, with a shot of Peter Reynolds sitting forlornly on a bomb-site with the caption underneath: 'THE BACK-GROUND OF DECAY WHERE YOUTH HAS TO BLOSSOM: If you are twenty-five and poor, with little more than a sandwich in the rubble, what does the future hold?' This satirical dig was close to a genuine caption in a recent issue of *Picture Post.*

I was unaware that the magazine was currently in a state of purge due to the very policy which I had lampooned. Inadvertently, I had contributed to the sacking of the editor, Ted Castle, and a staff conference where the formidable managing director produced a copy of *Panorama* to justify his action.

I was summoned to his office where he slammed the offending copy of *Panorama* on to his desk and demanded to know if I was responsible. Expecting to be sued myself, still unaware of the purge which I had precipitated, I confessed. 'Good man,' he exclaimed. 'How much are you earning?' This tough, shark-like man leant forward, his eyes glinting at the prospect of some hard bargaining. My moment had arrived and I lost it. I had started as a trainee copywriter in a venerable advertising agency where my salary was £4 a week, or slightly less; and, with a last gasp of my fatuous innocence, I told the truth. The powerful man groaned and lost all interest. 'Oh well,' he sighed, 'I think we can do better than *that*!' Which is how I joined *Picture Post* as a staff photographer rather than the boy-genius and potential-editor he was hoping for.

This proved a stroke of luck. In spite of the purges, *Picture Post* was still a fine magazine with such distinguished journalists as Fyffe Robertson, Robert Kee and Kenneth Allsop who became a particularly close friend. However, it was a photographic magazine and the photographers, such as Bert Hardy, were the stars. We were a mixed group without rivalry because we specialised in different areas. While the others abhorred the interminable waiting-about in film studios, I relished the glamour and the chance to become 'a friend of the stars', such as Dame Edith Evans who called me 'Snooper' and drove me into London every evening from the set of *The Importance of Being Earnest.*

Above all, there was the chance of travel: Salvador Dali in Spain; Robert Graves in Majorca; Brendan Behan in Dublin. I was lucky.

A Double Exposure in Port Lligat

SALVADOR DALI

'D'ACCORD' was the one-word telegram from Salvador Dali which gave me permission to visit his home in the north of Spain in 1951. The place must have changed terribly, but it was isolated then. In Barcelona I joined a freelance journalist called George Langelan, whose claim to fame was a horror story published in *Playboy* called 'The Fly', and his fluent French proved invaluable for Dali's English was poor.

We drove north to Cadaques and then to the small fishing village of Port Lligat. After that, as far as I remember, we walked on a rough track over a hill until we saw the dazzling white cubes of Dali's house on the edge of the water below. Originally a fishing shack, used as a storeroom for nets, it had been transformed into a luxurious home while remaining simple on the outside, joining up on different levels with another shack and a small fisherman's cottage. The front door was Dali's entrance to the jetty barely fifteen feet away, with a motionless sea beyond. As we approached, the walls were glaring white, a Roman bust stood on the terrace with the bleached skeletons of animals, and a tall, resplendent dove-cote rose above the red roof.

This was the perfect setting for Dali, enhanced by its remoteness. This was no accident: having found his base, Dali fought to preserve it, forming a friendship with General Franco who signed a deed in 1953 which declared Port Lligat as a 'beauty spot' to be placed under government protection with no further building allowed. Even in 1951 the bay seemed sacred but the order stated that the seclusion should be saved from the 'suffering [of] any lamentable denaturalisations which, without doubt, would militate against the specific quality of austerity which it is expedient to defend'. That *specific quality of austerity* was an apt description – I hope that it remains. So, due to Dali's support for, and consequently support from, Franco, this was Dali's landscape, his sea, his sky, the strange intensity of light reflected in so many of his paintings with the particular perspective of the rocks beyond.

Dali had lived there since 1931, a year after his marriage to Gala, the beautiful Russian who was married first to the poet Paul Eluard, so admired by the other surrealists that, when one of them produced a work which was particularly fine, the others would say,

Salvador Dali in Port Lligat, a landscape
which appears constantly in his work

'Ah well, he was in love with Gala then.' Eluard said she had a look which pierced walls;
Dali claimed he was impotent until he met her, though I should have thought she was the
sort of woman who might render a man impotent.

Always a man obsessed, she became his great obsession. After a visit in the late 1920s
with her husband, and other surrealists including René Magritte and Luis Buñuel, Gala
stayed behind. Driven hysterical by his desire, he resorted to almost tribal means in his
efforts to attract her: shaving his armpits to make them bleed, and then his knees
because he liked the look of blood; boiling fish glue and goat manure into a paste, fixed
with oil of aspic, which he used to cover his body.

At first she found him fascinating but loathsome. Then his fanaticism swayed her, and
when he threw himself at her feet, she cried: 'My little boy! We shall never leave each
other!' The climax was reached when they took a walk and he felt the compulsion to push
her over the cliff. Sensing that she was also under the influence of a strong emotion, he
asked her what she wanted him to do. 'I want you to kill me,' she replied, revealing her
horror of death and her wish that this might happen instantaneously. Robbed of his
impulse to do exactly that, Dali returned to his semblance of sanity, though it could be
said that their relationship remained surreal.

Yet I remember Dali as the gentlest of men. From my viewpoint as a photographer, he was sublime, a striking figure in tartan shorts, with a black and white sports shirt which looked American, and a white flower in his hair. He was a handsome man, though his appearance was calculated, I found it difficult not to stare, mesmerised, by the curved antennae of his moustache, wondering how he kept it up. Above this radar system, his eyes were as anxious as an animal's confronted by strangers.

As I had discovered, a photographer for *Picture Post* had a status denied to the journalists, often to their irritation. Invariably, the subject was keener to be photographed than written about, and this was certainly true of Dali who posed and preened outrageously. We rowed across the bay with a stuffed swan in the prow of the boat; he chained himself to an immense lobster pot; and took his afternoon nap in the chair designed by himself, holding a heavy iron key which fell on to a plate below the moment he nodded off. The crash woke him but he had experienced one perfect second of relaxation, better than a longer sleep, a trick taught him by monks.

At one alarming moment my Rolleiflex jammed as Dali hoisted immense wooden rowlocks above his head, but when the film was developed in London he appeared in a splendid, surrealistic double-exposure. In due course the photograph won a prize and the

In his passion for publicity Dali exulted in being photographed

editor called me into his office to ask: 'How did you do it?' I was about to say it was an accident but stopped myself in time. 'Well,' I hesitated, 'it certainly wasn't easy.'

Gala, enigmatic behind the dark glasses which she never removed, said little but smiled contentedly. Both seemed devoted to a lively, laughing boy, approximately ten years old, who was called Juan, the son of a local fisherman. Juan had posed for the Infant Christ in the painting where Gala represented the Madonna. At the time, I wondered if he was the substitute for the child she never had.

Dali's obsession with Gala was revealed in his paintings, her face even replacing Christ's in *The Last Supper.* In contrast to his shyness as a man, his arrogance as an artist was absolute. Explaining that Salvador means 'saviour', he told us he was pre-destined to become the saviour of art. 'Art is an expression of beauty. Ugliness is not art, and the beauty of ugliness is a falsehood, but ugliness can be attractive, especially to our baser sentiments. Hence the confusion.' He described Picasso as a 'destroyer' but meant this partly as a compliment. 'In his research into total ugliness, Picasso destroyed all the ugliness of modern painting.' Dali concluded: 'That is all – Picasso is not a builder.'

As for the old masters, he had an unreserved admiration for Vermeer, Raphael and Leonardo da Vinci. 'Leonardo had everything that a real artist should have. He was not just a man of science centuries ahead of his time, but a philosopher. Modern artists are

'Dali is the perfect fanatic'
(Sigmund Freud)

Salvador Dali

not men of science, but art without a deep knowledge of science is not real art.' Perversely, he described the *Mona Lisa* as the epitome of the attraction of ugliness: 'Leonardo had an Oedipus complex and the woman is a mother, her smile nothing more than a leering invitation.' He resented Langelan's comparison of Dali to Bosch: 'His strange little animal-men, human flowers and fish, are the creation of Flanders' mists, but Dali's shapes, animals, and monsters are all creations of light, intense light, rocks and clouds,

Dali at work on the *Crucifixion*

creations of nature.' He pointed to the trick of light at Port Lligat which gave the illusion that the distant shore was suspended, genuinely surreal.

Stating that great painters only exist in parts of the world where the light has indefinable qualities, he added: 'You in England have had good painters, but no great painters because you haven't got the right light.'

'What about Constable and Turner?' I objected.

Ignoring Constable, he dismissed Turner as the worst painter the world has ever known, to which there was no answer, or too many. 'All the really great painters have lived around the Mediterranean or Flanders.' He even had the gall – or courage – to describe Rembrandt as 'theatrical'.

I was becoming aware that Dali could talk nonsense, but liked him increasingly as he relaxed. By now the harsh glare of midday was softening, with bold shadows cast by the rocks in the late afternoon, and while the others stayed outside he beckoned and led me conspiratorially, past the stuffed white bear in the hallway, to his studio. 'My Christ is not yet finished, but sufficiently advanced. You shall be the first to see it.'

We entered the cloistered silence of the studio and he drew the curtains to avoid reflections for the canvas was still wet. Christ was caught by the same light we had left outside. His foreshortened body – a startling feat of perspective – floated over the same early evening sky above the familiar formation of the rocks. There was even the same boat we had rowed in earlier, with two fishermen beside it with their nets, one of them derived from a drawing by Velázquez. The composition was inspired by a sixteenth-century sketch by a Carmelite friar after a vision; as T. S. Eliot stated: 'Great painters never borrow, they steal.'

'Finished or not,' Dali declared, 'I shall show it in London this winter.' And he did. The scandal it caused is baffling today; it was denounced as sacrilegious because the face of Christ was hidden, which was less offensive than having it replaced by Gala's. When the Glasgow Art Gallery had the courage to buy the *Crucifixion* the following year for £8,200, the highest price ever paid by the Gallery for a work of art, though a bargain by today's inflated prices, an uproar occurred as the directors were blamed for extravagance. A few years later, the painting was attacked physically by a vandal and needed restoration. Even today it is condemned by the art historians, Peter and Linda Murray, in their *Dictionary of Art and Artists* as 'crude sensationalism'.

At the time I was deeply moved, partly because I was the first to be privileged to see it in an atmosphere enhanced by two spotlights and the music of Bach played on Dali's American pick-up.

'My wish,' he told me, 'is that my Christ should be as beautiful as the God he is.'

It is never easy to praise a painting to the painter's face, but as we walked back to the golden evening light I told him: 'You must be very happy.'

'I am too happy!' he exclaimed. 'And the best thing is not to talk about it.' He touched wood and smiled at Gala who returned like a shadow.

As we left, Dali's obsession with death was revealed as he assured us that he was always afraid of it, even of accidents in trains, cars and boats. 'Otherwise,' he proclaimed defiantly, 'I do not think I will die. I am confident that before my time is up science will have found a way to prolong life. I have so much to do . . . Oh, so much to do!'

And now, as I write this, Dali is dying and might as well be dead, and perhaps he will be by the time this book is published. After the death of Gala he existed in a reclusion similar to that of Howard Hughes, no longer in his beloved Port Lligat but concealed in a twelfth-century castle. Following the fire which swept through his bedroom and left him with terrible burns, he emerged only after a delay of two days. In hospital it was discovered that he was suffering from malnutrition, weighing less than seven stone.

At the same time, rumours claimed that Dali, now in his mid-eighties, was the victim of the biggest art fraud in history, with his name forged on thousands of lithographs.

Poor Dali. He worked so hard at being a sacred monster, with all the requisite obsession, that his showmanship ultimately jeopardised his genius. Not content with being the great surrealist painter, he needed to perform surrealistically in public too, earning him the sobriquet of the 'Clown Prince of Fools' which, surprisingly, dismayed him. Yet he could hardly complain: he once gave a lecture in a diving suit, and almost collapsed from lack of air; in Rome he emerged from a white egg painted with cabalistic signs, announcing: 'I am reborn. I am born from the egg. It is a perfect cube.' In London he appeared in a dinner jacket decorated with eighty-eight liqueur glasses each of which was filled with crème de menthe with a dead fly floating on the top.

The critics found it difficult to reconcile such behaviour with an artist capable of religious feeling, which is one explanation for their hostility towards the *Crucifixion*. Outrageousness was bad enough, but the shrewd commercial instinct behind it was worse, coming from a showman who shocked the public with such films as *Un Chien Andalou*, designed jewellery which sold for fabulous figures, and revealed his fetishism of ants, crutches, excrement and limp watches in such paintings as *The Great Masturbator* and *Persistence of Memory*.

If Dali was guilty of commercialism, he paid for it dearly when he was too weak to control his life. A former secretary has cast doubt on the authenticity of many paintings, claiming that 'a local artist painted most of the Glasgow *Crucifixion*'. Having seen Dali's devotion to that picture as he worked on it, I am glad to nail that lie. The touch of another hand would be apparent, for one can *feel*, as well as see, if something is dishonest in a painting.

This was Dali's Christ: his landscape, his incomparable light.

A Tantrum in Majorca

ROBERT GRAVES

When I travelled to Majorca to photograph Robert Graves, I was accompanied by the writer Robert Kee.

This was the best of it for Kee was a sympathetic companion with a wry sense of humour and a formidable intelligence. While his fierce integrity was admirable, my delayed adolescence was offensive. I was a prig personified. Like many people who behave badly, I have always had an exaggerated sense of moral rectitude. At that time it surpassed the Torquemada.

Occasionally you feel an instant rapport with someone, but this can work in reverse. I travelled in eager anticipation of meeting the famous poet, author of *I, Claudius* but, though my camera relished him on sight, I mistrusted him with an instinctive antipathy. This was not mutual. I was too insignificant for Graves to bother with, and he was too happy posing for the camera, though there was one incident which remains puzzling. Graves lived in the north of the island but we drove into Palma for a lavish lunch and an afternoon's bullfight. Instead of allowing us to choose what we wanted, Graves ordered every dish for us in his self-appointed role of 'Elder' which I resented, not because *Picture Post* was paying but because he avoided every dish on the menu which had set my taste-buds watering.

In the lull between lunch and the bullfight, I explained that I wanted to buy a present for my parents, and Graves insisted – kindly, as it seemed – on leading me to a small shop in a backstreet with the assurance that this was the place for miraculous bargains. Sure enough, it was crowded to the ceiling with interesting stuff but, as my eyes wandered, Graves made up my mind for me: a pile of white, or whitish plates of different shapes and sizes, worse than the 'seconds' you can buy at a discount at source. I assumed that their failure to match was proof of their antique value, which Graves vouched for enthusiastically. Certainly they looked old, some of them stained and slightly chipped, and I bought them readily though startled by their cost in view of Graves's argument with the shopkeeper as, apparently, he beat him down. Consequently, I returned to England burdened by this extraordinary choice, and far from being pleased my mother was shocked by the waste of money and effort, recognising them at once for the rejects they were – valueless. Had Graves misled me deliberately as a form of punishment? I cannot remember, but assume this came after the day when I had my outburst.

My morning had started idyllically. At the simple lodging house where I was staying at Deyá, I had been served a breakfast of sizzling ham and eggs in the pan they were cooked in, eating them outside as the mountains started to smoulder. The heat was broken later by a swim after an energetic climb to the rocks below, followed by an exhausting return to the top with the compensation of a lazy, al fresco lunch with all the Graveses. Robert Graves conducted the conversation as usual and produced several sex magazines sent to him from England which he quoted from at length to the delight of everyone present except me. The others were convulsed in particular when he came to the readers' letters, many of which asked for advice on how to pursue their perversions.

Robert Graves

At the bullfight in Palma, with Robert Kee next to Graves

Some of the letters came from apparently respectable couples (probably invented by the editor) which showed a touching naïvety rivalling my own. Maybe this is why my humour deserted me.

I have smiled at countless such letters since; indeed, I wrote for *Men Only* and *Cosmopolitan* though *Forum* comes closer to the magazines that afternoon. That I was genuinely shocked reveals the peculiar state I was in, for their laughter was natural as I realise now.

The incident was described by Martin Seymour-Smith in his biography: *Robert Graves, His Life and Work*:

Farson at that time seemed unhappy and awkward in company, and could not stand up to the often outrageous Oxonian jokes which were made (though not so much by Graves) about his Cantabrian origins of which he felt, understandably, entirely innocent. On one occasion, at dinner under the stars at the Lluchalcari Hotel, after undergoing a preposterous barrage of in-jokes about the propensities of Cambridge men – the novelist Thomas Hinde and his wife, both Oxonians, were present – he banged the table and shouted impressively that he had never in his life encountered such intolerance, cruelty, lack of the ordinary decencies and so forth. He then silently munched nuts for over an hour.

It is interesting how memory can play tricks on one, for this is not how I remembered it. When I met Thomas Hinde and his wife at Hatchard's Author of the Year Reception in 1988 – a less swanky occasion than I had anticipated – they remembered the incident with good humour and implied that Seymour-Smith had been stirring everyone up with a mischievous relish. Certainly, I cannot remember the Oxford–Cambridge banter, though I agree that 'Graves and Kee [a pre-war Oxford graduate] got on very well together'. Also, I doubt whether you can munch nuts *silently* for an hour. Seymour-Smith continued:

> At the end of the meal Graves, who had been as amused as anyone else, took him [me] aside and pointed out that the chief culprit – the man who had been making most of the jokes [Smith himself?] did not fully mean them, and that Farson should not take them seriously, or as directed at him (as they had been). Kee said that he found this gesture moving and deeply courteous. Certainly it marks a capacity for kindness and tact in Graves which is sometimes ignored. Farson was comforted, and eventually became a popular entertainer.

That is not how the popular entertainer remembers it, though everyone was remarkably tolerant considering my effect on the feast which must have out-Banquoed Banquo.

The entire assignment ended ironically: Robert Kee resigned from *Picture Post* on another matter of conscience, and the feature had to be written at the last moment by Graves's daughter, Jenny Nicholson, who described her father as 'this Picasso among writers'. No one could fail to photograph that impressive head successfully, and the lavish spread looked good.

Back in London a few years later, I interviewed Robert Graves on film for *This Week*. The jinx recurred. It was one of those mornings when everything failed: the camera, the lights, the director's temper, while Graves waited with growing and understandable impatience. By the time we started, the possibility of any vestige of rapport had gone. Two days later, the film editor came to me in a state of exasperation. 'The man's so damned clever that nothing he says makes any sense. As soon as he gets going with one idea, he's off on another.' This was one of my few interviews to be scrapped – a lost opportunity.

Playing Pinball on Brighton Pier

NOËL COWARD

Invisibility was one of the advantages in working for *Picture Post*. Like a butler, I moved unnoticed through family quarrels as if I were oblivious instead of observant. Photographers were presumed to be illiterate, so no one gave a damn what they said in front of me in the certainty that nothing would be taken down against them. Unlike writers, we did not resign on principle.

Picture Post means nothing to young people today but for many it was a weekly treat – eighty stimulating pages for threepence. It was created in 1938 by a brilliant Hungarian refugee, Stefan Lorant. He made editorial decisions minutes before the magazine went to press and kept his staff in an agony of tension, but he had a genius in selecting pictures and for printing the crusading feature which could sway the conscience. This made it as worthwhile as *Life*. In 1940, Lorant was convinced that England would be invaded by the Germans who would torture him to death, so he left for America, to be replaced by Tom Hopkinson who proved a worthy successor until his disagreement with the proprietor, Sir Edward Hulton, over a story brought back from Korea by the writer James Cameron and the photographer Bert Hardy.

Years later, James Cameron told me of television's debt to the magazine: 'It was a natural transition, though at first it was assumed that as radio was only concerned with speech, TV news would only be a matter of pictures. It came as a blinding shock that anyone could produce words to go behind them, but we had been trained to appreciate pictures and were never allowed to get away with a sloppy text. We were ideally suited for the medium. *Picture Post* writers brought a literate approach to television that had never existed before, and when this happened TV journalism started to grow up.' He seemed unaware that I was the first member of *Picture Post* to make the transition. Charles Hewitt, better known as 'Slim', was another photographer to make the move, though his role was largely behind the camera.

I asked Cameron if the *Picture Post* writers were the élite of Fleet Street. 'Not better paid,' he said, 'but they had more personal liberty which gave them a feeling of confidence. And they were not just good with pictures, they were bloody good writers. At

Coward proved surprisingly free from personal vanity, allowing me full access to his dressing-room

John Deakin consults his light-meter while the Master waits rigidly, dressed in his costume as King Magnus in *The Apple Cart*. Afterwards, Coward said, 'Never let that man near me again.'

'I'm just reading *Present Indicative*,' I told him. 'That's right, dear boy,' Coward clipped his reply. 'You must keep abreast of the classics.'

the end, editors tried to gain circulation with cheesecake but we didn't want to know it on those terms. Hulton's loss was TV's gain.' The magazine closed in 1957.

Probably unaware that I had joined the magazine after his 'resignation', Cameron told me that the photographers were 'notoriously stupid and ill-informed', but we had the last laugh for the magazine depended on us, and we were so pampered that one writer protested to the editor: 'You treat the cameramen like . . . well, royal children!'

Noël Coward was an example of someone who clammed up when confronted by the writer, in this case Robert Muller, yet proved totally at ease when I photographed him in Brighton where he was rehearsing for *The Apple Cart*. Revealing no star temperament whatever, except when confronted by Muller, he posed uncomplainingly on the Sussex Downs, playing a pinball machine on the Pier, lying on top of Margaret Leighton on stage at a dress rehearsal, receiving his guests, Graham Greene and Laurence Harvey, in his dressing-room after the first night. The only time he lost his composure was sparked by Deakin's tipsy arrival off the Brighton Belle, shortly before the curtain went up. It was hardly a propitious moment, aggravated by Deakin's insistence on their having a mutual friend in West Africa, a relationship which Coward denied with increasing irritability as he waited for Deakin to 'get on with it'. After Deakin had staggered off stage, I heard the Master berate the public relations officer: 'Never let that man near me again.' The unfortunate publicist escorted Deakin from the wings as the curtain rose, whispering that he could watch the play from a box. 'No thanks.' Deakin swayed alarmingly. 'I'm taking Mr Farson to the theatre round the corner to see *Soldiers in Skirts*.'

When Coward was fussing with the back of his wig for the part of King Magnus, his dresser tut-tutted, 'It doesn't *matter*. It's only the behind.'

A spring afternoon on Brighton Pier, an unlikely ambience for the Master

'I'll have you know,' Coward retorted crisply, 'that in its day my behind has been much admired and *much* sought-after.'

Mr Muller was hardly privy to such remarks, not that Mr Muller could have printed them then. A fund of theatrical anecdote, Coward entertained me with numerous stories over the days I shadowed him, one of which pleases me still. I have not heard it since though there were echoes in Harwood's play *The Dresser*.

A Shakespearean company went on tour from the West End, employing members of the local reps for minor walk-on parts. In one town an aged actor was given the role of messenger with a single, yet crucial line announcing the fate of the King's Army – a battle won or a battle lost, I forget which – before the curtain fell for the interval.

The old man approached and bowed before the King. Total silence followed as he 'dried'.

'Methinks you have a message for me?' the King improvised nervously.

'I hast?' queried the old man.

'Thou *hast*, go find it,' cried the King, gesturing frantically towards the wings. The aged actor withdrew, the prompter whispered the line, the actor returned. Again a ghastly silence as he struggled to remember.

'Hast thou naught to tell me?' cried the King in desperation.

Speech returned to the aged actor at last as he shook his head. '*Naught*!' And the curtain fell.

In view of his consideration towards me, it might seem odd that I include Noël Coward as a sacred monster. However, there is nothing to disallow kindness in the breed though there can be ruthlessness too. Coward was a professional to his manicured fingertips. Once he agreed to be photographed for *Picture Post*, he was prepared to co-operate to the utmost, and, perhaps, he recognised a dedication in myself. Otherwise he possessed that self-certainty essential to sacred monsters. When Tynan interviewed him for *Panorama*, he asked about 'star quality'.

'I don't know what it is, but I know I've got it.'

One night when he was playing Garry Essendine in *Present Laughter*, he came to the scene where he turns on his friends, berating them for their ingratitude. This had gone badly throughout the tour prior to the West End opening, and in Cardiff he found he was playing to an audience of deaf-mutes who did not care. Seizing the moment to improvise, he marched to the footlights and screamed: 'I gave you my youth! Where is it now? Whistling down the wind! *Où sont les neiges d'antan? Ici!*' He jabbed at his temples and continued madly in a tirade of French and Italian, finally throwing himself on the floor, pounding it with his fists and sobbing, so even *that* audience was galvanised.

After the curtain came down, he raced to the wings and asked the stage-manager if he had written any of it down. 'Not a bloody word, so I dashed upstairs and typed away like bloody hell!'

The element of risk is true to the sacred monster. As Tynan concluded: 'Above all he has energy. Even the youngest of us will know, in fifty years' time, precisely what is meant by "a very Noël Coward sort of person".'

Rousting in Dublin

BRENDAN BEHAN

My only regret when I went to Dublin was having to leave it. I sought the advice of John Ryan, a sympathetic young man whose family owned the Moo-Cow milk bars in the city, and whose sister, Kathleen, starred with James Mason in *Odd Man Out*. Part of the lure of Dublin, which captivated me on sight, was the ease with which one met people like Ryan, in one of the numerous bars. It was a city small enough to walk through yet grand enough to be a capital. I liked the panache: the elegant wooden bars where you could pause for a Gaelic coffee or a Guinness, those identical twins, and then walk down Grafton Street after a breakfast of soda-bread and bacon and eggs. I welcomed the zest for life which the British disapproved of, except in Soho, with the charade of racing out to the city limits after closing time at night, for the bona fide.

I saw the house where my great-uncle, Bram Stoker, was born: 15 The Crescent, at Clontarf, on 8 November 1847, and the mansion where his brother, Sir Thornley, held his famous parties. Ely House in Ely Place was filled with priceless furniture, described by Oliver St John Gogarty as 'one of the few remaining palaces of the spacious eighteenth century which exist in Dublin without having fallen into decay . . . filled with Chippendale, Adam, silver candelabra [which] match the silver jambs of the door, silver linings of great fireplaces under mantels of Siena and statuary marble'.

Sir Thornley was a surgeon, lavishing his fees on his collection. The novelist George Moore would tilt a new chair and ask innocently, 'A cancer, Sir Thornley, or a gallstone?' Sir Thornley had a secret, exposed one night when the dining-room door burst open and a naked lady ran round the dinner table with the startling cry, 'I like a little intelligent conversation!' The guests stood up politely until two female attendants seized some napkins to cover her as best they could, and led her screaming from the room. According to Gogarty, Sir Thornley sat there with bowed head while his guests struggled with small conversation. At last he broke his silence, rising as he implored them to 'keep this incident, mortifying as it is to me, from any rumour of scandal in this most gossipy town'. He knew his Dubliners and he knew his friends. Turning to Moore, he said, 'I conjure you most particularly, as you are the only one who causes me misgivings.'

Brendan Behan

Moore rose to the occasion: 'But it was charming, Sir Thornley, can't we have an encore?'

I was running out of time and money and asked John Ryan if he could think of any subject in Dublin which might bamboozle the picture editor of *Picture Post* into letting me stay on. He had one, tentative idea – a personality known throughout Dublin, a former member of the IRA who tried to dynamite a British battleship at Cammel Laird's in Birkenhead, and a promising writer whose stories Ryan had published in his erudite, literary magazine.

'Who?' demanded Harry Deverson, when I phoned him.

'Brendan Behan.'

'Never heard of him.'

'That's the point,' I persevered. 'He's unknown outside Dublin. He paints houses and writes.'

'Oh.'

Unlike the writers, Deverson had no intellectual pretensions and he protected his photographers as fiercely as a mother hen. He was a Fleet Street veteran, balding, bespectacled, with an uneasy, lop-sided smile, constantly on the defensive. Though seemingly ill at ease in my presence, he had looked after me from the outset. He gave me permission to stay on, though he was hardly enthusiastic about this unknown Irishman. 'I suppose you need some money?' he sighed, knowing the answer. 'All right, we'll send it. Be lucky.'

Lucky indeed, for this respite gave me the chance to remain in Dublin and follow in the wake of Brendan Behan for the following week.

It was true that Brendan was unknown beyond the city, but he was a figure inside it. Fame had yet to strike him down: *The Quare Fellow* was produced at Stratford East by Joan Littlewood in 1956, and the publication of *Borstal Boy* followed two years later, but it was evident that he was going to be something rich and rare. The promise of fame lay ahead like an ambush.

The photographs I took have a poignancy because they show him at his happiest and most innocent: those pudgy fingers at the typewriter, a glass of Guinness beside him at the table in McDaid's. Spirits cost too much. He sang in pubs in the countryside and hills outside Dublin, in a full, fine voice, commanding the stage, brooking no opposition. They were vigorous joyful songs even if they were about the Irish Republican Army. Many were used in his later plays, such as 'The Old Triangle' which opened *The Quare Fellow*:

Brendan's time in prison encouraged him to write seriously

A hungry feeling came o'er me stealing
And the mice were squealing in my prison cell,
And that old triangle
Went jingle jangle,
Along the banks of the Royal Canal.

He saw humour in everything. When he went swimming at Sandycove, he pointed to the notice: *Forty foot Gentlemen Only*; and clowned as Quasimodo at the top of a steeple beside the bells. He played with barefoot children, occasionally dashing up a ladder to complete some painting in order to pay for the next succession of drinks. We visited the actors Michael MacLiamnóir and Hilton Edwards, whom I had last seen in Paris with Orson Welles, and went to the markets at dawn. He slept majestically in a deserted chapel and by the end of the week he was black-eyed and bruised after a fight, but with his zest for life intact. He was one of the life-enhancers, constantly proclaiming defiantly: *'Fuck the begrudgers!'*

Beatrice Behan told me, 'He could establish communication with people in a way that I never saw anybody else do.'

'Fuck the begrudgers!'

'He genuinely enjoyed
entertaining people, and he did it
because he wanted to do it, not
because he was a showman'
(Beatrice Behan)

This was the happiest period of his life, before the ambush of fame

I saw him again over the years. Fame had claimed him. His Roman Emperor's face crumpling and his body bloated, he was laid out on a sofa while a party cavorted around him, just able to raise a hand in the old familiar greeting, 'How's the heart?'

In 1958, the year when *The Hostage* was produced at Stratford East, I interviewed him for *This Week*. He was neither drunk, as he had been with Malcolm Muggeridge, nor wholly sober, but in the dreaded in-between though he did his best to entertain: 'Do I spend £10 a day on drink? I should think you need £10 a day in London. I'd like to drink something which doesn't give me a hangover but doesn't give profits to the capitalists. I'd like to be a rich Red. I like the money, but I don't fancy it otherwise – it doesn't suit me.'

Ironically, it was after his death that I understood him better, when I returned to Dublin to make a television film called *Brendan* for the BBC's *Omnibus*.

We were shown an old newsreel with Brendan leaning over a Dublin bridge talking of the execution of Caryl Chessman, and this was frightening. His face resembled sponge-rubber and his voice was barely intelligible, all the more frightening because he was sober. What had happened to him to reduce him to this state?

Behan's story is one of betrayal, made all the sadder because this was unintentional. One by one his props were taken away until alcohol was the one support he could rely on, apart from a few friendships. When he was sent to Borstal in 1939, after his bungled attempt to blow up the battleship in the Liverpool Docks, he was excommunicated by his church. His religion was denied him. In Borstal, he discovered that the British weren't so bad after all. C. A. Joyce, who was Governor at the time, told me: 'I think he expected a reciprocal hatred and it rather knocked him back when he found that people weren't hating him.' So his faith in his politics was shaken. Possibly more than that, for he spoke occasionally in drink of the young Merchant Navy sailor who was drowned in the war after his release: 'You know what I'd like to do, I'd like to swim down to the bottom of the sea-bed and give old Charlie a chew.' His sexuality was uncertain.

Though his life was spent in the company of men, sentenced to fourteen years in Mountjoy Prison in 1942 for the attempted murder of a policeman, released after five to continue his male confinement in public bars, it was controlled by women. His two remarkable grandmothers came first, Granny Furlong who was arrested at the age of seventy-seven for gun-running and served three years in an English prison, and the unfortunately named Granny English who owned the slum property where the Behans lived rent-free. She was not an invalid but she spent the day in bed with her bald son beside her, receiving the tenants who came to pay their respects – and, more importantly, their rent. This curious bedridden existence was broken when she indulged in her favourite pastime of attending funerals, taking Brendan with her to the wake afterwards. Once, as they staggered home, an acquaintance stopped her and pointed to the boy. 'What a shame, such a beautiful child and him deformed.'

Granny English straightened up indignantly. 'He's not deformed,' she replied, 'he's drunk.' Brendan was six years old when he acquired his thirst.

When I made the television film, I asked his mother Kathleen if she had protested.

'Oh, you daren't,' she said hastily.

'Why not?'

'No. I could not.' I was prepared to leave it at that. The director, Richard Marquand, beckoned me into the next room and told me that I had to press her further. He was right, she was being evasive.

'I'm sorry, I don't understand. Why not?' I persisted, when we continued.

'I wouldn't like to fall out with her, now would I?'

'Even if she was turning Brendan into a drunkard, when he was only a child?'

'It wouldn't have stopped her. You couldn't have stopped her.'

'Was it because she had the money and held the purse strings?' I asked, cruelly. There was a pause and then the whispered answer: 'Yes.'

Then there was Joan Littlewood who presented *The Quare Fellow* at her Theatre Royal, Stratford East, on 24 May 1956. Unlike most of her productions, this was a straightforward presentation of a powerful play and it succeeded triumphantly. I suspect that this was one of the happiest moments of Brendan's life, before success turned sour. Then there came *The Hostage*. As I shall relate, Joan Littlewood loved the theatre with genuine passion but had little time for the written word. With *The Hostage*, she served up Brendan's play with all the trimmings and the hurly-burly of British music hall. Brendan, who was more intelligent than he contrived to appear, writing poetry in Gaelic and translating Marlowe, was wounded by this travesty as he told me in the pub opposite the theatre. He looked bereft and, allegedly, was unhappy with the frolics on stage on the first night. Conversely, when the West End production was flagging, he did his best to revive it by appearing drunk on BBC Television with Malcolm Muggeridge, and then by joining the actors on stage to indulge in a few boisterous frolics of his own, an interruption which delighted the audience and the box office where the receipts rose at once.

There are two ways of looking at this. Either Joan Littlewood tampered with a serious play and broke his heart, though hearts seldom break that hastily, or she transformed his untidy manuscript into such an unusual entertainment that her gusto gave it the huge, international success which followed. Whichever was the case, he lost something of himself in the process, while being forced further into the role of attendant fool.

What hurt him more was Joan's refusal to produce his last play, *Richard's Cork Leg*. With such dialogue as:

> ROSE: She's around behind.
> MARIA: I know she has, but where is she?

it is hard to fault her decision, but this time Brendan was denied even the hope of a box office, bowdlerised hit.

The next deprivation came with the books. Rae Jeffs, the publicist of Hutchinson's, sacrificed her career when she resigned to help Brendan with his final work, copying it meticulously from the tape-recorder. This was pure devotion, though fatal for him. No longer did those pudgy fingers *have* to press the keys, no physical exertion was needed, even his ramblings could be edited. No discipline was required. Conversely, it can be argued that the discipline had gone already and that if the books had not been taped they would never have been published.

Loyal to the end, Rae Jeffs described his deterioration to me. 'The last time I saw him I would not really have recognised him from the man I first met, and that was awful to watch. Brendan was a sensitive enough person to know that he was getting to the stage where he was having these imaginary conversations – I think he must have felt that his brain was going. He was not a fool, you know. No, Brendan knew he'd lost the power of conversation and also knew that his brain had these funny lapses. He was terrified of being committed.' When asked about the 'imaginary' conversations, she described how he sat in the lobby of the Hotel Chelsea in New York, a well-known death-trap for artistic folk, appearing to talk to people when there was no one there. 'He was leaning forward and offering someone a cigarette – which was very disturbing.'

When he woke in a New York hospital he was terrified that this was an asylum and discharged himself. A similar incident occurred in London when he left a hospital and stumbled, literally, into a home for alcoholics on a Sunday afternoon when the pubs had closed. Some saw this as good luck, but I believe it helped to kill him for he was subjected to the merciless antabuse treatment which makes the patient excruciatingly sick if he resorts to alcohol. The doses are increased over the following days until he begs the doctor never to show him alcohol again. It is a cure that pushes a man to the edge. Rae Jeffs told me that she brought him the reviews of *Brendan Behan's Other Island* but when they were alone he admitted that he was unable to read them. 'It's hard to say if the cure was responsible, but some pressure on the brain had affected his eyesight causing double-vision.' He discharged himself again and travelled to the vineyards in the south of France for the antidote.

When I asked how she felt about his deterioration, she said she thought she was facing the saddest man in Europe. 'Awful, because you can't really help an alcoholic. Brendan would say, "One drink is too many for me and a thousand not enough." He was a weak man and people would come up and say, "Come on, Brendan, have a drink," and I would keep on thinking of that remark of his, "One drink is too many . . . "'

'Was he a lonely man?'

'Very, very. I don't think anybody ever knew the complete Brendan.'

'Did he?'

'No, I don't think so.'

'Was the need to surround himself with company due to loneliness?'

'He needed the touch of human beings more than most of us. He was very frightened of the dark. That great remark, "I am a daylight atheist," was significant. He would never have any doors shut. He hated the night.'

Perhaps that is why he spent most of the day in bed towards the end, rising around ten o'clock at night in order to venture into the darkness rather than be left alone. Sometimes he would disappear for days. His beautiful wife Beatrice told me of one Sunday evening when he returned: 'The radio was on and we were all listening to it and they had a very good record of him singing "The Old Triangle", and he sat down and listened to it, and I suppose he was well jarred, but the tears poured down his face. He said, "Is that me singing?" I said, "Yes Brendan, it is." And the tears came out, you know, as much as to say, "This was me, and this is me . . . "'

He was barred from every pub in their respectable, residential neighbourhood in Dublin, except for one at the bottom of the road where he had an understanding. 'He was allowed to go in and sit down and ring for a taxi – our phone was cut off because he used such bad language on it (his obscenities were a part of his everyday speech) – and he was allowed to buy a drink for anyone on condition he was never served himself. Of course he got round this by going in with three people, ordering three drinks, drinking them all himself and going out again.'

Brendan was found on New Year's Eve in 1963 with his head gashed, covered in blood outside his mother's house. 'A man was going home from a party,' said Beatrice, 'and saw this bundle on the road and drove over to examine it.' Luckily it was someone Brendan had been kind to in the old days, one of the many, and he took him to hospital. No one knows what had happened.

After that he gave up, the golden tongue became inarticulate, the drinking was no longer a relief. 'He kept on drinking because he felt he was dying,' said Beatrice, 'and the drink just kept him going. He felt that if he lay down and went to bed that was the finish of it. Which is really what happened when he went into hospital again – he was only there ten days and he died.' On 20 March 1964.

At the funeral in Glasnevin Cemetery, his coffin, draped with the Tricolour, was borne shoulder-high by his former companions in the IRA, and a boy bugler from the Fianna sounded the Last Post. Though I am certain he would have condemned the terrorism of the IRA today, their loyalty to him cannot be denied. 'These were the people he went to in the last sad days,' Beatrice told me. 'They were the people he drank with, and ultimately they were the people who counted. No matter how outrageous or revolting he was, they would never walk away from him as most of the people who had wined and dined with him would. But then they were his own people, from the north side, working class. He didn't expect anything from anybody else.'

The tributes flowed. 'Brendan Behan was amiable and kind,' said Sean O'Casey. 'He had no bitterness or venom or literary jealousy. Had he lived another ten years he would have written more and perhaps better. It was horrible to think of a man of Behan's age dying, particularly when he had so much to offer.'

Joan Littlewood agreed. 'He squandered his life and his genius, but he took the world out on a spree.' She attended the funeral with the playwright, Frank Norman, who was told by Brendan's brothers, 'Yous'll always find a welcome in Dublin – you're the only ones to come over to pay your last respects. Sure, there wasn't even a wreath from the West End theatre or anyone else in England who made their fortune from Brendan's writing.'

So this is a story with a tragic ending. Not really. Rory Furlong, Brendan's half-brother, told me of his own feelings. 'Just his poem to Oscar Wilde, that's enough as far as I'm concerned to make a life worth living. If you think of his generosity and kindness to the old ladies in the market early in the morning, isn't that enough to make life worth-while?'

Don't ask too much of sacred monsters. It is enough if they leave a trail of pure delight behind them. Brendan's output was limited, but many a writer lives too long and writes too much. *Twenty Years A'Growing* by his fellow Irishman Maurice O'Sullivan is a masterpiece, compared by E. M. Forster to the freshness of the egg of a seabird, 'lovely, perfect and laid this very morning', but I doubt if he wrote anything else. *Borstal Boy* retains a similar freshness. Ken Tynan said, 'If the English hoard words like misers, the Irish spend them like sailors. Behan sends language out on a swaggering spree, ribald, flushed and spoiling for a fight.'

Brendan's remarkable wife told me she remembered him as 'the most entertaining man I have ever met. It was the fun and the jokes. It didn't matter where you were, he had this tremendous feeling for people. He could establish communication in a way I never saw anybody else do. He had a real feeling for people, lame, sick, rich or poor. This was a great gift he had.'

She said two things I shall always remember. When I asked why she stayed with him at the end, she replied simply, 'Fighting is better than loneliness.' And when Brendan was dying and told her the worst thing she had done was to marry him, she thought of the best of times, of their travels and the Blasket Islands off Dingle which he had celebrated in verse, and she replied, 'No, we had the *two* days.'

Life could not have been placid for Brendan. As a life-enhancer, he enriched others if not always himself. Like many a sacred monster he had the last laugh. He prophesied: 'I'll never live to see forty.'

'But you see,' said Beatrice, 'he lived till he was forty-one, so he cheated death by a year.' But it was far too soon.

A Summons to Arlington House
LORD BEAVERBROOK

Picture Post was running downhill and after two invigorating years I was included in the latest purge. Perhaps it would be more honest to say that I was sacked. By chance, Deakin had been in the editorial offices the day before, submitting some project which ultimately came to grief, and he was full of mischief when I met him in the Bunch of Grapes off Brompton Road on Saturday morning. Fortified with his first drink of the day, he informed me gloatingly, 'The editor was most impressed by me, but we had a few words to say about you.' Without comment, I handed him the letter I had just received. 'Oh my God!'

In those days you accepted the sack as part of life. There was no industrial tribunal to run to, no compensation or handshake. The lack of any such safety-net meant that you had to do your utmost in your job at all times and I am sure my dismissal was deserved. Soho was claiming too much of me.

I missed the security over the next two years, even more the back-up provided by Harry Deverson and the boys in the darkroom such as David Steen and Peter Bolton, both highly successful photographers in their own right today. Without them, I drifted.

First I was apprenticed to Baron Studios, following in the footsteps of Antony Arm-strong-Jones (now Lord Snowdon) but, though I liked the ebullient Baron personally, the set-up was too Mayfair posh and stiff for me and I moved to the Central Office of Information which proved even stiffer though far less posh. I struggled as a freelance, helped by Jane Stockwood, the features editor of *Harper's Bazaar*, which led to the commission from American *Harper's*, the most élite of all, to accompany Ken Tynan to photograph Burton and Bloom at the Edinburgh Festival.

My flourish as a photographer was starting to wilt. My Rollei was constantly in pawn. At least I had been given the chance to stretch a talent I did not know I possessed, but it was time to close that period of my life and I joined the British Merchant Navy and sailed round the world washing dishes on the S.S.*Orcades*.

I returned to writing. Though I remained a freelance, I was given my own place at the features desk on the *Evening Standard* among such lively personalities as Milton

Shulman, Alan Brien and Kenneth Allsop, with whom I frequently met up at lunchtime in the Cock Tavern in Fleet Street. Once again, life was full of interest, and I was asked to write an entire series on 'The Crisis in the Book Trade' which caused a fleeting stir because publishers tend to be prima donnas and yearn to see their names in print. Dozens of letters were sent to the editor, most of them attacking me.

One morning I was woken by a phone call from the deputy editor, Charles Wintour, who always seemed more powerful than the editor himself. 'Lord Beaverbrook would like to see you at Arlington House this afternoon at two-thirty.' I wanted to ask what madness this was, but he rang off abruptly.

Lord Beaverbrook! There was a sacred monster if ever there was one, but why did he wish to see me? In a state of nervous anticipation, I was punctual for once and shown into an attractive penthouse overlooking Green Park. There were three jars of honey with labels marked 'Lord Beaverbrook' on a table, and I was about to look at some papers beside them when Beaverbrook entered the hall, showing out his luncheon guest, a large man who puffed complacently at a big cigar.

This was a big moment for me. In the snakes-and-ladders of Fleet Street, a summons to Arlington House was a legendary move and other ambitious young journalists had emerged before me to be groomed as potential editors.

'Thank you so much for coming here,' said Beaverbrook in a strong Canadian accent. I murmured that it was a great pleasure. He was older and tinier than I expected, yet curiously sexual. His eyes were weak, but commanding, he had a deep suntan. He was intimate yet remote – alarming, like a malevolent pixie.

'And how long have you been on the staff of the *Express*?'

My heart sank, there had been a mistake. I explained that I was a freelance for the *Standard*.

'Yes, yes, quite so, that's what I meant.' He sounded irritated. He asked if I was married. I said I was not and felt as if I were covered in thick Max Factor make-up. The interrogation continued.

'Do you write every day?' I replied that I did.

'Do you work hard?' I heard myself reply, 'Yes, but not as hard as you do,' but he did not seem displeased by such archness.

'Do you intend making journalism your career?'

'I certainly intend making writing my career,' I countered with insufferable pretension.

He asked more questions and I mentioned the articles I had written for the *Standard* – 'Around the World with a Dishcloth', and my series on the book trade.

'How much are they paying you?' I told him the amount.

'For each article or the whole series?'

'For each article,' I replied with astonishment. He was certainly out of touch with current rates. Then we came to my father. 'Gifted man,' said Beaverbrook, 'doesn't work hard enough.'

I remembered the hours of struggle in the greyness of the early morning, the dozens of pages crunched up in balls in the waste-paper basket, the thousands of articles he had written, the books published. I flushed in his defence and replied that my father had been working exceptionally hard on his new book.

'Is it hot outside?' asked Beaverbrook, who could hardly be described as a good listener. I thought it was but, when his valet brought him a light overcoat and he led the way to his roof garden, he found it far from hot and demanded another overcoat, sinking into a deckchair peevishly, with two overcoats, a rug, and a peaked cap. As he looked as if he was going to doze off, I seized my chance, telling him what a relief it was to work for such a professional paper. He beamed, he chuckled, the rapport established at last. 'No, not every paper is professional, Mr Farson.' Then he caught sight of the shark tattooed on my left hand in Honolulu and stared at it intently, for nearly a minute.

'Thank you for coming to see me,' he concluded. 'I've liked what I've seen. What I've seen is good. I shall speak to the editor about you.' Calling for his valet, he said, 'Look after Mr Farson, James, I want you to look after him.' For a moment I thought I might receive a gift, a signed photograph or a jar of honey, but I was shown the door. Probably he did speak to the editor. A couple of days later, Charles Wintour asked me if I would mind vacating my place at the features desk. He was so polite I hardly realised that I had been given the sack, again.

THE ANGRY YOUNG MEN

There is doubt over the origin of the phrase 'Angry Young Men'. I cannot claim the credit for this, which should go to George Fearon, the press officer of the Royal Court Theatre which produced *Look Back in Anger*, and to John Osborne himself, but I brought the group together. Like most labels it was misleading – you could not have wished for a friendlier lot – but newspapers yearned for colourful people to write about in the drabness of the mid-1950s. I happened to know them, as Harry Ritchie has acknowledged in *Success Stories*: 'Struck by Osborne's new reputation and Colin Wilson's spectacular reception, a young freelance journalist, Daniel Farson, decided to write about the latest young writers. In two features published in the *Daily Mail* on 12 and 13 July [1956], Farson announced that literature's "Post-War Generation" had suddenly emerged. It was a classic example of a journalist being in the right place at the right time; Farson had already developed a friendship with Colin Wilson after happening to meet him the day *The Outsider* was first acclaimed, and had just written his feature on Amis for the *Evening Standard* ("The Crisis in the Book Trade", 4 May).'

Six Beers in Swansea

KINGSLEY AMIS

'Look!' said Kingsley Amis. 'There are llamas on the mountains!'

I peered through the lace curtains and sure enough three llamas and two elephants were heading up the street towards a mountain in the distance. This was my fourth hour in Swansea, hardly a pretty town but the home of the new humorous novelist, Kingsley Amis. He was waiting for me at the station barrier and hurried me to the buffet where he had abandoned half a drink (gin and French) and a friend (Dr Bartley, a colleague at the university where he lectured in English literature).

Dr Bartley wanted to remove a curiously shaped vase from the counter. 'It would look marvellous filled with green chartreuse,' he enthused. Amis explained that on Thursdays they always drank green chartreuse.

We lunched at a pub nearby. 'It's an odd day, sir,' said the barman. I agreed. While lecturer A. ordered two sherries and a stout, lecturer B. leaned across confidentially: 'We're awfully lucky to have this young man with us, but of course I disagree with everything he stands for.' We ordered a bottle of red wine. After lunch we had two rounds of port and then proceeded to Dr Bartlett's home, armed with a bottle of whisky. In those days, I hardly drank and thought the llamas were a momentary illusion until a small boy lifted up the window, climbed through it and told me that the animals were part of a travelling circus. 'Thank God for that,' I replied.

'Have a potion,' said his father, advancing with a bottle.

'Thanks,' I said, 'but better not.' I remembered with alarm that I had not asked a single question. 'My train leaves at five,' I added.

'Nonsense,' said Kingsley Amis, 'stay the night at my place.'

When we arrived at his home it was late afternoon. He showed me to a small room with a sloping roof and pointed to a bed. 'Flannel sheets,' he announced, and disappeared.

I woke with a sudden start – it could have been an hour later. Beside me in the gloom stood an extremely attractive blonde. We looked at each other with surprise and she departed. All I need, I thought, is to set fire to the flannel sheets to become the complete

'Look, there are llamas on the mountains!'

Amis anti-hero, reviled so curiously by Somerset Maugham after *Lucky Jim* won the Maugham Award which encouraged young writers to travel: 'Mr Amis is so talented, his observation so keen, that you cannot fail to be convinced that the young men he so brilliantly describes truly represent the class with which his novel is concerned,' Maugham had started deceptively in the *Sunday Times*' 'Books of the Year' column the previous Christmas. Then he had put the boot in: 'They do not go to university to acquire culture, but to get a job . . . They have no manners . . . Their idea of a celebration is to go to a public house and drink six beers. They are mean, malicious and envious. Charity, kindliness, generosity, are qualities which they hold in contempt. They are scum.'

I wondered, what would Willie make of me now, tucked up with a hangover in flannel sheets? Six beers, indeed! What about the green chartreuse?

Amis referred to Dixon as an 'anti-chap', unknown in Maugham's youth, and by attacking him so violently Maugham had drawn attention to the book which became a bestseller in its first year in Britain though it flopped in the States. Amis had started something – he had given seediness a good name.

'What does it feel like to be the founder of a movement?' I asked him at dinner as we ate under-cooked pork chops and frozen peas under a forest of laundry in the kitchen.

'I still can't believe it's happening to us. I used to snatch at three guineas for a poem; now we get two-figure, even three-figure cheques.' With no private income of his own, he explained the difference *Lucky Jim* had made. 'Born 1922, middle-class background and grammar school stuff. I won a scholarship to Oxford in '41, war service as a lieutenant in the Royal Corps of Signals, back to Oxford in '45 and married '46.' His wife, Hilary, or Hilly as he called her, was the beautiful girl I had seen standing by my bed. 'From Oxford to Swansea at £450 a year with a yearly increase of £50 and children's allowances. We were pretty well on our uppers, when we had another kid we were desperate. Only in the last eighteen months have we lived as well as we want.'

The thought of this prompted a move before closing time. So we said goodnight to the two boys, Martin, eight and a half who spoke with a Welsh lilt and said his favourite book was the 'Bi-bel', and Philip, seven and a half. Their baby sister slept in a cot upstairs.

'Let's go for a walk.' On the way he pulled a Dylan Thomas face as he imitated the deafening climax to a Dylan Thomas lecture delivered on an unfortunate visit to Swansea.

Like Brendan Behan when I photographed him in Dublin, all was promise as we hurried into his local for 'six beers'.

Kingsley Amis being interviewed by Martin Amis in Swansea

A Shock in Sloane Square

JOHN OSBORNE

'In the theatre,' I wrote in the *Mail*, 'this cynical post-war type is exemplified by John Osborne's *angry young man* Jimmy Porter,' possibly the first time that the phrase had been printed. 'Who is John Osborne? He is twenty-six and was a struggling, unsuccessful actor. "For the past two years," he told me, "I lived on £2 a week. The Labour Exchange knew me so well it was like my club."'

He wrote *Look Back in Anger* in three and a half weeks and the managements returned it with rude letters or did not reply. When he had given up hope it was accepted by the Royal Court Theatre where it shocked audiences to such an extent that many people left in disgust.

'Why has your play caused such controversy?' I asked.

'It's about real people and audiences aren't used to seeing that. It's so fashionable to be indifferent to human beings nowadays. I hate the smart people at cocktail parties who do nothing and stand there destroying things.'

The play was not an instant success. Ken Tynan lifted the flagging spirits of all concerned with the famous conclusion to his review in the *Observer*: 'I doubt if I could love anyone who did not wish to see *Look Back in Anger*. It is the best young play of its decade.' Yet it was not until extracts were shown on the powerful new medium of television that the play took off.

I admired Osborne's astringency, interviewing him later on television when he spoke scathingly on the debutantes' ball, but we did not become friends as I should have liked. I introduced Colin Wilson to Kingsley Amis over a gloomy lunch in a Leicester Square pub opposite the statue of Sir Henry Irving, and mentioned that *Look Back in Anger* had been described as 'an Amis sort of play'.

'I'm astonished,' said Amis. 'I don't like glum chums. Amis likes laughing. I'm sick of all these people who claim to be more mixed-up than the next man.' He looked at the statue of 'old nonsense' and downed his beer. 'Amis is very keen on human qualities. Amis likes love and affection.'

I took Colin to the Royal Court and heard him fuming in the darkness: 'If I was in the

John Osborne outside the Royal Court Theatre in Sloane Square

same room as that insufferable Jimmy Porter I'd give him a jolly good kick in the pants. I'm sick of mixed-up kids.'

I invited John Osborne and Mary Ure to a wild party at Wilson's room in Chepstow Villas where the word 'genius' was passed around like Kleenex. Mary Ure, who was playing Alison in *Anger* and married the playwright the following year, burst into tears when Colin spoke dismissively of the play, proclaiming loyally that Osborne was the greatest playwright since Sheridan. The young playwright Michael Hastings was sick in a corner, muttering, 'Hastings, Hastings, not a good enough name for a genius,' and Osborne surveyed the scene with sly detachment.

In spite of my bracketing them together, the Angry Young Men had little in common, and each survived because of his individual talent. At the time, however, they benefited from the label for this was the last time that writers were celebrated in Britain as if they were the pop-stars of today.

Colin Wilson in particular was taken up and momentarily destroyed by the media when they tired of him, and I played a shabby part in that process.

A Horsewhip in Bayswater

COLIN WILSON

It was a Saturday afternoon in May – the same month that *Look Back in Anger* had opened at the Royal Court – that I met Colin Wilson for the first time, in David Archer's Soho bookshop. I showed him the *Evening News* which contained the first review of his book *The Outsider*: 'At twenty-four Mr Wilson steps immediately into the ranks of major writers.' It was a happy beginning to a friendship. On Sunday, *The Outsider* was acclaimed by the two leading critics in England: Philip Toynbee for the *Observer*, and Cyril Connolly, who wrote in the *Sunday Times*, 'This is one of the most remarkable books I have read for a long time.' On Monday Colin was famous.

Without a full-time job of my own, I witnessed the 'celebrity' treatment he received and shared it vicariously, meeting him daily at Chepstow Villas in a house which threatened to collapse at any moment. As I entered his chaotic room, my stomach heaved at the sight of the horrid, dented saucepan brimming with stale, left-over grease in which he cooked sausages and mushrooms over a vicious primus ring. A shaky table was covered by a plastic cloth littered with unwashed plates and chocolate biscuits, now to be replaced by bottles of vintage wine and long-playing records. An Einstein quotation was scribbled on the wall next to a pin-up of Nietzsche and various loony-looking girls wandered in and out enigmatically. It was a sort of intellectual, boy-scout Bohemia which I thought my life had by-passed, and I listened cross-legged and happy as Colin expounded brilliantly on subjects I only half-understood.

In retrospect, my series in the *Mail* was perceptive – I even referred to the 'great contemporary influence of Francis Bacon', still comparatively unknown at the time – and described Colin, under the heading I MEET A GENIUS WITH INDIGESTION, as 'that rare person, a man with vision. He has enthusiasm for the future and a determination to help in shaping it.'

'What is an Outsider?' I asked him.

'We're technically too rich. We've moved too far from life. The Outsider is the frustrated creator in conflict with a civilisation that has become too complex.'

'What advice do you give to the post-war generation?'

'Discipline. You must have self-discipline.'

He has remained true to this philosophy, that we are capable of stretching ourselves beyond the limits we accept. As recently as April 1988, he confirmed this belief in the *Literary Review*: 'I have always felt strongly that the basic problem of human beings is the sheer *triviality* in which we are entangled,' making the point that it was 'an incredible piece of irony that the success of the book dumped me in the same wagon as Amis, Wain, Osborne, Tynan, Sillitoe and the rest'. As for Tynan, 'He spent his life chasing after the "famous", worshipping success and preaching a rather muddled sort of Marxist collectivism. *The Outsider* was literally horrifying to him. It represented a condemnation of everything he stood for.'

Meanwhile, Colin was famous himself and manna to the media, photographed by *Life* in a sleeping bag on Hampstead Heath where he stayed when he cycled from Leicester to London at the age of sixteen. This image was reconstructed, and you could see from the cover that he was reading one of my father's books.

As Ken Allsop related in his book *The Angry Decade*, I introduced Colin to my father when we drove to North Devon in Ken's open sports car. Not only was there an instant rapport, they became genuinely fond of each other and I was proud of them both though frequently surprised by Colin's naïvety. Pointing to a pitiable, dying rabbit, Ken remarked, 'Myxomatosis.' 'What's that?' asked Colin. On a subsequent visit, my father announced that he wanted a drink, and though he knew of my father's alcoholism Colin hurried upstairs to his bedroom and returned with a bottle of brandy. 'You may be a genius,' sighed my mother, 'but my God you're a bloody fool.'

The newspapers loved Colin. The image was ideal; he was instantly recognisable with his spectacles and polo-neck sweater. The copy he provided was entertaining and hit the front pages the following February when his girlfriend's father burst into a dinner party brandishing a horsewhip as he uttered the cry, 'Wilson! The game is up. You're a homosexual with six mistresses!' Concerned for his daughter's welfare, for Colin was separated from his wife and child, John Stewart had discovered a journal which he assumed was Colin's private diary. In fact they were highly salacious notes for his novel on a sexual psychopath, published later as *Ritual in the Dark*. While Colin rolled on the floor with laughter, a fellow guest, Gerald Hamilton (the original Mr Norris in Isherwood's novel), sneaked out and phoned the press. A genius and an irate father with a horsewhip! What editor could ask for more? The newspapers interviewed the weeping parent who explained: 'I went with a horsewhip to drag her home. Neither her mother nor I could reason with her and I wanted to teach Colin a lesson. She thinks he is a genius.'

Colin and Joy fled to my parents' home in North Devon but the press pursued them and they were photographed for the front page of the *Express*: 'Tousle-haired Colin Wilson, 25-year-old author of *The Outsider*, moved into a new hide-out last night with his girlfriend, Joy Stewart. Soon after dawn they waved goodbye to author Negley Farson and wife Eve, at whose home they stayed the last two nights. And their second "flight" in three days was on.'

Finally Colin made an exclusive deal with the *Express* and moved to Ireland.

The poloneck sweater and glasses were the boy genius's manna to the media

Characteristically, he thought it only fair to give extracts from his journal to the *Mail*, which was naïve, for these looked less hilarious in newsprint.

Then it all went sour. This was partly due to Colin's belief that he could use the publicity to his advantage, unaware that it was using him. Daphne du Maurier warned him that he would not receive a good review for the next ten years, and Victor Gollancz, who published both my father and Colin, urged him not to publish a word for the next three years. Privately, he wrote to my father:

> I'm desperately worried about Colin. Ever since the first big success, I've been trying – with a really tremendous expenditure of time and energy – to save him from a disastrous future: but he has defeated me. I am fond of him,

and still believe in him: but the trouble is that he has got into such a financial mess that he just can't wait until he has something really important to say, but must go dashing off and writing the first thing that comes into his head . . . you know, better than most, how important the long crystallising, simmering process is.

These were the words of a devoted publisher, but Gollancz had a shrewd commercial instinct and found himself in a maddening dilemma. Colin was a bestseller. Though Colin protested in his review of *Success Stories* that *The Outsider* raised his income that year 'to about that of a 1950's bank manager', he admits that it sold 40,000 copies. Gollancz had no wish to lose such a profitable author but he detested the manuscript of *Ritual in the Dark*, writing to my father again:

> It is a horribly nasty book – indeed, I should go so far as to call it a foul book – and one that I would not dream of publishing in any ordinary case. [However, another publisher was eager to do so.] The trouble is that I shall have unquiet nights anyhow, with the prospect, in the one event, of having to publish so nasty a book and, on the other, of depriving Colin of what might turn out to be thousands of pounds.

Scrupulously fair to Colin, he conceded:

> For all this, it has a great deal of merit – a strong narrative gift, the power to evoke excitement (of an exceedingly unpleasant kind) and a kind of desperate, if adolescent sincerity. Moreover, the basic idea – that even a multiple murderer is seeking to enhance life – is a horribly perverted form of truth.
>
> Any unprejudiced person reading this book could have no doubt of Colin's ultimate possibilities . . .

In the end, Victor Gollancz's commercialism conquered and he published *Ritual*.

My series in the *Mail* launched me on a new phase as a television interviewer and Colin was my first subject in a short film made for *This Week* which I scripted myself. In the *Sketch* the next morning, under the headline 'COLIN (I'M A GENIUS) WILSON GIVES ME A PAIN', Herbert Kretzmer continued, 'He admitted he might be a genius. "Every writer works under that assumption," he claimed – a fact that will be received with certain surprise by dozens of writers with a more humble approach to their craft.' Kretzmer concluded with a reference to Colin answering the telephone – 'Colin Wilson speaking': 'I would have given a lot to hear a voice replying, "So what!"'

Unaware of the damage it might be causing him, I was thrilled, but Colin's constant proclamation of his genius started to grate and, when I chaired a live discussion on Shakespeare between Colin and Wolf Mankowitz, the latter did not conceal his dislike. 'Why do you feel such animosity towards me?' asked Colin beforehand. 'Because you're such a damned bad writer,' Wolf replied. After the discussion, Mankowitz was so furious that he refused to speak to Colin, ridiculing him later at a symposium held at the Royal Court when Colin described the bard as a 'thoroughly second-rate mind'. Inevitably, people took offence though Peter Simple retaliated with wit:

> Shakespeare, Mr Wilson notes,
> Was a hack who churned out quotes.
> Poor old Will, he never tried a
> Method used in *The Outsider*;
> Though his plots might be on loan,
> His quotations were his own.

Colin was the target for malicious envy, having achieved so much so soon, but at times he asked for it. Gate-crashing a dressing-room party on the first night of *A View from the Bridge*, he informed Olivier that he was writing a play for him, and told me there was someone there 'called Monroe – I didn't think much of her'.

Previously, we had lunched in Sloane Square with George Devine, the charming and intelligent director of the Royal Court, and Colin left with the impression that he had been commissioned to write a play for him, which he delivered several months later. After two months' silence, *The Death of God* was returned with a mere rejection slip which was inconsiderate, but Colin wrote an irate letter to Devine which was understandable except that he sent copies to the press. 'I am a busy writer with a great deal to do and you know that I regarded the play as practically commissioned by you. It looks as if the Royal Court has lowered its standards all round. You were certainly under no obligation to accept my play, but you were clearly under an obligation to give me a full account of its faults.' He continued, stressing that he was not complaining on his own behalf but for several playwrights who had been treated shabbily, including Michael Hastings, Sandy Wilson, and his friend Stuart Holroyd. Woken in the middle of the night by the *Daily Express* for his reaction, Ronald Duncan, who was on the board of directors, replied, 'The play was bad. It was all argument and no drama. Mr Wilson cannot understand why we have not accepted him as the new Bernard Shaw he regards himself to be. What he should really be is a publicity man for a detergent firm.' Such was Colin's charm and innate good nature that they became close friends, but the publicity was damaging with Colin being retitled as a 'petulant' rather than an angry young man.

His friends were alarmed. Kenneth Allsop predicted: 'Ever since *The Outsider* appeared . . . there has been an ominously growing ambush awaiting Colin Wilson's next book . . . The rotten eggs may be about to fly about his shaggy head.'

This was where I played a vile part in his downfall. Colin had irritated with such boastful statements as 'The day must come when I'm hailed as a major prophet' which were said half-humorously but taken literally, and I failed to realise their effect in print when I recorded an interview on my new Vortexion tape-recorder when we stayed in the twin-bedded annexe at my parents' home in North Devon.

'You have said you want to be an atomic bomb on the minds of our time. What is your philosophy?'

Answer: 'You can only define a philosophy in relation to the climate of thought in its own time. Now, as far as I'm concerned our civilisation is an appalling, stinking thing, materialistic, drifting, second-rate. I feel that television and the newspapers give the second-rate an infinitely bigger chance than ever to express themselves and make money.'

'Yet you are always glad to appear on television, and you've made the front-page often enough.'

Answer: 'I suppose so, and I intend to keep on doing so. Any real man of genius must be prepared to take on the most difficult forms of self-expression, such as the newspapers.'

'And, in this, you think of yourself as a genius?'

Answer: 'Oh, of course. I mean one makes that assumption in any case. It may prove untrue but I've got to work on that assumption.'

'But I don't think most people assume they have genius?'

Answer: 'This is why the age produces so much lousy writing.'

Perfectly fair; indeed, his views on the 'materialistic, drifting, second-rate' are even more valid today. Unfortunately, the interview reproduced in a small literary review, *Books and Art*, was taken up by the *Sunday Express*, and that word 'genius' stuck in people's throats yet again. I tried to excuse myself by saying that the headline – 'COLIN WILSON EXPLAINS MY GENIUS' – was not my own, also that my favourable comments had been cut, but the harm was done. 'Rather shattered about that article of yours in *Books and Art*,' he wrote on a postcard. 'Can't you see how much this damages me, especially just before a new book is published – and on top of this stupid Royal Court affair?'

To my father, he wrote:

> I have been feeling pretty gloomy about the rejection by the Court. And I presume you saw the attack by that slimy bastard Duncan in yesterday's *Mail*? . . . I'm afraid it was rather naughty of Dan to do this in *Books and Art* on me, and giving the *Sunday Express* an opportunity to be so bitchy. It is true that I said it, but rather rash of Dan to quote me as saying it in a Beaverbrook paper!

He raised the fear 'that it will make the critics sharpen their tomahawks' and this was realised with the publication of *Religion and the Rebel*, dedicated, incidentally, to my father and me. The critics exercised their retribution, especially those who had praised him before. 'Unhappy sequel,' wrote Toynbee. 'A deplorable piece of work,' wrote Raymond Mortimer, deputising for Connolly in the *Sunday Times*. 'Muddlesome, inexcusable.' When it was published in America, *Time* chortled, 'Egghead, scrambled.' *Books and Bookmen* labelled it 'Flop of the year'. This was a literary lynching and Colin left for Cornwall where he has lived ever since.

Colin Wilson – at peace in Cornwall

As Colin recognises today: 'My own abrupt fall from favour with my second book was an unpleasant experience at the time, but I soon recognised that it was the best thing that could have happened. While preaching that *The Outsider* has to stand alone, I was being made the object of the silliest and most empty-headed kind of publicity. Now I had to live up to my own theory, which meant working alone and getting on with my real business, which is thinking and writing. In the thirty years since the débâcle I have done precisely that. I have often thought that perhaps you actually did me a favour by writing the piece in *Books and Art*, which seemed at the time such a disaster. In a way, no "serious" writer is cut out for success – at least, the kind of success he can easily get nowadays.'

He does not suffer from such envy abroad and is close to being a cult personality in Japan and America. There is a marvellous man in Melbourne called Howard Dosser whose idolatry is obsessive. He has the biggest collection of Wilson in the world, surpassing even Wilson's own. While others take to the beaches or visit art galleries, Dosser heads for the second-hand bookshops in Tokyo or London, whisking his stalwart wife past the fashion shops as he lavishes the family funds on some rare Wilson edition. When I stayed with the Dossers in Melbourne in 1986, it was several weeks before the arrival of the great man himself for a lecture tour organised by Dosser. This event was enthused over at dinner on my first night in Australia to such an exhaustive extent that at last I burst out: 'Can't you talk of anything but Colin Wilson?' His family, silent until then, applauded. 'Thank God,' said his son, 'we've been waiting for someone to say that.'

Wilson told me later of Howard Dosser's introductory speech at La Trobe University: 'We are not only in the presence of one of the great minds of the twentieth century,' exulted his disciple. 'We are in the presence of *the* greatest mind of the twentieth century.' With his deadpan humour which people take too literally, Colin added: 'Of course I agreed with every word he said, but I did think he might have put it differently.'

No one can deny Colin's perseverance, and his generous nature remains intact. He married Joy Stewart, becoming reconciled with her horsewhipping parents, and befriended such critics as the late Ronald Duncan with whom he collaborated. His children are supportive and intelligent, and he relaxes by taking his two amiable labradors along the coast near his house in Cornwall, crowded with books and gramophone records.

He is an excellent host and the best of friends. There is no need to feel sorry for Colin Wilson; he is one of the most fulfilled men I know.

A Fish In Finchley

LINDSAY ANDERSON

When I mentioned to Glenda Jackson (something of a sacred monster herself) that I was on my way to see Lindsay Anderson, she laughed and called him 'The Old Growler'. This was said with affection but Lindsay found her comment incomprehensible: 'Good Lord! I've never worked with her – I wonder if we'd get on . . . I wonder!'

His eyebrows are raised in constant surprise at the effect he has on people. At times this is disingenuous for he knows full well that his lacerating wit is rarely forgiven by his victims. 'I am serious,' he insists, 'and I may be critical, but I'm affirmative.' Always pouncing on favourite words, playing with them like a cat with a mouse, he repeats: 'If anyone looks at what I've done, they'll see I have an *affirmative* feeling about people. The trouble is they get scared.'

In spite of his brilliance as one of our most imaginative directors, with such film classics to his credit as *A Sporting Life*, *If* and *O Lucky Man!*, he is rarely seen at those interminable award ceremonies when everybody thanks everybody. 'They bust a gut trying to ape the Americans but it's like the Pier Pavilion at Westcliffe-on-Sea compared to the Hollywood Oscars. Sometimes they invite me, but as I'm never given anything I don't go.'

On one memorable occasion, when he was pressed into presenting an award, he was told that the film had been funded by Channel 4. He did not care for it, but told the TV 'celebrities' at their separate tables, 'At least television has done something for us to be grateful for. For I'm sure we all agree that television is the greatest single disaster in the history of mankind.' He laughs as he remembers, adding the typical qualification: '*Mind you*, when the programme went out they cut that line, inevitably yet idiotically. After all, who cares?'

Like most outspoken people, he seethes with indignation when the victim turns. When he directed Alan Bennett's play *The Old Crowd* for television, he was mystified by the hostility of the critics and the particular virulence of Clive James who accused him of being the only man who was capable of making Alan Bennett unfunny. 'Then someone reminded me that I had described Clive James as the thinking man's Rolf Harris. That did it for me!' It does not occur to him that just for once Clive James may have been right. There is an element of naïvety and self-destruction in his tilting at established windmills, with the irony that such a champion of free speech should be honoured in Buenos Aires and Warsaw while regarded with suspicion in his own country. To this, he points out that England is not his own country: 'I take an uncompromising view and put that down to my Scottishness. The English don't like the Scots.' He pauses and thinks again, as he is apt to do in conversation: 'It's not so much that I don't like the English, just that they don't like me. Why do they like Jonathan Miller? Because he's a good egg, he's not going to do them any harm.'

Knowing few people who enjoy their indignation more, it is hard to think of Lindsay as a renegade, intent on harming everything we hold dear, but there has always been a rebel trying to break loose, cursed at the outset in being born in Bangalore in 1923, son of a Scottish Major-General, when his sympathies really lay with the working class. A distinguished journalist actually described him as 'cruel' when they were fellow-under-graduates at Oxford where Lindsay coincided with Kenneth Tynan, took part in uni-versity productions, and replaced John Schlesinger to sing 'My Sister Ruth' in a Sunday-night revue called *Oxford Circus*, largely composed of material by Sandy Wilson which had proved successful at Oxford. He wrote on films for *Panorama*; founded the film magazine *Sequence* with Gavin Lambert; and began his career as a film director when he met a lady whose husband manufactured mining machinery and needed a short film to mark the fiftieth anniversary of the company. 'I told them that they were mad because I knew nothing about making films. But I took it on and that's what started me off.'

Meanwhile, he was, characteristically, with the angries yet against them. In those days, before the surrender to television, there were plenty of parties and political meet-ings. At one, organised by *Marxist Today*, Lindsay had prepared no speech but got up and attacked the art critic, John Berger, as humourless and pompous. Berger was un-likely to relish such wit, and Ken Tynan was outraged, accusing Lindsay of 'betraying the Left' in an irate postcard, warning him not to degenerate into 'a scold'. Lindsay replied, also by postcard: 'You always were a cunt, take care you don't degenerate into an arsehole.' Yet he was startled when Ken took offence: 'He didn't really like me in case I said something nasty, and he wouldn't like that from someone who might be intelli-gent.' Lindsay's flippancy was calculated to upset.

Another fracas occurred on the first night of *The Tenth Chance* by Stuart Holroyd at the Royal Court Theatre on 9 March 1958. Towards the end of the play, which ran for only one night, Elaine Dundy marched out followed by her husband, Ken Tynan. Chris-topher Logue shouted that the play was 'rubbish!', only to be countered by Colin Wilson who yelled back that Logue should leave as well. In the bar next door afterwards, Wilson and his acolytes, Holroyd and Bill Hopkins, turned on their critics. Logue was pushed under a table and Wilson shouted the warning, 'We'll stamp you out, Tynan, just you wait.' The contretemps made the front-page of the *Express* the next morning.

This was the last angry gasp, for a climax had been reached with the publication the previous year of *Declaration*, 'an anthology of "Anger"' published by Tom Maschler at

Lindsay Anderson on a film-set near Crystal Palace

Cape which was scorned by the critics though it sold 25,000 copies. John Osborne, John Wain, Lindsay Anderson, Kenneth Tynan and Doris Lessing contributed, and so did Colin Wilson, Stuart Holroyd and Bill Hopkins as a separate group. Wisely, Kingsley Amis abstained: 'I hate all this pharisaical twittering about the "state of our civilisation" and I suspect anyone who wants to buttonhole me about my "role in society".'

With an unattractive arrogance, I turned on my former friends in a review for *Books and Bookman*:

> The really heartening thing about *Declaration* is its complete failure. Not its commercial failure, for I believe the first edition has sold out, but its failure as a statement of any real significance or permanence. It would have been too awful if this conceited and remote little document had been acclaimed as the voice of a generation, but the opposite has happened. For the first time we see the 'angry young men' in their proper perspective. They not only disagree, they actively dislike each other and they are not nearly angry enough, there is instead a note of sullen petulance. *Declaration* marks the end of the 'Angry Epoch'.

This was cool considering that I had bracketed the unlikely throng in the first place. John Osborne had attacked the Royal Family as 'a gold tooth in a mouth of social decay' which I described as 'pungently phrased' but 'churlish and rather childish', and suggested that his attack on class-consciousness was more class-conscious than the people he criticised. I mocked Colin Wilson's 'movement' – 'trailed by Stuart Holroyd and, inevitably, his literary dog, Mr Bill Hopkins, whose inclusion in the book is one of its mysteries'; and, surprisingly, condemned Lindsay Anderson 'as the most remote of all'.

> He talks of 'the people' as if he actually knew the people. Intelligent when he writes on films, he becomes embarrassing when he writes this unforgettable phrase: 'If I have made a forty-minute film about the people of Covent Garden, I do not want to be told to cut it to eighteen minutes . . . Those good and friendly faces deserve a place of pride on the screens of their country and I will fight for the notion of community which will give it to them.'

I asked if Anderson realised 'how odiously condescending' this sounded. My peevishness was largely due to a strike in Covent Garden at the time, fully covered by ITN news which showed 'those good and friendly faces' more realistically. Defending television, now that I was a part of it, I commented: 'Because these television coverages have to be done in a matter of hours, whereas Anderson usually takes months or years, the result may not be so distinguished but I do think it has a greater honesty. Anderson and the other contributors to *Declaration* should watch television documentaries and they might be shocked to discover they are no longer the pioneers.'

That we are friends today proves that Lindsay does not hold grudges. He even conceded that he wrote about the Covent Garden workers 'sentimentally'. Inviting me to see an advance cassette of *The Whales of August* at his flat off Finchley Road in 1988, he opened the door suspiciously like a furry animal out of *The Wind in the Willows*, though more predatory than Mole with greying tufts of hair apparently uncombed since the night before, a toe peeping through a bedroom slipper, a glimpse of pyjama top above his sweater. The floors were piled with books and the walls festooned with pictures, prints and posters, with laundry waving on the balcony outside. It was a friendly burrow, without the bachelor chic of an interior decorator, but pleasantly well worn like himself. Insisting on cooking a trout instead of going out, he did so as if this was a game of chance. I had brought a bottle of champagne and after this was drunk he peered into his fridge, emerging with a bottle of wine and a look of mild surprise: 'It's been there several weeks. It's English.'

'Medium sweet?'

He peered again and looked up admiringly. 'How did you know?'

The gentle, elegiac *The Whales of August* is an unexpected contrast to the earlier films until one remembers Anderson's delicate handling on stage of David Storey's *Home* with Gielgud and Richardson: 'Anyone who's surprised that I accepted the chance to direct such a film doesn't really know me or my work. If your indignation's valid, it's got to be compensated by warmth of feeling.'

With no violence, no sex and little plot, the film's leisurely pace may be unfashionable but it has secured a place in the history of cinema with the casting of Bette Davis, Lillian Gish and Ann Sothern and with Vincent Price as the juvenile lead – a geriatric outing with panache. As Bette Davis is *the* sacred monstress of Hollywood, I asked if she was hell to work with. 'Challenging! You don't direct Bette, you suggest. She tends to deride your ideas and then accept them, but I respect her talent and admire her guts. She's had a hard time – a stroke, broken hip and double mastectomy which makes her even more irascible. She's always being pursued by temperamental demons and has had to argue with a lot of fools. The trouble is that, even if you are not a fool, she treats you just the same. She started by liking me, then became suspicious, but we ended as sort of friends and of course you forgive her everything. She's a great artist with a size and intensity that's undiminished. For her alone this film will be unique – nothing like it will happen again.' With Lindsay's direction, and a lifetime's discipline to draw on, she asked for no concessions in her austere portrayal of the blind sister. She looks awesome, and sounds as strong and caustic as ever. A glorious last stand.

Never prepared to compromise, Lindsay Anderson has made more enemies than Dickie Attenborough has gushed acceptance speeches. He is an individual in a conformist's world who has been labelled 'difficult'. He echoes this with hurt bemusement: '*Difficult!* It's getting dangerous if you're outspoken. You're known as a professional outsider and I've paid for it. If anybody talks in public as we all do in private, they're immediately labelled *difficult*. In America you'd be invited to appear on chat-shows.' But it means that his reputation can work against him. 'If you were a big producer,' he asked, 'you wouldn't want to invest a lot of money in me?'

Such comments as his verdict that Attenborough's *Gandhi* is 'approximate to a child's history of India' could not have endeared him to the British film establishment, but he is out of sympathy also with the young film-makers. 'My enthusiasm for the new British cinema is less wholehearted than I would like it to be. But my reservations are not because they're disrespectful but because they're half-baked.'

He anticipated the trend of films which delighted in showing the shabbiest side of British life, like *Sammy and Rosie Get Laid,* and perhaps he was ahead of his time with *If,* the culmination of his anarchy in which his handful of schoolboy heroes takes on the entire establishment (though one episode of *Grange Hill* is almost as violent today), and his allegory of British decay with *Britannia Hospital.*

'I'm a sort of interesting marginal character. As far as the critics and film-makers are concerned, a film like *Britannia Hospital* does not exist, it didn't happen.' He admits to a total disaster in Britain though recognition came from abroad.

'Does that hurt you?'

'It's something I've long since learnt to live with.'

'Does it surprise you?'

'Not in the least, though I was disappointed not to receive more support for a radical point of view. I miscalculated. Unfortunately, the British don't know what you're talking about, but the idea of making a film which does NOT relate to the perilous world we live in would be too boring for words.'

He'll enjoy the last laugh, I'm sure of that. There is talk of a sequel to *If* which made Malcolm McDowell a star: 'I take it for granted that Lindsay is one of the great directors, though the film establishment is jealous of him because he's an anarchist. I hope he does a sequel to *If* for I'd love to do it.'

Over the trout and English wine, Lindsay talked about the earlier, angrier days and it is good to report that he has not mellowed. I left the sacred monster of the British film industry cheerful in his discontent.

A PATCH OF TELEVISION 'FAME'

Television is the great corrupter and I discovered in time that it is all too easy to believe in oneself as someone of importance, to see the penalty of instant recognition as something to be proud of. I signed autographs; judged a beauty contest at the LSE, and was pelted with paper darts, which was amusing, at least; made guest appearances and ghastly speeches; and was drifting into showbusiness as the 'popular entertainer' referred to by Martin Seymour-Smith in his biography of Robert Graves. I was moving away from the writer I wanted to be. There is more satisfaction, as I have learnt since, in the publication of a single book than making a hundred telly progs.

Conversely, I had the luck to be in at the beginning of ITV with the freedom to make my own frontiers in my documentaries and discover how far I could go. It was a rare opportunity and I relished it at first.

The corruption was insidious. When I resigned people could not understand why and reacted as if I had done something morally wrong or been given the sack, but the hollowness of television fame was brought home to me in a vile manner.

'DAN FARSON'S FATHER DIES.' No one recognised the irony of the headline in the *Evening News* more than myself though the gossip columnist in the *Daily Mail* the next morning asked 'What is fame?' This was cool considering that the *Mail* also ran a news item about whether a scheduled interview between my father and me would still be transmitted the following week. My father had written a series of articles on Africa for the *Mail* in the 1930s; had sailed to Murmansk as their War Correspondent in Russia in the Second World War; and contributed articles until his death. Yet there was no feature article on him in the *Mail*, no obituary, just the news item and the columnist's comment 'What is fame?'

I realised then that television fame is a mockery.

A Last Resort in Yugoslavia

NEGLEY FARSON

'DAN FARSON'S FATHER DIES.' All my life I had been Negley's boy. He was so much larger than life that his presence overshadowed mine. One reason for this was his alcoholism which became a preoccupation between himself and my mother who fought desperately to prevent it, conscripting me to the cause. The cause was worth it.

He was an extraordinary man whose life was one of unusual progression, from American athlete to contemplative thinker. That he was different from the outset, adventurous yet sensitive, may have been due to the eccentric personalities who forged his growing-up, especially his grandfather, General Negley, whose name he adopted, a colourful figure who was one of the four generals who rode with Sherman as they burned Georgia from Atlanta to the sea. In saving one battle he shot so many of his own men as they turned and ran that he was court-martialled, and though the General was acquitted my father grew up in an atmosphere of puzzled disgrace and poverty. He told me once that he preferred 'hurt' people, and he had known them.

At the age of twenty-three he sailed for England on the eve of the First War to join an engineering firm in Manchester. 'Before I had been in foggy, dirty, grimy Manchester one week, I had fallen completely in love with the simplicity and substantiality of British life. I found more dignity in "small" lives in Manchester than I ever found in any city in America.'

From there he joined a firm selling munitions to the Russians and spent the next three years in St Petersburg during the last days of the Tsar. What luck he had! He saw Lenin haranguing the crowds and one morning in 1917 he heard the first rumble of revolution under Kerensky as horsemen with swords charged these same crowds and the workers struck back. My fearless mother, who shared my father's wanderlust, was a British VAD nurse in the Anglo-Russian hospital housed in the palace of Crown Duke Dimitri and told me of the night when Prince Yusipoff and Dimitri burst in after midnight, covered in blood and so wild the doctors thought they were drunk until they realised they were hysterical. They had murdered Rasputin and Dimitri fled to the Caucasus at dawn.

High tide on Putsborough Sands with the Grey House in the background

My parents may have passed each other on the Nevsky Prospekt but it was in a London hospital, after he crashed his plane in Egypt when he was in the Royal Canadian Flying Corps, that they were introduced by mutual friends who knew how much they shared in common. The day they married they sailed for America and halfway across the Atlantic a wireless message informed him that his job in South America had fallen through: 'I had just £100 in the wide, but now very interesting world.'

Two idyllic years followed on a lake in British Columbia where my father fished and hunted for food, and wrote the short stories which kept them alive. Finally he knew it was time to leave or stagnate, so he took a job selling Mack trucks in Chicago in fierce materialistic contrast. He was successful but chained; high wages did not compensate

Negley Farson

for the freedom on the lake. One stifling Sunday when there was no wind in the windy city and Janet Fairbank had failed to invite them to Lake Geneva, he took an atlas and planned a journey over a dinner of lobster salad, his favourite.

'We're only going to live once,' he said profoundly. 'Hear, hear!' said my mother. So he chucked up his security and left for Europe. They sailed from Rotterdam on a small boat called *The Flame* on 15 June 1925, travelling down the Rhine and the Danube until they emerged in the Black Sea just as the ice closed in. The stories he sent the *Chicago Daily News* were aimed at emigrants from the various countries he sailed through, but appealed to a wider public and he joined the staff as Foreign Correspondent.

Foreign Correspondent! What glamour that title evokes, a legendary type which is now extinct and often made news in the course of reporting it. My father was one of the best. *Time* called him 'the great extrovert'. The *New Yorker* described him as a 'phenomenon of our time – the star-billing American foreign correspondent, an interesting creature who flourished most luxuriantly in the 1930s . . . The men of Farson's breed – if such a congeries of eccentrics and prima donnas can be called a breed – were not so much serious as cynical; "I know," he says, speaking of his job, "of no profession more calculated to kill one's enthusiasm for the human race." They were personalities (the titles of their books are indicative of the objectivity they brought to the world scene – *Personal History*, *The Way of a Transgressor*, *I Saw* . . .) and they were egoists and snobs – achievement snobs, that is, the reverse of money or position snobs. And many of them ultimately became bored, and many became drunks.'

My father never lost his enthusiasm. Never was he bored. His drunkenness is undeniable. He claimed it started when he ran the London bureau for the *News*; after he had filed his despatches he hurried to the Savoy where he drank three double whiskies in a row to calm his nerves. He suffered from exaggerated guilt as well and this drove him to try every cure and took him to the edge of insanity. If his books make him sound too decent, if the jungles are too green, the wildlife too noble, and the mountain air of the Caucasus too pure, he paid for them when 'meteor lights flamed through the sky of my mind and torn faces laughed at me'.

When Colonel Knox acquired the *Chicago Daily News* and came to London, he heard reports of my father's drinking and recalled him to America on the grounds that he had absorbed the British point of view to an extent where he was no longer objective. My father resigned. He was broke, sick from alcohol, unemployed, and it was the best thing which could have happened to him for his only choice was to draw on the vast reserve of his experience and write the story of his life.

To achieve this, we escaped from London and travelled across Europe – a longer journey in those days – in our battered Ford. Our destination was a lake in the north of Yugoslavia. Getting there was a nightmare.

Recently I came across the following letter which I sent to my grandmother from a hotel in St Malo. I assumed this described the start of that journey until I checked the date and realised the letter was written two or three years later. However, *all* our journeys started in this way. The start of our drive across Europe would have been identical, for this was the pattern of my childhood.

> Dear Gran
> It will be all right when we are in the car, now Pops is drinking rather a lot. He spent a lot of money in taxys, oh ill be so glad when we motor. We had a lovely cabin last night. Mummy is very tiered, oh I think she is so brilliant she

is managing everything ever so well. In the train Pop was nice in the boat he drank. We are both trying to be good till the car, then it will all go *perfectly all right*. I think that Pops is trying not to drink. He's spending to much money on taxis. He will Im sure be perfect later I think he wont drink much now. He is getting medicine and stuff. Dont worry for now onwards *it'll be perfect*. I am helping Mummy as much as I can, she is taking everything ever so well. I'm so glad we go in the car now onwards. Best Best love from yours Danny. P.S. Don't worry because I think It'll be perfect now.

The effect of these reassurances on my grandmother must have been shattering! Unless I confused the date (29 July 1937) and it was in fact the earlier journey in 1934, I was ten. When we drove to Yugoslavia I would have been eight.

We reached Vienna. There were days in a hotel bedroom large and dark with heavy, red plush curtains and brass bedsteads. My father had disappeared and my mother was constantly on the telephone. Sometimes she would leave, while I was told to stay in the room, and return several hours later. One morning there was a sudden activity of phones ringing and people knocking at the door. After whispered consultations, she gave me a slip of paper and some money and told me to go to a chemist nearby to collect some photos which were being developed. Instinctively, I sensed that this was an excuse to get me out of the way and I started to argue until she repeated the directions with such impatience that I did as I was told. I think I found the shop, certainly I remember running back to the hotel. It was on the other side of the street and I caught sight of my father being carried into the entrance on a stretcher, my mother beside him. I raced across to join them, ignoring the shouts as I missed the traffic.

We continued to drive. I usually lay on the floor in the back, covered with a blanket as my parents imagined I was fast asleep in spite of their arguments, the shouts from my father, my mother's tears, and the sudden silence as they remembered I was there, which alarmed me more than the noise.

One day was particularly bad. In her non-stop battle in which she never weakened, my mother pleaded with him not to stop for a drink and when he lost his temper it had been unusually violent. My mother's sobs sounded more hopeless than ever. Then that silence.

There were whispers and we stopped. I looked out hopefully but there were just a couple of houses and a small shop in a landscape which would encourage me to emulate Edvard Munch if I tried to paint it today.

Turning round, my father handed me some money and asked me to fetch some matches from the shop. I scrambled out eagerly and ran up a glistening white path to the shop at the top, which was empty of people. It was a long, wooden store, one of those which sell everything that is crucial in a small community. The counter was littered, ropes and tools drooped from the ceiling, but there was no sign of life. I banged and yelled. It seemed a long time before a young woman came in, and when I cried out *streiches* she burst into giggles and went out again. A few moments later she returned with several people, presumably her family, and while I kept on shouting *streiches* a motherly woman smiled at me kindly. The others kept on laughing and I suppose that a small English boy demanding matches in such a remote place was funny to them, but I thought irrationally of my parents leaving without me. The older woman must have noticed the animal panic in my eyes for she gave me the matches suddenly and I raced, almost falling, back to the safety of the car, appalled at having taken so long, shocked to realise I had not even asked for change.

Half-sobbing with relief, I thrust the matches through the window and climbed into the back. To my horror my parents turned round to say how clever I had been to get them and how we were going to stop at the next town for ice-cream and cake. Obviously they had made an effort for my sake, but I was not expecting that. I remembered the anger and despair when I left them and the sudden change of mood was inexplicable.

Still, there was ice-cream to look forward to.

And then we arrived at the lake and unpacked all our luggage for the next few months instead of a single night in a strange hotel. And my father found his true self again.

Lake Bohinsko lies at the most northern point of Yugoslavia, the source of the River Sava. There were no houses around it, just two little hotels owned by a religious order. Ours was the Saint James, named after the painted church nearby. The cost of full board for the three of us each day was less than the price of one of his double whiskies at the Savoy.

Every fortnight we climbed to the top of the surrounding mountains where a cable car goes swiftly today, and I wore boots with heavy hobnails made by the cobbler, with a rucksack on my back. We passed edelweiss, chamois, glaciers and fields of snow and burnt in the sun. We stopped the night, sleeping in the hay in one of the log chalets – Vogel, or Planina na Kraj, or The Hut of the Seven Lakes, one of which was rippling with snakes. In the spring when the lake was flooded with the melting snow, I looked over the side of the rowboat into an underwater world of wild flowers and carpets of blue gentian.

My father fished for trout and we cooked them in butter afterwards in a sizzling frying pan above a wood fire which I had gathered and built. Rowing back at night, counting the shooting stars, we felt that physical tiredness which is almost a sensual state of well-being.

Sorting through old notes recently, I came across a typewritten sheet apparently abandoned by my father in which he recalled that time; and I had hoarded it, remembering too:

> When I was trout fishing up in those marvellous streams that leapt and danced down through the forested valleys of the Dinaric Alps, I often sat by the bank, wondering what sort of life I would go in for if my book really did hit the jackpot. I thought writing the book would help me to find it. It did, in a way. I saw that if there was anything that could be called a pattern in my life, it was like the tacking of a ship at sea, a constant beat to windward, to get the moods I had known surf-casting along the Atlantic . . .

The words poured out as my father typed on a small table in the gravel courtyard outside the hotel, served constant coffee by the courteous Joseph, while my mother gave me lessons and I built a tree in the wood behind us in the afternoons. My one regret was the lack of brothers or sisters – what a difference that would have made in such surroundings.

At last the book was finished. He hit his jackpot. *The Way of a Transgressor* was an instant bestseller in 1935 both in America where it topped the lists, and in Britain where it was published with brilliant promotional flair by Victor Gollancz. Now virtually forgotten, though occasionally reprinted, the *Transgressor* has a freshness which makes it even more readable in these unromantic days. It is now a period piece. At the time the impact was tremendous. 'It's wild stuff and astringent, like berries on uplands where there is wind from the sea,' wrote H. M. Tomlinson. 'I know of no international journalist . . . who has written a personal chronicle so exciting, so authentically romantic, yet so revelatory of what forces have been surging through the world . . . A grand picture of a grand man who found every hour exciting,' wrote Sinclair Lewis.

'DAN FARSON'S FATHER DIES.' There was so much to look back on with happiness, though his drinking continued. Ironically, the *Transgressor* gave him the freedom to travel and take his mistress on a disastrous tour of South America starting with his arrest and imprisonment in a Panama gaol. When *Transgressor in the Tropics* was published, one reviewer commented: 'If *The Way of a Transgressor* was the binge, this is the hangover.'

In a desperate attempt to recover his sanity which he feared was slipping away, he committed himself to the care of Dr Bumke in Munich and emerged with such miraculous willpower and new resolve that he crossed Africa without resort to alcohol. My mother joined him and he dedicated *Behind God's Back* to her – 'She was better than any man' – but gangrene infected the wound in his leg from his plane crash in Egypt, and an overdose of morphine proved disastrous for he returned to the solace of alcohol.

The three Farsons in the Yugoslavian mountains

Lake Bohinsko

It was several years after the war when he committed himself again, this time to the state asylum in Switzerland, where the head doctor told him: 'Mr Farson, keep your conflicts. It is better for you not to be a normal man.' This was the wisest advice ever given to him and he seized it gratefully. The drinking continued erratically but mattered less. Perhaps the constant battle provided a necessary friction. It could have defeated him but he had the strength ultimately to survive it supported by my mother to whom he was married to the end.

Colin Wilson wrote of him: 'Farson was the only man I have ever met who seemed cast in a bigger mould than other men. Unlike Hemingway, who tried hard to play the archetypal hero, and who, as a consequence, often struck false notes, Farson's impressiveness was completely natural and unselfconscious . . . he was interested in everything. This was the quality that made him one of the world's greatest foreign correspondents and – in my own opinion – one of the best writers of this century.'

Negley Farson died in 1960 at his home in North Devon. That morning he tied labels on his luggage for yet another journey abroad, and took his dog for a walk on Putsborough Sands pounded by the Atlantic surf. He told me once, 'This is the perfect place for journey's end.'

He was reading in his armchair in the afternoon, my mother opposite, his cat on his lap, his dog at his feet, when he died within seconds. He was seventy and I could not grieve. He had done the things that most men dream about.

Knees-Up in the East End

JOAN LITTLEWOOD

When she left Langan's Brasserie late one afternoon, several of the staff lined up to speak to Joan Littlewood, although she had not set foot there before. Although satiated with celebrities, they knew instinctively that she would be fun and, plainly touched by the warmth of their welcome on one of her rare visits to London, she did not disappoint them.

When she collected her shopping from the cloakroom, it included a vast bag of dog biscuit. 'For Jacques Tati' she informed the startled waiter, explaining to me afterwards that this was her name for the stiff-legged mongrel she had befriended in Vienne, near Lyons, where she was living at the time in a state of vigil following the death of her friend and partner, Gerry Raffles, who helped her run the famous Theatre Royal at Stratford East.

She had confided to me earlier that afternoon: 'If I started to cry, the tears would last for years. I have lived like a ghost for five years now, and I really do not want to come back to life.' Her total abandonment of the British theatre to which she had dedicated her life remains so extraordinary that outsiders find it hard to comprehend, and so the subject is avoided, yet the roll-call of those she helped is long and unexpected: Barbara Windsor, Harry Corbett, Brian Murphy, Roy Kinnear, Nigel Hawthorne and Richard Harris whose impersonation of Winston Churchill opening a lavatory prompted the Lord Chamberlain to take the company to court where it was defended by Gerald Gardiner, later the Lord Chancellor, free of charge. When a young northern girl saw a photograph of Joan Littlewood and her actors as they left after a small fine, she thought, She looks a right character, and sent Joan her play *A Taste of Honey*. Other playwrights besides Sheila Delaney included Brendan Behan and Frank Norman.

The most unlikely Littlewood discovery was Michael Caine who sat at his corner table that afternoon before he was barred by his partner Peter Langan who is indeed a sacred monster himself, highly respected by his staff, in spite of his wild antics, as I discovered one evening after he collapsed in the Colony Room and I brought him back to the Brasserie in a taxi. Safely slumped at the back of the bar, he received his waiters like an

Emperor granting an audience, listening to their problems attentively though barely conscious, offering advice while telling them to be sure to remind him in the morning. Their problems ranged from the permit of a visa which had been refused, to the failure of some delivery, with courteous concern on both sides. My God! I thought, as I was plied with champagne, if they treat him like that he is far from the fool that he pretends to be.

On this afternoon, however, he was conspicuous in his absence and had not yet fallen out with Michael Caine who stopped Joan as we passed. She appeared not to remember him. 'I worked for you at Stratford East, Joanie,' he reminded her.

'Oh yes,' she exclaimed, 'and you were bloody hopeless. What have you been doing since?' Michael Caine gulped like a dyspeptic toad, uncertain whether she was teasing him or not.

'Oh, I've done all right, made some films, you know.'

'Good,' she replied airily as if this was the first she had heard of it, and moved on.

Many years earlier, in 1955, I had seen Joan Littlewood on the unlikely stage of the Queen's Hall in Barnstaple at the North Devon Festival organised by Ronald Duncan where I introduced Ken Tynan to my parents whom he treated like provincial bores. The play was *Mother Courage* and, after a row with her leading lady, Joan had taken on the part herself, playing it magnificently with Frances Cukor as her daughter (unless my memory plays tricks). As I discovered subsequently, few people knew of this excursion and she hated being reminded of it, presumably because the casting was too close for comfort.

After that I saw Joan intermittently but it was when I moved into the East End of London that we became close. I was among the first, if not the first, to move into Limehouse simply for the joy of it, though Antony Armstrong-Jones moved to Rotherhithe on the opposite bank at the same time, in a house which had formerly been a pub called the Little Midshipman. My rented flat above a barge yard had been another, tiny riverside pub – the Waterman's Arms – and I fell in love with this aspect of the Thames where guests were occasionally rash enough to dive into the water from my balcony. That is another story, but my genuine affection for the place and the people was something I had in common with Joan Littlewood and brought us together when she appointed me Adviser to the Director on her first film, *Sparrers Can't Sing*, which she made on location. A more idiotic designation could hardly be imagined, for Joan was not the person to want advice or seek it, and the last to take it. Instead, I received urgent notes instructing me that she needed 'three tarts and a dozen merchant seamen for a punch-up and a striptease in a suitable Cable Street caff by midday'. This was not the easiest of commands. I solved the tarts by telling the wives of three local friends that they were going to be in films and would they appear in their fanciest clothes, and accosted some merchant seamen in Charlie Brown's whose vanity made them accept without demur. I gained the impression that Joan was disappointed to discover I had not been beaten up in the process. In her turn, she appeared in a dustman's jacket embroidered with red lettering: 'Borough of Hackney' and the inevitable woolly cap.

As a result of her habit of using anyone around her, I was told to play the minor part of

Joan Littlewood

a ship's officer which I did with such giddy empathy that my performance scarcely reached the cutting-room floor. Still, if they show *Sparrers* on television, you'll see me among the credits as the alleged 'Adviser'.

Gradually I noticed a curious thing that Joan was flawed in the area I had least expected. Outwardly the tough Marxist realist, she romanticised the working classes into the roles that she wanted them to play – lovable Cockneys with cloth caps and mufflers and knees-ups and outside toilets. Surprisingly, she was as out of touch and as out of date as Lindsay Anderson and his 'friendly faces' in Covent Garden. Only with *A Taste of Honey* did she approach reality.

Her theatre was found, with difficulty, at the end of Angel Lane, a delightful market that actually resembled a film-set and fulfilled her fantasy of Cockney cheerfulness with sleek, black eels slithering in wooden boxes. One morning I was chatting to a stallholder with literary pretensions who was telling me about his interest in Proust when he was transformed by a flurry of convulsive shouts and obscene gestures, 'Up yours too!' and 'Good to see yer, yer old cow.' After Joan had returned the compliment with similar Cockney capers, continuing happily on her way to the theatre, he leant over the fruit and veg and apologised confidentially: 'Excuse me, but Joan *does* like us to talk like that.'

In spite of fierce disagreement with the aged cameraman – 'He's used to lighting Anna Neagle' – she established total control and received devotion for she had the ability to look someone straight in the eye which gave the impression that this was the one person she wanted to meet at that moment. Like most sacred monsters, she wove a web of conspiracy into which you were drawn unawares. She used people shamelessly with her spellbinding charm, astonishing the technicians by her appetite for hard work. She spoke to the children in the film as if they were adults, and the villains as if they were naughty children. After moving into Limehouse I had been taken to the Kentucky Club where I was introduced to Ronnie and Reggie Kray who ran it. Unaware of their criminal activities, accepting them naïvely as the self-styled 'civic businessmen' they claimed to be, I was fascinated by the Kentucky which was small and chic with Regency flock and white leather banquettes. The girls were mute but immaculate, the men wore blue suits, white shirts and dark ties, and when I fell down the narrow stairs Ronnie Kray tended to cringe: 'Watch your language, Dan, there's ladies present.' This was the etiquette of the East End. I took Joan to the Kentucky when we were looking for a suitable location and she and the Krays took to each other at once, though they were shaken by her language. Delighted with the Club, she filmed one of her 'tarts' dancing in a slit-skirt to the jukebox while the Krays watched aghast at this travesty which outraged their propriety.

I was dismayed also, for Joan had missed the point.

Joan attempted to realise her dream of building a Fun Palace on the Isle of Dogs to rival that of the old Vauxhall Gardens, an imaginative venture which failed for lack of support. I attended a conference at which she explained her ideas, flanked by Tom Driberg as a sort of *éminence grise,* a former chairman of the Labour Party and much loved by his many friends though I found him sinister, subversive and, almost certainly, a Russian spy. I could not understand the point of the meeting, which accomplished nothing, though a brochure hints at what might have been: 'Joan Littlewood presents the First Giant Space Mobile in the World, it moves in light, turns winter into summer for your delight.' With brilliant designers at her disposal, such a grandiose scheme deserved to succeed, but she was ahead of her time. Imagine the triumph such a pleasure garden would be today, enhancing or at least distracting from the new building which overwhelms the Isle of Dogs, a Tivoli Garden to rival Copenhagen, except that no one really wants to linger in the new East End. Instead, she resorted to the role of fairground barker for the local children, inventing 'games' to keep them entertained, until she returned triumphantly with *Oh What a Lovely War!* which opened at Stratford East in 1963.

When I returned four years later, she led me round the theatre, now painted in bright psychedelic colours, pointing to painted footprints on the pavement which led to the pub opposite. 'That's our tiger,' she explained. Over the road stretched bedraggled bunting reading MUSIC HALL except that some of the letters had fallen off so the message was unintelligible. Gradually I realised that she was presenting her actors upstairs in the pub where a hat went round afterwards. The Theatre Royal was leased to someone else. Considering her impact on twentieth-century theatre, this was sad. After the usual vicissitudes attending any musical, I had sent her a script on Marie Lloyd and she had asked to see me. Now she revealed that she wanted to produce it – Marie Lloyd fascinated both of us: the great sacred monster of music hall.

The next few months were among the most traumatic of my life. Anyone who has been closely involved in a musical will know that some of us go slightly mad in the anticipation, but with Joan there was no question of 'slightly'. She threw me on a roller-coaster of elation and despair. To start with, my suspicions were confirmed by Gerry Raffles, the general manager of the Theatre Workshop, that the company was in the doldrums and I needed to raise half the backing which I managed to extract from generous if unfortunate friends. Then the agents moved in and contracts were exchanged in a charade of bargaining as if we had a Drury Lane hit on our hands already. There was an evening before the rehearsals began when I was asked to dinner at the splendid home in Blackheath where Joan lived in unexpected luxury with Gerry Raffles and his elegant American secretary. During the filming of *Sparrers*, I had turned down an invitation to join them at Portsmouth one Sunday to go sailing on Gerry's yacht, a refusal which I had recognised later as churlish and unwise. Now I was being accepted as one of her 'nuts' and as we seemed to agree on the presentation of *Marie* I returned to Limehouse in ecstasy. The rehearsals started the next day.

I knew of Joan's reputation, of the audience rising in anger at the first night of Lionel Bart's *Twang!* in Manchester, with the actors still being given their lines, and the violent argument afterwards when Bernard Delfont walked out in disgust, taking his money with him. I knew that she signed her notes J. Hell, but I was unprepared to find the stage peopled by actors doing extraordinary things, with a grown woman being dragged across it howling like a baby. I smiled, assuming this was a new scene for the transfer of *Mrs Wilson's Diary*. Then it dawned on me, this was *Marie*. Not a word of dialogue remained. No one had warned me that this was how she worked.

The next morning I played an old man in a queue in one of their games, and my collaborator, a BBC director called Harry Moore, the gentlest of men who wore a constantly martyred smile, arrived in the stalls and sat there white and aghast. Joan noticed him, but did not speak. I had tea with some of the actors in the caff which was managed by two old women who screamed endless messages – 'Joanee! One of yer young fellers been in for yer' – which killed discussion, and though I had grown to hate the good humour of the place I thought I got on rather well with the cast which included Nigel Hawthorne as a theatre manager; Avis Bunnage as Marie; and Jimmy Perry who played Alec Hurley and continued to greater success as the scriptwriter of *Dad's Army*. By the next morning the shock was starting to fade and Joan took the trouble to explain certain points to Norman Kay, the composer of the new music, and me. She wanted a song for a character loosely based on Fred Barnes who was ruined after a scandal involving a sailor in Hyde Park, and for once she accepted my suggestion that instead of making this character a female impersonator it would be funnier to have him dressed immaculately in a white suit while he sang cowboy numbers which 'got the bird'. I wrote the lyrics for the song which was meant to be terrible but proved the most popular in the new score, so much so that on one occasion during the run Joan glared at me and said, 'Why can't *you* write lyrics like that?' She was unamused when I reminded her that I had. It was called 'The Great Outback':

> I'm on my way to the great outback
> And the wide open spaces
> Where the sun glares down and cracks the ground
> And the men have dusty faces.

I had phoned these and equally awful lyrics through the night before and, as we sat in the stalls and read them through, Norman Kay gave a deafening bellow as he realised he had misheard 'yearn for a girl's embraces' as 'yearn for a girl *in braces*'. I sobbed with laughter too, partly with the relief that everything seemed to be going well. Joan Littlewood stopped for a second on stage and looked down at us over her half-specs.

Studying her notes later, hurrying from one actor to another, she beckoned to me. 'It's no good. I can't go through with it. It's not going to work.' I gave an uneasy smile. 'I'm miserable,' she continued, 'you're miserable.'

'But Joan,' my throat was dry, 'I couldn't be happier. I agree with everything you've suggested.'

'I can't work this way. I'm an egomaniac, no I'm not, it's just that I'm too old. I don't care if I break people's hearts. This is the only way I can work. I did this with Brendan and Shelagh and my other nuts and it worked. Wolf Mankowitz expected me to stick to his script but I can't work like that.'

All this was said softly as she looked at me over those half-spectacles with their thin metal frames. 'I don't think you know a thing about the theatre. I don't believe you can write dialogue. Norman comes here and has the audacity to tell me what to do. [When asked for his opinion, he had suggested that one scene might be "tightened up".] Harry sits there looking like death and upsets the actors. I can only work my way. I thought you understood that.' The words came rapidly like machine-gun fire yet anyone watching from the stalls might have thought we were having a friendly talk. In his innocence, Norman sat there beaming.

Joan was called away, but she came back to make sure that the corpse was lifeless. 'And you, you're too concerned.'

'Wouldn't it be awful if I wasn't?' I managed to say.

'I mean it. I'm dead serious.' She gave me a cold look and walked away. The rehearsals continued without us. We were barred from the theatre.

Of course she was right. Our presence was intolerable, except for that of Norman Kay who had to present the new score. I *was* too concerned. We had worked too hard and too long on the script, when she would have been happier with a few pages of outline to build on. We should have trusted her and let her get on with it. Unfortunately, in her detestation of the written word which did not exclude Shakespeare – 'Bill wasn't a bad old hack but we don't respect him' – and her dedication to the actors which was inviolate, she allowed them to improvise dialogue which was even worse than my own. Also, she had one weakness: if a scene failed to work, such as a dreadful coffee-stall sketch which bore no relation to music hall, she would not admit this but shifted the actors to enter left instead of right, or played it at a different pace rather than change it. One matinée I found the production transformed – successful at last – and, when I realised that scenes had been cut due to the pressure of having two performances on the same day, I made the mistake of urging her to leave them out from then on. After that, they were reinstated even for the matinées.

She had genius, there's no doubt of that. It's the price the writer has to pay. In spite of all the traumas off-stage, and the last-minute cancellation of the first night for the sake of publicity, it came tantalisingly close to success. With a few bold strokes, Joan achieved effects as spectacular as those of any Drury Lane production with revolving stages. There were moments of magic that only she could produce. Her taste was impeccable when it came to costumes and sets.

After the first-night cancellation, the critics were invited instead to a Saturday performance, which is not their favourite night in the theatre, and Joan and Gerry had filled it with old-age pensioners in the hope that they would join spontaneously in the choruses of such Marie Lloyd numbers as 'My Old Man' and 'Oh Mr Porter'. Robert Carrier, one of the unfortunate backers, told me there was so much coughing and wheezing that he felt he was in the walrus house in a zoo.

Even so the critics were fair. Milton Shulman wrote: 'The book seems to have been mauled in the production'; *The Times* made a surprising comment on the *lack* of 'the usual reports of disagreement between Joan Littlewood and her writers', adding, 'the story-line is consistently sabotaged by the impulse to keep things lively'. Frank Marcus voted it the best musical of the year.

In spite of the cold and pre-Christmas preoccupation, the old music hall theatre glowed with nostalgia. The show improved steadily and the one person Joan never spared was herself, surveying the scene nightly from various concealed points in the auditorium, like a phantom of the opera. The transfer was not in doubt. It never is, until too late. Agents bargained over percentages on our behalf and the time ran out. The West End manager who intended the transfer changed his plans at the last moment and no alternative had been prepared. The lease of the theatre had been sold to another company due to take over on Boxing Day.

On Christmas Eve I phoned Joan and Gerry suggesting a farewell drink and we met in a crowded Aldgate pub teaming with colourful Cockney characters who might have been figments of her imagination. No longer the need for the task-master with the shadow-boxing gestures and sinister half-specs, she looked like a young girl. She wore a dashing mink cap which the local children had given her after she spoke up for them in the magistrates' court earlier that week.

'Didn't like to ask where they'd nicked it!' she smiled proudly.

Throughout these years, one man stood beside her – Gerry Raffles. Joan conceded: 'We did everything together but, when we had a success, I got the credit.' They formed Theatre Workshop after the war, largely subsidised by his money, and, after eight years of hard, penniless touring through Europe as well as Britain, they reached London in 1953 where he rented the small, perfect Theatre Royal for £12 a week. From then on, he battled away from his office, pacifying agents and petulant playwrights with his constant good humour. He was a huge man and hugely popular. Not only did he save the theatre from being demolished by property developers, he managed to buy it a piece at a time. 'He's one of those men,' said Joan, 'from two hundred years ago, sitting there with a gun on his knee and holding them all at bay. And, by God, he's done it.'

Today the area is known as Gerry Raffles Square. 'He never told me of these troubles he was having, but always kept them away from me so I could direct.' They were inseparable and, though it was not in either of their temperaments to be sweet to each other in public, there were moments when she spoke so impatiently that I hoped, with the insolence of an outsider, that she would be able to forgive herself. He died suddenly near Vienne in the summer of 1977 when he was returning with his beloved boat up the Rhône, while she went ahead to England.

As he had left no will, Joan was shocked when people he had done business with for years came banging on her door in Blackheath demanding their money while she was in a state of grief. Conversely, the local shopkeepers sent their children to her with gifts of food and cigarettes. She staged a curious afternoon's performance in his honour outside, but did not leave the house herself though we spoke on the telephone. Unable to forgive herself, she left England the following year, going first to Aix-en-Provence where she taught drama, then to Vienne where she started her vigil and remained there apart from the time when she became so ill that a friend arranged for her to fly to America for medical help.

One cannot fault such loyalty and such grief because one cannot comprehend it in another person unless one is closely involved. The setting of Vienne had no significance: Gerry Raffles had just happened to be passing on his boat. Joan shunned the old part of town, preferring to live in the industrial outskirts, first in a hotel room, then in the flat of one of the cleaners. One of the few privileged friends allowed to visit her compared the bleakness of the place to a set out of *Oliver!* Most of her friends had no idea where she had vanished. Ken Tynan had a rough idea and told me of his fear that she might drown in the Rhône near the spot where she had planted a cherry tree, on the anniversary of Raffles's death. He was relieved when he received a curious letter apparently written by a concierge about a strange English lady who lived upstairs. Her humour was intact.

Then something happened which was so extraordinary that it has gone largely unnoticed. The Baron Philippe de Rothschild, in his late seventies, and 'still grief-stricken' after the death of his wife Pauline, heard that Joan 'was in a similar state, having a year earlier lost her great man: Gerry Raffles'. He remembered the productions of their Theatre Workshop which he had admired and sought her out. At the end of May he motored alone from Paris to Vienne.

> [Joan] had stayed in hiding, isolated, living near the river bank where Gerry died. I wanted to help if I could. Joan was standing in clogs and slacks outside a small, whitewashed hotel not a hundred yards from the River Rhône, suspicious, reticent, not to say hostile. I talked. We lunched together and afterwards I read her passages of Marlowe's *Tamburlaine*. First one phrase, then another roused enthusiasm or sharp criticism. It took time but I felt that a ray of light might be slowly moving in her distressed mind. I had been shocked and startled by her appearance, but it was not long before I was overwhelmed by her knowledge of the Elizabethans, her sense of theatre, her humour.
>
> I managed to persuade her to visit Mouton. That was the experience which was to promote our everlasting understandings and misunderstandings. Joan loved the place . . . Perhaps she found a little solace at Mouton, above all.

These words are taken from the Baron's Preface to his autobiography (with the lamentable title of *Milady Vine*) largely written by Joan Littlewood. They came to London for the publication and gave a party which was curious in so far as her 'nuts' were assembled, though uncertain why; an aged trio played tunes from *My Fair Lady* under the impression that she had produced it; and the wine was so bad that I mentioned it to a hired waiter, adding that I ought not to complain.

'Oh, sir!' He gave a sigh worthy of Eric Blore. 'If I were sir, I'd be complaining. It doesn't do one good to serve at venues like this.'

Needless to add that everyone had been hoping for the rarest vintage Mouton Rothschild or champagne, instead of the usual plonk.

Joan looked unchanged. I think she was wearing her woolly cap as she introduced the Baron as the fourth Marx Brother and asked him to dance. Wisely he refused, for his family seemed unamused enough by her collection of 'nuts' and 'clowns'.

Apart from this odd departure from France, the Marxist came to Mouton and stayed. The Baron involved her with his activities: the placing of a new statue, the preparation for a visit from the Queen Mother. Joan wrote an essay for a brochure introducing a new wine named after the Baronne Pauline, and they shared their passion for good wine and the theatre.

Her irreverence was restored: when a team from *Playboy* descended for an interview with the Baron, she descended to a grand dinner in the Château Rothschild wearing two bedraggled rabbit-ears and a pompom on her behind.

The Baron concluded his Preface: 'Joan, my love to you. It is Mouton, your home for ever, if you wish, which begs you to carry on, not to stray too far from the one you call the "Guv". Never stop being the Joan I met in Vienne on the Rhône.'

And now the Baron is dead too. Wherever Joan may be today, I wish her well without the risk of seeming impertinent, for this is a sentiment shared by all of those who have had the luck to work with this most sacred of monsters.

Lunch at the Hyde Park Hotel

SIR OSWALD MOSLEY

When I was successful on television, I suggested a series on people who were still alive but would claim their footnote in history: Magda Lupesco, the red-haired beauty who cost King Carol his Romanian throne, living in Estoril; Kerenksy in New York; Ethel le Neve who had sailed to New York with Crippen, now living anonymously in the suburbs; Prince Yusipoff, who murdered Rasputin, and so on . . . Even if the interviews were shown after these people were dead, they would form a fascinating basis for a television archive.

This ambitious project was turned down flat because of the expense, so I suggested Sir Oswald Mosley instead. There was a rumour that he was dying from phlebitis and I thought we should seize the opportunity while we could, especially as we could do so at virtually no cost. The reaction took me by surprise, for it was one of outrage.

'Are you a fascist?' I was asked by the Head of Features at Associated Rediffusion. 'If you found Hitler alive and well in Notting Hill, wouldn't you want to interview *him*?' I retaliated. 'Politics have nothing to do with it. We ought to film Mosley because he is part of contemporary history.' I thought then, as I think now, that the way the British absorbed him and spat him out without harming a hair on his head was a tribute to our innate tolerance, but I was damned if I was going to be so specious. It was something we ought to do. Perhaps I was naïve. Even my father grumbled, 'I don't know why you want to get mixed up with people like that.'

No one in Associated Rediffusion was prepared to discuss it further so I took the idea to Granada where it was approved by Sydney Bernstein on condition that I hired an 'outside crew' and that Granada's name would not be involved.

At that time Sir Oswald Mosley was boycotted by the press, virtually dead to the outside world. Welcoming the unexpected chance I offered him, he invited me to lunch at the Hyde Park Hotel. Because of the boycott, I assumed he was a traitor, unaware that he had taken several papers to court when they called him that, winning damages every time for the charge could not be substantiated. That might have been another reason for the boycott. Because of it, I expected to be confronted by an ogre. The first surprise was his stature for he was a formidable figure, erect in spite of a slight limp, with an attractive foxy face. After a lifetime of charming people, he shook me strongly by the hand and, while he put me at my ease instantly, he did so as the seigneur to the serf. The second and greater shock was his keen sense of humour. I had not expected laughter from a would-be 'dictator'. I was mesmerised throughout, as he intended, especially when he paused on the steps of the hotel as we said goodbye.

'This might interest you, Mr Farson,' he told me, staring me straight in the face with his piercing eyes. 'My wife and I were lunching in Venice recently and after we left the restaurant a friend of ours overheard an English couple talking about us.

'"He doesn't look so bad," said the husband. "I don't think he'd have put us in the gas-oven."

'"No," the wife agreed. "But *she* would have." Goodbye Mr Farson,' and he strode into the busy street, unrecognised by the passers-by, as I looked after him speechless, wondering why he had told such a story to a total stranger. It puzzles me still.

Then Granada had cold feet and I needed to reassure them. Then Mosley had his doubts, insisting on a chance to reply in the final programme to any attacks made against him. In return he would guarantee no libel action. This seemed reasonable enough but Granada told me angrily that they could give no undertaking whatsoever, and as Mosley would have had the last word this was reasonable too. In the end we decided on a long, single programme and Mosley, in his desperation for publicity, agreed to our terms though he warned me that he would attack if anything was falsified.

I lunched with him again at the house he rented, or was lent to him, in Cheyne Walk, with Lady Diana Mosley and her sister the Duchess of Devonshire who gossiped ceaselessly throughout the meal while Mosley attempted to impress me with his plans for the future of the world. I remember that the first course was excellent scrambled-egg on toast, a very aristocratic starter.

The interview was remarkable and developed into a duel. The revelation was Mosley's continual thirst for power, and his conviction that he would have become Prime Minister if it had not been for the war.

Finally, I asked him if he thought he would gain power again – which he did – and quoted Lord Elton's dictum that power corrupts, and absolute power corrupts absolutely.

'Only small men,' he replied. 'Power never corrupts *great* men.' He smiled with his teeth bared and there was no doubt as to whom he had in mind.

The interview proved too strong, even for the archives. I doubt if a trace of it remains. Malcolm Muggeridge was the next to attempt it, and his interview was banned as well. When the BBC filmed him, and vetoed it too, Mosley went to court where he had a sympathetic hearing from the judge who refused to lift the veto but remarked that if a man was constantly attacked for his views (by then the boycott must have ended), it was only fair to allow him to defend himself. Soon after that, James Mossman interviewed Mosley to great effect on *Panorama*.

I was disappointed in my own failure because I thought that Mosley's was a salutary story. We agreed that I should write his biography and I grew increasingly fascinated the more I uncovered of his early years. This time, Mosley insisted on waiving libel rights provided he was given the chance to reply in the final chapter, and the publisher, scenting a strong selling-point, agreed. That same evening I went to a cocktail party where I discussed Mosley's life with someone who asked me what had gone wrong after I described Mosley as one of the *potentially* great figures of contemporary British politics.

'I believe he was flawed.'

'What sort of flaw?'

'*Vanity.*'

This was published in the *Evening Standard* the following day for the stranger I was talking to so indiscreetly was a gossip columnist. That was the end of the association with Mosley.

Lunch at the
Temple de la Gloire
LADY DIANA MOSLEY

The interview with Sir Oswald Mosley occurred in 1959. On Easter Saturday in 1988, I lunched at the Temple de la Gloire at Orsay. Returning to Paris, which I had fallen in love with (like everyone else) when I was young, I dreaded to find that the city had changed. Instead, I was shocked, in the most delightful way, to see that it was enhanced. The old buildings looked lovelier, the views across the Seine were open with scarcely a tower in sight, and only then in the far distance, unlike the dusty debris of the blitzed building-site which London resembles today. I love London, but Paris is crisp by comparison. I walked across the Pont Royal with the couple who had travelled with me, through the Tuileries Gardens to the Orangerie at the end before the Obelisk of Luxor, which houses the joyful Guillaume Collection of Modigliani, Soutine, Renoir, Douanier Rousseau and Cézanne at their *best*, with the reward of the circular room downstairs which I had seen in black and white photographs but surpassed all anticipation. Monet's ageing obsession with the water-lilies fascinates as an aim in life, and as my eyes first absorbed those tremendous screens, so close to abstract yet so far, I felt the sheer elation of being alive. Corny perhaps, but what a start to the day! Afterwards we took the Métro to Lozère where the grey Citroën was waiting with an American guest, Stuart Preston, who had arrived on an earlier train, driven by the Irish chauffeur who, with his wife, has looked after Lady Diana devotedly since her husband's death.

The area has been compared to Woking, which makes the Temple all the more eccentric, worthy of its fairy-tale name. The proportions of the house are perfect but small, though *small* is an inadequate description for something so elegant, built for one of Napoleon's generals to celebrate his victory at Hoenliden in 1800. There is a portico outside which leads on to a lawn and a lake with swans at the end, all surrounded today by suburbia. Sir Oswald called it 'our funny little house' and it was ideal for them both. We were shown upstairs to three connecting rooms, the largest 'cube' in the centre, with a high ceiling and superb Empire furniture, though sparse. Lady Diana was waiting for us.

She is such an extraordinary woman that it is hard to remember that most people hate everything she stands for. Linked, irrevocably, with the politics of her husband, she continues to speak out passionately on his behalf as I discovered when I quoted from a biography of Edward VIII which stated that Sir Oswald Mosley told his solicitor in Brixton prison in 1940 that 'Hitler had already appointed him as co-leader of Britain, ready for when the invasion came'.

After a lifetime of controversy and libel, she is not surprised by inaccuracies but this enraged her. 'It's a *complete* lie.' She tends to emphasise her words. 'He never would have become a leader, but if he *had* thought like that he wouldn't have been so *mad* as to tell a solicitor. Remember, there was always someone listening. He wasn't a half-wit, you know. It's not only *monstrous* but silly.' As proof, she quoted his statement in *Action*, *before* he was imprisoned, in which he asked the members of the BUF to defend Britain if invasion came. 'Never, *never* would he have co-operated against his own country.'

Ironically, Hitler came into contact with Mosley only through his affection for Lady Diana and her sister Unity Mitford and not because he recognised him as a British counterpart. 'The last time they met was three years before the war which hardly suggests they were *chums*!'

Her indignation was uncharacteristic. Usually, her reaction is one of constant laughter. Though too courteous to say anything against him personally, she was entranced though bewildered by a recent visit from the late Russell Harty who claimed that Hitler had gone to her wedding reception clutching a bunch of daffodils.

'Daffodils in *October*, I ask you!' Peals of laughter.

The concept of Mein Führer tripping into the Goebbelses' home with a bunch of daffs is bizarre, if merry. 'If he *had* brought flowers, they would have been orchids,' she assured me.

There was a curious summing up in Harty's television interview with Lady Diana which had been shown several weeks earlier. 'Can it be conceivable,' he asked himself, as he was wont to do, 'that a friend of Hitler's could be a friend of mine?' When I told her this, she leant forward with delight: 'But did he *answer* the question?'

At the age of seventy-eight, she is the loveliest of the Mitford sisters with those famous cheekbones and swanlike neck. Her eyes are cornflower blue and she looked remarkably well considering the terrible operation a few years ago when she was flown to London and spent seven weeks in hospital to have a tumour on the brain removed. Today, her hair restored, her recovery is complete with the compensation that former migraines have gone. Far from living in isolation, she entertains a flow of visitors, assisted by the Irish couple, with a son and daughter-in-law in Paris, grandchildren and even great-grandchildren. Politics apart, it is impossible not to admire her unless you find it impossible to put the politics apart.

For a stranger like myself, the conversation over lunch was astounding, with pieces of history thrown in as casually as comments on the weather. 'When I was seventeen I crossed the Channel with Winston who dropped me off in Paris, which was *so* kind of him as it saved the expense of a nanny or a chaperone. He was on his way to Rome to see Mussolini for whom he had the *greatest* admiration.'

Diana's notorious friendship with Hitler has obscured her closer relationship with Churchill which started in her childhood: 'He was always talking about war, even then.' Clementine Churchill was her cousin. This makes her imprisonment in the war so surprising.

When a German invasion was imminent, Lady Mosley was arrested without any charge brought against her, except for the well-known fact that she supported her husband. Understandably, with the tension of the time, habeas corpus had been suspended. Two policemen and a woman took her away for questioning, over the weekend, as she assumed, and startled her by asking if she wanted to take her youngest son with her. Fearing for his safety in the blitz, she refused though it was a sacrifice to leave behind the eleven-week-old child. It was three and a half years before she saw him again. By then he was almost four and her other son, also by her second marriage to Sir Oswald, was five.

Many people will think that she got off lightly, that she should have been shot and would have been in another country. It is a tribute to the English sense of fair play that this was not considered. There was no question of treachery, but people might have thought there was in the panic of the moment. 'Did you ever feel in danger?' I asked her.

'Not for me, but for *him*.'

Although she is devoid of rancour, her imprisonment has left a lasting impression and she talked of it in vivid detail. Many of the memories are hilarious, such as the occasion of a visit from her sister Unity when Diana had cried, 'Darling, you've brought *grouse!*' only to discover that the objects left on the radiator were Unity's gloves. Fortunately, one of the other 18 B internees was a former Major-General who was expert at plucking the birds brought to her by her family and friends.

Mention of Unity made her momentarily sad. 'We were so happy that she was alive,' said Lady Diana, referring to Unity's suicide attempt in Germany at the outbreak of war. 'Later we realised that she was not the Unity we knew. It wasn't the bullet, but the infection.'

Because they were technically on 'remand', she was allowed to wear her own clothes unlike the women convicts who were forced to wear soiled clothes previously used by others. Even so, the conditions were grim – 'terrible food on plates rimmed with age-old grease, stained blankets and the cold' – made worse when a bomb smashed the local waterworks, the lavatories overflowed, and she was rationed to one pint of water a day, to drink or wash in. 'I washed; our faces were black.' I did not like to suggest that her choice might have been fortified by the bottles of port in her hampers from Harrods.

Interviewed by her solicitor at the time, she was so angry that she complained about the conditions. 'What a pity,' he mused, 'that you don't know anyone in the War Cabinet.'

'*Anyone!*' she exclaimed. 'I know them all, from Winston down, and every one of them should be put against a wall and shot!' Ill-advised words. As Mosley warned her: 'It's fatal to say anything in fun.'

Years later, meeting Churchill on the Riviera, Daisy Fellowes asked him why he never saw Diana Mosley. 'Because she wanted me shot in the war,' he replied gruffly.

Lady Diana Mosley with the Temple de la Gloire in the background

When she was told of this, Diana wrote to him saying that she disagreed with his policies but never wanted him shot. 'I was *so* angry that afternoon,' she admitted, 'and if I had submitted you to those conditions, you'd have wanted me shot.' Silence. Then a telegram from Winston thanking her, followed by 'such a kind letter'. Could I see it? Of course, but it was lost in the fire which destroyed her home in Ireland. Equally frustrating, Hitler's signed photograph in a silver frame, which he presented on her wedding day, was in a drawer – 'somewhere'.

Yet Churchill had been solicitous on two occasions, overruling his Home Secretary, Herbert Morrison. Once he gave a direct order that she should be allowed a bath daily: 'How could I? We were lucky to have one bath a week and then the water was usually cold and filthy, so I couldn't accept a favour denied to the others.'

Churchill's other concession established a precedent, remarkable in wartime when he had so much to occupy his time. Her brother Tom, who was killed in the war, told her he was dining at Number Ten that evening and asked if there was anything in particular which she wanted. One thing above all: to be reunited with 'Kit'. This was granted on Churchill's orders a few weeks later, allowing them generous quarters in prison with convicts to clean for them. 'They were *so* kind,' she told me. 'They gave us sexual offenders because they never steal anything.' Chatting to the friendly governor one day, she had the gall to complain that a button was missing on her husband's orange-coloured overcoat.

'I rather thought that was the wife's job,' said the governor stiffly.

'*Me!*' she protested with aristocratic hauteur. 'Kit wouldn't think of letting *me* do that. He says that a button can only be sewn on properly by a *tailor*.' It went unsewn.

Her comments over lunch had the fascination of eye-witness veracity: how Eva Braun's prettiness resembled Unity's; how she admired the Goebbelses' suicide, though she could not have brought herself to kill the children even though they would have suffered if alive; of Goering – 'such a pity he didn't come to the Coronation, the crowds would have *loved* him with his uniforms and everything'. And, of course, Hitler, with his fine, neatly brushed hair and white, well-shaped hands, whom she has described in her autobiography, *A Life of Contrasts*. She remains convinced that Churchill was a warmonger, pushing England into a war that could have been avoided, and that Hitler did not want to invade England, hoping for a settlement with Lloyd George as an English Pétain.

Regretfully, she concluded of her two close friends, Churchill and Hitler, that 'it was such a pity that they came together at the wrong moment'.

I started to argue and suggested, with hindsight, that Mosley's aping of Nazism with the black shirts, lightning insignia and parodied parades was a fatal miscalculation of the British.

Naïvely, or evasively, she replied that people love parades and uniforms. I decided to change the subject, preferring the laughter to the raking of ashes.

When loyalty is that inviolate, it deserves respect.

THE END OF 'FAME'

'DAN FARSON'S FATHER DIES.' A year later, my mother died too, as she had wanted to every day since they were separated. It seemed that she had died in an accident, falling down the stairs of a friend's house in London where she was lunching. Reading of her fall in the papers, Sacheverell Sitwell sent me a letter suggesting that I read a book on Elizabeth and Essex which claimed that Essex was innocent of arranging the murder of his wife, as rumoured at the time. The book suggested that Essex's wife was already dying from cancer and it was the first step on the staircase which killed her and precipitated the fall. I believe this is what happened in my mother's case, that she was already dead when she fell. I had to identify her body and attend the inquest, with the inevitable publicity surrounding unnatural death. This time it was 'DAN FARSON'S MOTHER DIES IN FALL', as broadcast on the six o'clock ITN news. I was unaware of this until I was stopped in the East End by an old man who greeted me with the words: 'See the old girl's snuffed it.'

Now that my parents' home in North Devon was empty, I felt it was absurd to go there for only a few weeks' holiday each year. I wanted to find out if I could write, so in 1964 I resigned from Associated Rediffusion after a battle to break my contract, and gave up the tenancy of the Waterman's Arms, the pub I'd taken over on the Isle of Dogs. It had proved so successful that it became too crowded after eight-thirty when it was difficult to reach the bar to buy a drink – a perverse form of success which cost me dearly though the Waterman's had provided many happy hours. With the licensing laws of the day, it had been impossible to make a profit in such a short time.

My decision to leave London was a rash one, and desperately unwise from every practical and financial point of view, but the television notoriety had soured me. It is easy to distort an emotion, however unwittingly, when you recall it years later, but a letter I came across recently, which I wrote to my parents in 1959, confirms that my distaste for television fame was genuine from the outset: 'You'll find it hard to believe but this staggering thing of being recognised wherever one goes is torture and sheer unadulterated hell. One feels one is being hunted. In a pub, bus or on the street, to have constantly to smile back at people who make fatuous though probably well-meaning remarks gets one down.'

In 1964, five years after writing this letter, I retired with relief to Putsborough Sands in North Devon where the writer, Henry Williamson, was my neighbour.

An Eightieth Birthday at Ox's Cross

HENRY WILLIAMSON

Henry looked magnificent in his old age, like one of the lean, windswept beeches he had planted in the field at Ox's Cross fifty years earlier, except that he remained erect. His hair was white and his eyes watered but they were riveting; he expected you to look at him when he was talking. Sometimes they blazed with impatience. He had never tolerated fools but by now fools were frequently intolerant of him, a solitary old man in a grey raincoat sitting in the corner of a pub, cupping his hands together as he imitated the cuckoo.

'Cuckoo, indeed!' they'd murmur.

Sometimes he accosted such strangers to inform them that he was a great writer, which scared them off. I liked the fact that he was neither tamed nor mellow. He remained as cantankerous as ever though there were moments when I was touched by his growing vulnerability. I had known him since my childhood when he brought me to the verge of angry tears as we raced through the empty Devon lanes in his Alvis while he assured me that Hitler was 'a good and misjudged man'. Always he sought and found an affinity with children, playing with them like fish on a line though his special attention was reserved for girls.

My father and Henry were fellow-members of the Savage Club where their bad behaviour fuelled a long-running feud which they enjoyed, concealing a genuine mutual admiration. Henry had a habit of descending on the Grey House, my parents' house on Putsborough Sands, to read aloud interminably after dinner in a sepulchral voice from his latest manuscript. This exasperated my father who revelled in good conversation, driving him to his bedroom where he clomped about noisily above us as a form of retaliation. Once, after discussing Henry with some guests, we discovered on going outside that he had eavesdropped, for the initials H.W. were carefully composed in twigs and leaves.

'My God!' exclaimed my father. 'Henry's been here. Tarka the Rotter, that elfin son of a bitch!'

The effect of Henry on animals was devastating and it is significant that *Tarka the Otter* was dedicated to the Master of the Cheriton Otterhounds. (He had taken me on an

The hut which is preserved by the Henry Williamson Society

otter hunt when I was a boy, and I was delighted that the day proved unsuccessful.) My mother claimed that she knew when Henry was coming down the drive because the hens squawked with alarm, the dog dived under the chair, and the cat flew out of the window. When our mutual friend, Barry Driscoll, came to Ox's Cross with his wife and child to illustrate a new edition of *Tarka*, he was dismayed when Henry burst into their caravan after midnight demanding milk.

'I'm sorry, Henry,' Barry explained, 'but we've only just arrived and we haven't had time to do any shopping. Have you run out?'

'No,' said Henry savagely, 'but the village is full of Jews and they've taken all the milk.'

After he had stormed out, Barry lay there aghast, thinking, 'Oh no, not already.' Ignoring the vexed subject of the milk the next morning, he remarked brightly that a wonderful thing had happened: 'After you left, I heard a willow warbler and it seemed so right, in your field up here at Ox's Cross.'

Henry looked at him coldly. 'I do hope,' he said in his soft, sinister voice, 'that you haven't come here to talk about bloody animals.'

After Henry kicked Barry Driscoll's dog, Titus, Barry threatened to punch him if he did so again, and a new relationship dawned. Henry relaxed, caressed Titus, and set out deliberately to make Barry's twelve-year-old daughter fall in love with him. Barry told me: 'It could have ruined her life, this outrageous flattery! He'd say, "I'd like to read you a passage and ask your opinion," and he'd read aloud to her for two or three hours. "Don't you want to come down to the beach with us?" No, she preferred to stay with Henry. Such was his power that he got her to listen to the *entire* recording of *Tristan* without complaint.' There were no sexual implications whatever, but at last Pippa had to be rescued by her parents, much against her will for by then she was spellbound by Henry's intensity.

As the years passed on my return to Devon, many of them lean for both of us, Henry was frequently alone which explains why he sought my company. He tried to be congenial, even if it went against the grain, and could be absorbing company. Because his humour was schoolboyish – he called the Prince of Wales the Pragger-Wagger – people often failed to detect it. He greeted food as if he were unused to it, which may have been the case in this late period in his life. 'Is this *sugared* tea?' he asked me. 'It's very nice.' He was always grateful when something interesting was placed before him instead of the usual pub pasty. 'I feel rather wan,' he admitted, 'I've gone down to ten pounds.' Once, seeing him huddled in his raincoat, I asked if he was cold. He shook his head. 'I don't feel anything. I don't expect I'd feel it if you hit me.'

Yet his physical stamina was exceptional for a man in his seventies. At first, when he came to see me on most days in the week, he navigated his MG down the narrow lanes from Georgeham as if it were a tank, defying any vehicle approaching from the opposite direction. After a contretemps with my neighbour, a retired colonel who took umbrage when Henry sprawled his car across the drive, he came down to visit me on foot. 'I'd have biffed him one,' he told me indignantly after his quarrel with the colonel, 'but I thought he'd biff me back.' On one occasion he walked from Ilfracombe where he stayed when not at Ox's Cross, a distance of ten miles or more, and arrived gasping, 'I hope you've got the wood for the coffin!'

Our relationship benefited from my lack of reverence. Plenty of Williamson's admirers made the trek to North Devon to sit at his feet and listen to him, but I was unfamiliar with his work, though I revere it now, and this led to an easy, straightforward rapport. I felt a growing affection for him, however difficult he could be. People told me how he spoke out on my behalf when I was criticised, for both of us were regarded as undesirable aliens in this narrow-minded community, and this pleased me greatly. One day when I was working, I found Henry in the porch where he had been sitting patiently for at least an hour. 'You should have called me,' I told him, but he replied, solemnly, that he had heard me typing and would never disturb a fellow-writer.

At this period in his life he revealed that 'people always seem to be going out when I call on them', although he made an effort to be agreeable. Years earlier he had shocked me when he kicked my dog Littlewood (named after Joan) when she nuzzled her snout against his knee while he was reading aloud – always a sacrosanct moment for Henry. Now he stroked her great-granddaughter, Bonzo, ruffling her fur the wrong way as he whispered, 'Poor little doggy-poggy, poor little man,' while she watched him wide-eyed and askance. One evening he arrived ebulliently, declaring that it was too long since he had seen me, and I did not have the heart to point out that he had called that morning.

Henry was growing old. Two crucial events lay ahead: the completion of *A Chronicle of Ancient Sunlight*, his epic account of England from the end of the last century to the present day; and his eightieth birthday.

One brilliant spring morning in 1968 I met him by chance on the beach and he announced that he had finished *The Gale of the World*, the last and fifteenth volume of his epic. He looked dazed, now devoured by doubt: should he have written it as an auto-biographical series, rather than as fiction. I thought it an extraordinary admission after so many years of irretrievable effort. Having completed the manuscript at his cottage in Ilfracombe on the previous Sunday afternoon, he had added a postscript as if he could not bear to let it go: 'I got up from my writing table overcome by emotion, crying out words of grief and amazement while walking aimlessly about the rooms of the cottage empty except for myself, disturbed by feelings of a lost freedom which also had been a tyranny during the two decades now closed behind one.'

The *Gale* was such a weird novel that Ken Allsop, to whom it was dedicated, could not bring himself to write Henry a letter of praise. Meanwhile, my neighbours implored me not to read it because Henry was so 'cruel' about my late mother and father. I bought it at once to discover that Henry had taken his revenge for all my father's drunken insults over the years by portraying him as an alcoholic American writer, Osgood Nilsson, who had written an autobiography called *Sinner's Way*. My father's own autobiography was *The Way of a Transgressor*, and this was a feeble disguise. My mother was shown unfairly as a tiresome gossip, but if there had been wit I should have minded less. Instead, there was a new note of bitterness. Colin Wilson responded loyally in his review for *Books & Bookmen*:

> There is an acid portrait of Negley Farson as the American writer, Osgood Nilsson of whom he writes primly: 'Self-knowledge, in relation to the defects of others, was denied him; so he remained a second-rate or superficial writer.' Williamson could be describing himself. If Williamson had simply portrayed Farson's alcoholism and capacity for virulent abuse, he would have been perfectly fair; but he shows Nilsson involved in acts of calculated meanness; and, whatever Farson's faults, he was never mean. Unfortunately, Williamson was; and it is because this can be sensed in the later volumes that *A Chronicle of Ancient Sunlight* ends on a level that is so far below its beginning.

That beginning had been splendid. The first two volumes – *The Dark Lantern* and *Donkey Boy* – are among the finest books of our time, evoking the turn of the century with astonishing detail, but the *Gale* is bilious by comparison and smutty in its description of Philip Maddison's sexual frustration or Laura's memory of her abortion:

> Am I like that really? Wanting revenge, because my father raped me when I was a child, was it punishment for coming on him when he was frigging the nanny-goat behind the hedge? If I wrote that, no one would believe it. Mother

found out and I had to sleep with Granny ever afterwards . . . Was it when we started to walk upright? Animals are shapely, compared with women after twenty-five. Black brassières and French knickers – trap for John Thomas Esquire – and finally cancer of the breast, from too much mauling. God, I am human bait, nothing more . . .

In one respect it was admirable that the old man had so much spunk in him, and he remained irresistibly attractive to numerous young women. Other readers, and they were sparse, found the book loathsome because of Henry's glorification of Sir Oswald Mosley, thinly disguised as Sir Hereward Birkin. Altogether it was a sad business for it meant that his great work received no recognition.

When I met Henry on Barnstaple Station a few weeks later, I had forgotten his vindictive portrayal of my parents and we walked across the bridge together for a drink at Mugford's. It was market day, when the pub stayed open all afternoon, and Henry should have heeded the warning: like father like son. With a sudden flush of filial loyalty, I remembered the *Gale* and tried to think of something which would hurt him in return. With unerring aim, I struck his Achilles' heel, remembering a remark made to me by Oswald Mosley: 'We like Henry so much, but he will take it all so seriously.' The effect on Henry when I repeated this was appalling. He left the pub trembling and sent me a series of letters over the next few days, starting with the reproof, 'I am most sorry that you felt you had to speak (almost in public) as you did in Mugford's tonight,' continuing, by way of explanation, 'And I can only repeat, *with truth*, that I have never had to "get my own back" on your father Negley. I understood him. And how alcohol disturbed his judgement, and released at times a sense of his own social superiority: as when he produced in public General Negley's photograph in order to say to one or another of his pub-stooges, "You never had a general in *your* family, you're a no-good man." '

This was truer of Henry's Osgood than my father, but, characteristically, Henry's letters became increasingly defensive, protesting that 'Nilsson is *not* a bad character', then 'Good for Goodie Nilsson!' Next he resorted to self-pity: 'I am sorry – to repeat – you have been distressed. I will not trouble you again with my presence, Dan. In any case, I am weakening fast, and have lost the will to live. It's time to go. Bless you, Dan.' After this finality, he added the postscript: 'I shall be away tomorrow, else I'd come and see you, hoping to ease your unhappiness with my *sincere* belief that I had "nothing to get back" to poor old Negley.'

Finally he made the surprising admission:

> I believe what you said re O.M. He spoke to *me* like that, once, at Nicky's wedding reception at the Savoy (1947 or 1948). I begged him NOT to form another party – 'European Union'. I wanted him to write his memoirs instead. He was NEWS! but bad news. He let loose a sarcastic glance at me and said, 'Your place in our Movement, Henry, is to stand by the Savage Club window as we go past down below, and to say, "I shouldn't be surprised if there wasn't

something in it."' Well, I didn't mind that. I'd asked for it. But twenty years later, Diana said, 'You did advise Kit to write his memoirs and keep quiet – I remember.'

Our clash was short-lived and our friendship became the stronger because of it.

As Henry's eightieth birthday approached – 1 December 1975 – I realised with alarm that he was depending on the honours he was bound to receive. In jocular mood he had written to a friend, 'My only hope seems to be to try to accept things and become a Grand Old Man of Letters. Oh dear. Perhaps not even grand. A Hardy without Hardy's simplicity.' Henry's self-deprecation was seldom convincing, and he added in the inevitable postscript: 'Some critics write that *A Chronicle of Ancient Sunlight* will be the greatest novel in the world. *If* I can finish it, it might be a lesser English classic . . . ' In the event, it passed without notice. Now he had a second chance with his birthday, and the English respect for longevity.

HTV agreed that we should celebrate the occasion with a short film. Henry was shown walking across his landscape: the great field at Braunton, the burrows, Saunton Sands, and the old lighthouse near Bideford Bar where we picnicked beside the breakwaters and my dog Bonzo stole his food. I wrote about Henry for the *Sunday Telegraph Magazine* and this produced a score of congratulatory letters which he carried in his battered leather briefcase.

The omens were good as the great day drew nearer when the honours would be announced. It was inconceivable otherwise. Lady Diana Mosley confided to me: 'Most people loved Henry's books but hated the politics. Of course I approved of the politics but I'm afraid I couldn't do with the books.' She admitted to an aversion to books about animals, but for several generations *Tarka the Otter* was part of the pleasure of growing up, devoid of the usual sentimentality. The four volumes of *The Flax of Dream*, with such delightful titles as *The Dream of Fair Women* and *Dandelion Days*, evoke the peace of England between the two great wars, immortalising the innocence of the North Devon countryside in particular. The last true literary figure in English literature, apart from J. B. Priestley, Henry Williamson was in the tradition of his heroes: Richard Jefferies, Thomas Hardy, John Masefield and John Galsworthy, who had presented him with the Hawthornden Prize for *Tarka* in 1928, with a cheque for £100 which enabled him to buy the field at Ox's Cross.

Henry had anticipated the occasion from the outset of the year, writing me a forlorn yet hopeful letter on 9 April 1975, from his cottage in Ilfracombe:

Time, 10.55 a.m. Condition – pallid, burnt out (feeling) as 1 December approaches. A failure, henceforward. Sitting in this little room with tall windows facing north and east. And that is all.

Dear Dan, the flow has stopped. It was drying up after my 15th volume of *The Gale of the World*, 15th and ultimate volume of *A Chronicle of Ancient Sunlight,* dedicated to Kenneth Allsop. As a 16 year old, bicycled from Hertfordshire to Devon to call on the author: and years later 'couldn't take' *The Gale*. (Masefield's opinion – 'You have written more classics in the English language than any man now living.' Well, well . . .

Dan, *in confidence*; I feel I am only litter left. Litter on tables here – scattered – HERE I CHANGE MY MIND, from sloth and near-despair to start again. And I pick up, from the round mahogany table (all a-litter), your letter. With your help, dear neighbour, I feel I could start again – a fresh start.

David Cobham, bless him and his dear companion-wife, gave me a chance on film. [*Tarka the Otter*]

Now the son of dear Negley Farson offers a new hope. Thank you, Dan! (I changed my mind over your dinner party: and glad I was to find such a cheery atmosphere.)

I did hope that 1 December would be kept dark: but what's the odds? *Times* and *Telegraph* keep tabs on such items. But it's rather like prophesying one's own doom – but no! Heart and lungs etc. are sound . . .

Blessing upon you, Dan'l Farson! And many thanks! Yours, Henry.

The letter was typical of his sporadic self-pity, which he rather enjoyed, followed by new resolve. The deprecation of 'I did hope that 1 December would be kept dark' was sheer hypocrisy.

The great day arrived and it was dark indeed. Nobody came to honour him. There was no knighthood, no Order of Merit which he regarded as his due. A lonely, bewildered figure in the hut at Ox's Cross, his hurt was palpable. I was reminded of the contrasting scene in Maugham's *Cakes and Ale* when they paid homage to Edward Driffield, unmistakably Thomas Hardy, on his eightieth birthday: 'I think you'd have to go a long way to find gathered together such a collection of distinguished people as got out from that train at Blackstable. It was awfully moving when the PM presented the old man with the Order of Merit.' The only people to leave the train at Barnstaple were Henry's sons.

What had gone wrong? Why did a writer whose books portray English life with such compassion go to his death unhonoured? How had he offended? The answer lies in two names – Hitler and Mosley – but the key to everything lies in the First World War. Understand that, and you understand Henry.

The formative moment was the Christmas Truce in 1914 when the soldiers on both sides surged across the No Man's Land in Flanders in sudden, spontaneous sympathy, played football, exchanged schnapps and cigarettes, and showed photographs of their loved ones. I remember Henry talking of one German soldier who sang 'Silent Night' as dusk fell, joining in himself in his surprisingly high voice – 'Heilige Nacht'. He was shocked to discover that the 'huns' believed they were fighting for a worthy cause, just as he was, and that they were perfectly decent men. At midnight they retired to their trenches and received their orders to recommence the slaughter. From that moment, Henry was convinced that the 'cousin nations' should never go to war again.

Few men could have survived the trenches to return the same as before, unless they

Henry Williamson in skittish mood on the signpost at Ox's Cross

were unbalanced to begin with, and though Henry was unscarred physically he was in turmoil within. He quarrelled with his father, a pedantic man who became exasperated by Henry's constant praise of the German soldiers until he could bear it no longer and accused his son of being a 'traitor', a cry which echoed through the rest of Henry's life. Ordered to leave their home in Blackheath, Henry set out for Devon on his Norton motorbike and arrived at the village of Georgeham in 1921 where he rented Skirr Cottage by the stream, beside the church, for £4 a year. Gradually he recovered as he walked through the landscape which I think of as Williamson country today, gaining the new identities of naturalist and writer. And he began to realise that the experience he had been through in the war was noble as well as fearsome, never to be regained. In *A Dream of Fair Women* he wrote:

> Never again to have such friendships? Or to see the white flares beyond the parapet at night and hear the mournful wailing of gas-horns over the wastes of the Somme battlefields? Gone, gone for ever. His heart ached: the splendid bitter days of the war dimmed the sunlight as he lay on the beach of shells, among the dried weed and black brittle cases of dogfish eggs cast up during old storms, and corks and rusty tins, all the littered drift of the sea.

Years later he startled me when he spoke of the First War as 'rather nice'. Sensing my astonishment, he confirmed, 'It wasn't such a bad war really. Beautiful. Here and there we found some mercy and kindness and that is what made the war generally, apart from the physical wounds, rather a nice one.'

This was in his eightieth year when his mind returned to the Great War like a needle stuck in the groove of a record. By then he had obliterated the brutality, remembering only the finer qualities which war can create, but in 1930 his *Patriot's Progress* was one of the most powerful anti-war books, together with Sassoon's *Memoirs of an Infantry Officer*, Remarque's *All Quiet on the Western Front, Goodbye to All That* by Robert Graves, and the poems of Wilfred Owen. *Patriot's Progress* is scarcely acknowledged today, yet Henry's words scorch with their anger, confirming the claim by Arnold Bennett that 'of its kind [it] has never been surpassed'.

In his *The Collapse of British Power,* Corelli Barnett condemns didactic anti-war novels, quoting Williamson in particular, for giving 'a highly subjective, unbalanced and misleading version both of the Western Front and of the British army's reaction to it. For the war writers were not in the least representative of the men of the British army as a whole; they were writers and poets, and with few exceptions they came from sheltered, well-off, upper or upper-middle-class backgrounds, the products of an upbringing at home and at their public schools which had given them little knowledge or understanding of the real world of their time, but rather a set of unpractical idealistic attitudes. They were indeed flowers of English liberalism and romanticism.'

Corelli Barnett has the grace to concede that he is sitting in judgement on men who endured ordeals that he fears he himself could not support, but detests their implicit pacifism: 'The catastrophically far-reaching effects of the war books on British opinion, and hence on British policy, were compounded by the unlucky coincidence of their historical timing, for they straddled the very turning-point of the inter-war period.' He goes on to explain that the books appeared at a moment when the Great War seemed forgotten, with the new 'world situation' in which a second war was a definite possibility. 'What began as an epitaph ended as a warning. As a warning, the war books seemed to say that war was so terrible and futile that the British ought to keep out of another one at any cost.'

Certainly this was Henry's reaction, and it would be naïve to expect a different re-action when the anti-war mood was echoed, not only by other writers, but in the melan-choly of Elgar, the war memorials of Lutyens and the paintings by Nevinson and Nash with the ironic disillusionment of such titles as *We Are Making a New World.*

The likelihood of a second war came later, while in the mid 1930s Henry's pro-German sympathies were reflected by many Englishmen. In 1935 Henry wrote to T. E. Law-rence, living in obscurity as Aircraftsman Shaw, suggesting a rally of ex-soldiers at the Albert Hall followed by a visit to Berlin to see Hitler. Lawrence was sufficiently in-terested to discuss it, and sent Henry a telegram on 13 May: 'LUNCH TUESDAY WET FINE COTTAGE ONE MILE NORTH BOVINGTON CAMP'. As Lawrence rode back from the post office, his motorbike skidded as he avoided some children playing in the road and he died from his injuries five days later. Rumours of a Zionist plot and a sinister black limousine racing away from the crash can be discounted although Henry perpetuated the myth until I asked him outright if this was true, when he had the honesty to deny it.

'I believe,' wrote Henry later, 'that had he lived, Lawrence would have confirmed the inner hopes of every ex-serviceman in England: that the spirit of Christmas Day 1914, already hovering in the air, would have swiftly materialised and given . . . a vision of a new conception of life.'

Searching for another leader to endorse his views, Henry found him in Sir Oswald Mosley, but it was his foreword to a new edition of *The Flax of Dream* which proved fatal to Henry's soaring reputation. Significantly, this was dated Christmas Day 1935 and harks back again to the truce: 'The seed idea of *The Flax of Dream* was loosed upon the frozen ground of the battlefield . . . The fulfilment or materialisation of that idea has been the mainspring of life ever since; for many years in a solitariness of desperation; now with hope, because the vision of a new world, dreamed by many young soldiers in the trenches and shell-craters of the World War, is being made real in one European nation at least . . . I salute the great man across the Rhine, whose life symbol is the happy child.'

That was the most disastrous sentence ever written by Williamson. This was when he gave offence. Henry's attitude towards Hitler strayed into fantasy. He attended the Nuremberg rally, describing the event in *Goodbye West Country* (1937): 'I wandered about, saw Hitler quite close, talking to several people. He was very quick in his head movements. He spoke rapidly. I got the idea his natural pace is much swifter than the ordinary, his eyes falcon-like, remarkably full of life . . . Amused myself by wondering what I should say, if by chance of Time's wheel, the minor country writer was brought up before Hitler. I'd have nothing to say . . . '

Years later, in his softest voice, he deceived himself, or his memory was confused, when I asked whether he was comparing Hitler with Jesus: 'I am in a way, of course I am, because Hitler was human and Jesus was human, he wasn't just floating about in coloured pyjamas or something like that! Hitler told me there must never be a war with England; if so everything would come to an end. There were tears in his eyes. He was a very emotional man.' Henry had tears in his eyes as well when he recounted this balder-

Even as an old man, Henry retained his mesmeric attraction

dash; like many a shameless liar he treasured his lies. He convinced himself further that Hitler was one of the soldiers who had taken part in the Christmas Truce: 'He has the truest eyes I have ever seen in a man's face, he is an ex-corporal of the Linz Regiment which opposed my regiment under Messines Hill on Christmas Day 1914. We made a truce then, which must never be broken.' Henry had confused the Linz Regiment with Hitler's *List* Regiment, named after its commander. It hardly matters now, and when we made that film by the breakwaters near Bideford Bar he made a rare admission after praising Hitler as a great man: 'But so many great men turn out to be fiends and devils because they go too far. He wanted to avoid the war with us, but he went the way to get it.'

In his contrary way, Henry was a patriot. He wished to avoid a second war with Germany because he believed it would cost us our Empire and reduce Britain to a second-rate power, but once war was declared he told me he was prepared to take up a pitchfork to defend the Norfolk farm he was cultivating at the time, should the Germans invade. He wrote to a girl: 'It is better to die yourself than cause the death of others.' He was interrogated briefly by the local police when it was rumoured that he was a German spy, painting arrows on his fields with lime in order to direct the German bombers, but to his dismay he was released as a harmless eccentric.

If he had skipped off to America like Auden and Isherwood, if he had been supplicatory like Wodehouse and Chaplin, if he had recanted, he would have received his honours on his eightieth birthday, but that was not his way. Soon afterwards he collapsed and was sent to Twyford Abbey on the outskirts of London where he could be cared for. One day he was found naked on the platform of the local railway station, presumably yearning to go somewhere – perhaps to Baggy Point which I could see from my window in the Grey House. He had told his son, Harry, at Ox's Cross: 'I want to go out on Baggy Point at a very low tide and climb as far out on the rocks as I can and go to sleep in the sunshine and be washed off and drift out to sea.'

This was not to be, though it would have been so right. His mind almost obliterated, he died at the Abbey on 13 August 1977.

It is time to forgive him.

RIP

A 'Hopeless Case' in Soho

GERALD WILDE

When I ventured into Soho in the early 1950s, I found myself surrounded by sacred monsters. Most of them were painters and Gerald Wilde was the craziest, someone I tried to avoid at first as he advanced, wild-eyed and menacing, demanding drink. When we collided it was usually a brief encounter as he was ejected from the Caves de France by the barman, Secundo Primera, the gentle brother of Primo. If the pub was double-doored, like the York Minster, he'd be thrown out of one door and reappear through the other, like the couple in a weather-vane. On these occasions Wilde made a considerable noise, voluble to the point of unintelligibility, and I was young enough to admire someone who dared be so outrageous, described to me romantically as 'the incantation of Bohemian excess'. Even so I found his appearance alarming: a snowfall of cigarette ash on his shoulders, a garish shirt, a bootlace tie, an overcoat falling to his ankles, and that singular wide-eyed stare. I discovered later that it was singular indeed because he had lost the use of his left eye through an accident when he was six.

Allegedly reticent when he was sober, he indulged in skirmishes with the police when he was drunk, being under the delusion that they were persecuting him though they were remarkably forbearing. The art critic Tim Hilton described him as 'never good company [who] would disappear when you gave him money'. After Wilde returned from the mental hospital in Epsom where he received electric shock treatment in 1954, he was 'just as crazy as before'.

Inevitably he is confused with the eccentric artist Gully Jimson in Joyce Carey's novel *The Horse's Mouth* published in 1944. In the film, Jimson was played by Alec Guinness and the massive murals were painted by the artist John Bratby. Wilde was Jimson personified, exasperating his patrons by the trail of havoc in his wake, yet it was not until five years after publication that he met Carey in Oxford. They did so late at night at a party. Carey was suddenly aware of a 'queer noise' and saw a strange figure across the room.

> At first glance, in the dim light, Wilde seemed like a spectre. His long, dead-white face with its hollow cheeks was like a mask of bleached skin on a skull,

his arms seemed but bones, hanging loosely in the sleeves of an enormous coat whose crumpled folds gave no room for flesh. The arms, too, were extremely long, so that the bony hands almost touched the floor. It was as if this skeleton had but half risen from the grave.

All this figure was in violent and continuous agitation, and with a movement that seemed by itself preternatural. It was this shivering, shaking which, more than anything, gave at that moment the sense of visitation from another world.

Carey started to rise to his feet, uncertain whether Wilde was trying to speak to him, though aware that he was staring and that his stare was urgent. Then Wilde flung out his arms and plunged forward, knocking over a table of glasses which seemed to baffle him. His admirable hostess escorted him to bed and returned laughing. The glass was swept up, the carpet mopped, and the party continued as before.

After this encounter, the more surprising considering that Wilde was sober, the two men felt a mutual attraction: Wilde excited at meeting his 'creator'; Carey rewarded by seeing his character brought to life. 'Wilde was a painter who thought of himself as a Gully Jimson,' he wrote afterwards, 'and seeing me unexpectedly he wanted to explain, all at once, his feelings about the book, about Gully . . . ' They had a number of 'polite conversations' when Wilde aired his views in a soft voice, eager to agree. 'We could agree quietly that a really original artist is never popular; that he . . . is lucky to get [recognition] in his lifetime.' Carey himself had no doubts about Wilde's paintings, paying him the ultimate compliment of buying several himself: 'You cannot classify Wilde's art. It is not representative; and neither is it abstract. He came to us out of a dream that he could not even describe, or explain – he could only paint it.'

Wilde was considered 'a hopeless case' but such friends and patrons as Carey, Peter Watson and Kenneth Clark persevered in their efforts to help him. Wilde foiled them every time.

Once he appeared in Soho in a smart new overcoat in contrast to his usual shabby, second-hand cast-offs. This magnificent coat – which could have been cashmere – cost £30, a considerable sum of money in the 1950s, and there were cries of admiration when he made his entrance at opening time. By one o'clock he had sold it for £2. His pursuit of drink was thwarted only when friends locked him up in a room, for it was seldom that he had a studio or home of his own. With the cunning of the alcoholic, he revealed a flair for escape worthy of Houdini. Once he found a rope, attached a large, expensive easel to the end, and lowered it from the upstairs window before climbing down himself. Within minutes the easel had been sold for a few shillings and Wilde was happily ensconced in a pub.

Meary Tambimuttu, the founder of Poetry London and a figure in Fitzrovia, treated Wilde like a performing dog. Starting a fund for 'Gerald Wilde the Mad Artist' in the Wheatsheaf pub, he proclaimed: 'He's starving and with no money, you know.' Julian Maclaren-Ross related the episode in his *Memoirs of the Forties*: 'I'd never until then heard of Gerald Wilde the Mad Artist but I put something in the hat and was then intro-

Gerald Wilde

duced to the Mad Artist himself: sitting at a table guarded by Tambi's supporters, with only a glass of mineral water before him and seeming not noticeably insane: just pale, dispirited and sad.'

Tambimuttu went around the pub collecting from the customers but, when the hat was filled with coins and Wilde dared to stretch out a tentative hand towards it, he was shouted at reprovingly – 'as one who corrects a too-presumptuous or greedy child, and Gerald Wilde relapsed remonstrating in a rapid inaudible mutter, this incipient mutiny being quelled at once by a glance from Tambi's celebrated eyes.'

The poet assured Maclaren-Ross that Wilde was on the wagon – 'It's not good for him to drink and he has work to do' – so he followed the usual procedure of sending him back to his flat with instructions to paint. After Wilde had shuffled out accompanied by the friend who would return with the key, Maclaren-Ross echoed, 'Lock him up!' 'Yes,' explained the poet, 'you must be severe with Gerald. If you give him money he buys drink with it and does not work,' whereupon he delved into the hat and bought a round from the collection. At their regular café after closing time, he ordered steaks – paid for again from the collection – and demanded donations of food from the other customers ('for Gerald Wilde the Mad Artist who is starving, you know'), proffering a paper bag into which they dropped their scraps – enough to reward the Mad Artist for his work.

Tambimuttu went away for the weekend, which proved a long one, and returned on the Tuesday to find the flat door hanging on its hinges and the books gone from their shelves. The Mad and Hungry Artist had become ravenous after four days' starvation and sold the books after phoning a taxi, embarking on a drunken spree.

Tambimuttu got the treatment he deserved, but Wilde did have the unfortunate habit of giving his paintings away to strangers which made it difficult to assemble an exhibition. In addition to being given away, sold for drink, or simply abandoned, much of his work was destroyed in the Blitz, and it wasn't until he was forty-three that he held his first one-man show at the Hanover Gallery in 1948.

A hopeless case, yet redeemed by a touch of genius. Catching Wilde on the wing, as it were, there was rarely the chance for a serious conversation, and the more I learn about him today the more I regret the missed opportunity. To my layman's eye, Wilde's paintings seemed tiresomely abstract at that time and I undervalued him accordingly until Lucian Freud reproved me sharply when I expressed some doubts recently. One reason for the neglect of Wilde's work is the difficulty of placing it in a specific category as people like to do, although in 1984 the critic John McEwan paid the astonishing tribute: 'Many now consider him the outstanding painter of his generation [Sutherland, Piper] in England, and the only abstract expressionist.'

His qualifications were impressive: seven years at the Chelsea School of Art with Graham Sutherland, which led to a lifelong friendship with Henry Moore. Writing of Wilde's one-man show in 1948, David Sylvester claimed that Wilde was then at the peak of his powers: 'He had evolved on his own, independently of the great Americans, a form of abstract expressionism. Violent and vertiginous, the paintings have a feeling of chaos held in miraculous balance, a chaos faced, all but embraced, and somehow held at bay. It is an art which has the exhilaration of a disaster just averted.' Today, I find his work more invigorating than that of Jackson Pollock.

For someone so unreliable, Wilde revealed a sense of pattern and even a momentary discipline when he was commissioned to design scarves for Ascher in 1944. The fabric he designed for a silk-screen printed dress made by Molyneaux was worn by the Queen in 1947 – an unlikely juxtaposition! Wilde soon grew impatient with commercial success and rejected security to return to the police-cells and the pubs where 'he would begin to whirl his arms with a curious clockwork motion', according to Maclaren-Ross, 'as if drink wound up some mechanism inside him. Later would come the stage of staggering and clutching painfully at people's arms while shouting imaginary grievances into their faces.'

In a particular moment of despair, Wilde himself wrote that 'life is pure unadulterated hell', yet he had the last laugh. To an extent he played a game: 'If we didn't face the threat of fall, we couldn't dance at all. My life may be miserable, but I'm not.' Far from burning himself out, he died on the morning of his eighty-first birthday, though he had been identified as a dead tramp in 1970 by the *Daily Express,* which corrected the report two days later with the heading 'I'M FEELING VERY WELL SAYS "DEAD MAN"'. After his genuine death in 1986, *The Times* described him as Oscar Wilde's grandson and it seems correct that he should have baffled even from the grave.

A photograph taken in 1980 shows him looking avuncular with a charming smile, for he gained a period of calm due to the support from the October Gallery which represented him for the last ten years with regular one-man shows. The latest posthumous exhibition was held in 1988 and brought him new recognition. Wilde was a brilliant colourist and William Feaver claims that his 'lashings of mustard yellow, scarlet and grey plunged in blackness outdo the mannerisms of those artists, like Graham Sutherland . . . ' Wilde himself made the wilful boast that Francis Bacon had 'ripped off [his] colours in the early days', according to Corinna MacNeice of the October Gallery, but she implies that he became obsessed with Bacon, dwelling on the time when Bacon bought him a half of bitter while Bacon himself drank champagne. As Bacon is notoriously generous, pouring his bottles of champagne into the glasses of his friends and strangers until they spill over, this is unlikely unless Wilde had expressed a preference for bitter or Bacon deliberately tried to rid himself of Wilde's bad company. The latter is possible, for although Bacon recommended Wilde's work to me once, he had changed his mind when I mentioned him later, describing Wilde as a 'dreadful bore' who banged on his door at four o'clock in the morning demanding money for drink.

At the end of his life Wilde found a sort of contentment when he stayed in the Stables at Sherborne House in Gloucestershire. He adopted a cat and apparently knew requited love for the first time in his life.

Corinna MacNeice recalls that Wilde greeted visitors triumphantly, fists in the air: 'I won out. I won out! They said alcohol would kill me but I defeated alcohol! . . . I have been searching for the miraculous and I have found what I needed.'

A Lace-Maker's Niece in New York

FRANCIS BACON

There can be little doubt that Francis Bacon is the greatest sacred monster of them all. Everything he does is on a larger scale than most, yet he has scarcely changed since I first met him in Muriel's Colony Room in Dean Street in the early 1950s.

A few months later he was so broke that he asked if I could sell a painting of Pope Innocent X for £150 within the next few hours as he needed the money urgently. I was able to sell it to a college friend, and to my surprise Francis gave me £15 as a commission. In 1987 one of Bacon's paintings sold for over £1 million at an auction in New York, yet we can drink together in Soho in a pub where he is seldom recognised and where once he was offered a job 'doing up' someone's house, when the stranger learnt that he was a 'painter'. At such moments, I savour the irresistible fantasy of escorting Toulouse-Lautrec to the Moulin Rouge.

Having written so much about Francis Bacon elsewhere, I hardly dare to here in case it smacks of trespass or sycophancy. However, as the theme is sacred monsters, I shall show the monster roaring, and I doubt whether he will find this any more objectionable than my more usual praise. His own suggestion for the title of this book was *The Seducers* – ' *"seduire, c'est tout"*, as the French say' – and Bacon, like the best of the sacred monsters, is a seducer himself. This could be one reason why he objects to the biography for which I have been offered formidable sums of money by numerous publishers, protesting on the one hand that he is 'just a painter' so there is nothing to write about, while letting slip tantalising glimpses on the other. 'It could upset the children of the parents I've seduced' – with a reference to the patron who took him to South Africa, travelling first class while Francis was put in steerage.

'More fun in steerage?' I suggested.

'Far more fun!' he agreed, emphatically.

My friendship with Francis Bacon has been a series of skirmishes. The first came at midnight in the Gargoyle Club after our meeting in Muriel's. My drunken companion staggered over to the corner table where Francis was sitting with Peter Lacey and demanded a drink. Afterwards, I went over primly to apologise.

'It's bad enough,' cried Francis, 'that we have to pay for your friend's drink without having to put up with your boredom as well.'

I placed the appropriate money on the table, which I could ill-afford, and left ignominiously. When we laughed about it in Muriel's the next afternoon, our friendship was forged. As Francis put it: 'If you can't be rude to your *real* friends, who can you be rude to?' Every time he said this, I felt there was an answer although I could not find it. Francis spoke from experience. His 'turning' can be entertaining when you are not at the receiving end, and, although the temper is shocking because the words are meant to hurt, they can be disarming when wide of the mark. In one tirade, he swung round at me. 'And as for your father's second-rate books –'

'But you haven't read any!'

'I don't have to. I *know* they're second-rate.'

Three of his ripostes were aimed at painters, seldom his favourite people.

In Muriel's one afternoon, the distinguished wildlife artist Barry Driscoll (who visited Henry Williamson at Ox's Cross) asked him: 'Tell me, Francis, if you weren't an artist, what would you like to have been?' With deceptive artlessness, Bacon replied, 'A *mother*.' Driscoll should have left it at that but was rash enough to quote this some time later. Bacon swung round with imperious reproof: 'I never said such a thing.' Turning to Driscoll's two sons who happened to be standing near by, he demanded, 'Do you like your father?'

'Yes, of course,' they stammered nervously.

'Well I *don't*. I think he's an absolute bastard.' Since then, he greets Driscoll with a beaming smile without giving the slightest indication that they have met before.

There is a nice story, related by George Melly, concerning Francis's gallery in New York which persuaded him, against his instinct, to accept an invitation to a lunch given in his honour by an influential hostess. Arriving in a vile temper, he was placed carefully next to a beautiful but dull young man, and lapsed into silence. Trying to please him, the hostess said that he was sitting next to the nephew of Jackson Pollock. 'Oh.' Francis regarded the pretty boy with even less pleasure than before but he spoke at last: 'So you're the old lace-maker's *niece*, are you?'

Recently, Julian Schnabel phoned him on a visit to London. 'I'm Schnabel, you're Bacon. We should get together.'

'*No*,' said Francis with his usual emphasis, and hung up.

More serious are the friendships he has lost. The saddest rift of all concerned Graham Sutherland.

No Monster at Menton

GRAHAM SUTHERLAND

Of all the artists I have known, Graham Sutherland troubles me the most. We met in 1954 when we were fellow visitors at the Voile D'Or, a delightful hotel-restaurant at Saint Jean, Cap Ferrat, owned by a British film producer. I had stopped with an Australian acquaintance on our way to Italy. Travelling with friends is fraught enough, but to do so with an acquaintance is decidedly risky, and one night, when I staggered back in the early hours from Villefranche, I awoke in daylight to discover I was on my own. Fed up with my louche behaviour, the Australian had departed although he had the generosity to leave me some francs for my return to England and had paid my hotel bill for the rest of the week. So I settled down and relaxed. I remembered this coastline, so close to the Villa Mauresque – indeed Maugham sped past in his car one day without recognising me in my civilian clothes – and wrote to my mother though I did not reveal that I had been jettisoned as I deserved:

> Thank heavens the Sutherlands are here for I should feel extremely lonely now that my colleague has gone, not that he was scintillating by any means!
>
> The Sutherlands are two of the nicest people I have ever met, astonishingly friendly and kind. We lunch together every day and often dine, and I have gone house-hunting with them for they wish to settle down here. We went and saw Chagall the other day, who's as big and phoney a showman as Sutherland is not. Graham S. talks endlessly of the Churchill episode which is absorbing – he *hates* it! (Churchill hates the portrait, I mean.) Ustinov is working near by and turned up yesterday at the hotel. We had a long chat and he has asked me to come to see him.
>
> Above all, away from the perils of Soho, I feel saner than I have done for years. I realise it would be mad, now that I've got somewhere, to throw up photography [I did so soon afterwards]. Sutherland and Bacon are really so extraordinarily enthusiastic about my photography and so keen to boost it that I feel most bucked . . . I suddenly found I had captured something,

experienced a sudden thrill realising I had for the first time pulled it off photographically. Sutherland says I should paint, and it is fascinating talking to him about painting, especially as I have done so often with Bacon and I suppose they are the two leading British painters working today. I have been lucky in making such interesting friends, and in the Sutherlands' case such charming ones. They have warmly invited me to stay in England. I do think, fantastic though it is, that they quite like me.

Perhaps I had the zest of youth; certainly we 'hit it off' from the moment when Kathy asked what had happened to the Australian, bursting into laughter when I told them I had been abandoned. They had that rare charm and curiosity which made me feel at my best, and, although their thirst for gossip about their friends was insatiable, this sprang from genuine interest. Apart from the meals together, I went with them in Graham's comfortable Citroën to see the houses which had been recommended, one of them a mysterious, tumbledown château on top of a hill, which I fell in love with but was hopelessly impractical. Instead, they settled for a modern bungalow outside Menton which I found unsympathetic.

Finally it was time to return, and the Sutherlands drove me back to Paris, stopping en route at Douglas Cooper's colonnaded palace, the Château de Castille, where each bedroom and bathroom was decorated with the work of a single painter – mine was Miró. I kept quiet which was not difficult for Cooper never stopped talking. When Deakin saw him leaving an exhibition of Michael Wishart's in Bond Street a few weeks later, muttering 'Messy, messy messy', he mentioned that I was a friend of his.

'Oh *him*!' said Cooper dismissively, 'we didn't find *him* very funny.'

'How odd,' replied Deakin with the loyalty he reserved for friends under attack, 'he's been very funny about *you*!'

Douglas Cooper, both a sacred monster and an *éminence grise* in the art world, had become rich from sheep-dip in Australia, and was powerful as a critic. At that time, Sutherland was desperate for Cooper's approval, believing this would establish his reputation as a greater painter than Bacon. Consequently, he was anxious to please, and that was the trouble. Bacon didn't give a damn.

Cooper had turned against Bacon, even acquiring some early furniture which Bacon had designed, in order to make fun of it before his friends. Yet his wholehearted support for Sutherland remained in abeyance. However vindictive he felt towards Bacon, Cooper was not going to commit himself until he was certain. Sutherland spoilt his chances a few years later when he made the mistake of painting Cooper's portrait. Like many ugly people, Cooper was excessively vain and did not forgive him. Also, he was suffering from cirrhosis of the liver so his behaviour frequently became irrational.

On my return to England, I kept in close touch with the Sutherlands, staying at their pleasant home at Trottiscliffe in Kent, called the White House; hence the Villa Blanche became the name for their new house in France.

Many artists blossom when they become *déraciné*; such as Tissot and Whistler when

they came to England, but in retrospect it was a mistake to move to a landscape so alien to that of his beloved Pembrokeshire in Wales with its twisted trees and rocks and thorns which he made his own. Why did they feel the urge to move? Partly, I suspect, because of the glamour of the Côte d'Azure which they relished after so many years of hardship and penury. Now they were a part of high society.

Writing from the Villa Blanche, Kathy described a visit to see Margot Fonteyn at Monte Carlo:

> . . . G. has always thought her dancing quite incredible, and so off we went in evening clothes to a 'gala'. We were set upon by reporters who remembered G. from the Tate Gallery affair [the scandalous occasion when Douglas Cooper attacked Sir John Rothenstein, the director of the Tate Gallery, at a private view] and in the interval we were introduced to Onassis by Margot's husband. So we went to supper with them all in the nearby nightclub. He is a nice man (O.) and we were enthralled to meet so rich a man. Caviare and the lot, and bed by four a.m. Next night we went to see his yacht – it is quite stupendous, de luxe and quite good taste (two El Grecos) and such films to see! R.A. Butler, looking rather guilty in such a milieu, was there, and that sot Randolph C. who plunged straight into that dreary old portrait stuff, over and over again. 'Would G. write to the old man' etc. I must say it is tedious to have it all raked up again.

In many ways the effect of the Churchill portrait was calamitous, earning Sutherland a brittle notoriety. Dismissed publicly by Churchill on its unveiling in Parliament as 'a remarkable example of modern art', destroyed wilfully by Lady Churchill, controversy has diminished the power of this portrait which would be respected today as one of Sutherland's best. Churchill, however, had a special reason for hating it, apart from his comment that it made him look as if he was straining on the lavatory. He suspected a conspiracy, for Jennie Lee was on the committee appointed to choose Parliament's gift to Winston, and she was married to Nye Bevan, the political adversary who had described the Tories as 'scum'. Nye Bevan had formed an unlikely friendship with the framer Alfred Hecht, frequently staying as a guest at Hecht's house off the King's Road. When the vexed subject of a suitable gift for Churchill arose, Hecht advised a portrait by Sutherland and Jennie Lee agreed. At first Churchill and Sutherland took to each other with their mutual passion for paint but the old man became increasingly suspicious as he realised the chain reaction which went from Sutherland to Nye Bevan, and convinced himself that he was the victim of a plot.

The fuss over the Churchill portrait became oppressive; the move to the south of France and the glitter of high society detracted. But it was the influence of Francis Bacon which, however inadvertently, proved devastating.

To understand this one has to remember that they were the closest of friends at a time when Graham Sutherland was considered the most exciting contemporary British

Kathy and Graham Sutherland at Cap Ferrat

artist. Certainly, Sutherland was of early assistance to Bacon who was self-taught. Sutherland had long experience. Born in 1903 in London the son of a barrister, he worked as an engineering apprentice on the Midland Railway in Derby, leaving after a year to study at the Goldsmith School of Art until he was twenty-six. To start with he scraped a living as an etcher, influenced by the Romantic style of Samuel Palmer, until he made his name with his individual interpretation of the twisted shapes of nature in the landscape of Pembrokeshire. These were echoed in his paintings as a war artist in the Second World War.

Bacon painted when the mood seized him; Graham was disciplined. Francis flouted convention, but Sutherland needed the consistent loyalty from his wife, Kathy. Bacon has stressed that nothing in his work matters until his *Three Studies for Figures at the Base of a Crucifixion* (1944), but he had exhibited as early as 1933 and Herbert Read had shown remarkable perspicacity by including a Bacon *Crucifixion* in *Art Now* the same year. As Bacon was an atheist and Sutherland a devout Catholic, the manipulation of the image of Christ could have been disturbing and it was noticed that in Sutherland's copy of Read's book, from which he was excluded, it was Bacon's illustration which was the most heavily thumbed. In 1937 they exhibited at Agnew along with John Piper, Victor Pasmore and Bacon's older friend, the Australian Roy de Maistre. All these years, Bacon must have been acquiring knowledge for his pre-war friendship with Sutherland was one of support rather than rivalry.

In his biography of Sutherland, Roger Berthoud describes how the friendship resumed at the end of the war when Bacon moved into Millais's old studio in Cromwell Place in South Kensington, with his old nanny to whom he was devoted. By 1945, the Sutherlands dined there once a week. 'It was a large chaotic place,' writes Berthoud, 'where the salad bowl was likely to have paint on it and the painting to have salad dressing on it, but the wine and food were good and the conversation, Kathy recalled, marvellous. Bacon used the studio for gambling sessions (then illegal), and Nanny would be the hat-check girl.'

With his characteristic unselfishness, Sutherland recommended Bacon's work to two powerful patrons: Sir Kenneth Clark and Sir Colin Anderson, the shipping millionaire who bought the 1933 *Crucifixion*. At Sutherland's suggestion, Kenneth Clark came to Bacon's studio. Outwardly a glacial man with a tightly rolled umbrella, the Director of the National Gallery commented, 'Interesting, yes,' and left.

'You see,' said Bacon, 'you're surrounded by cretins.'

That evening Clark told Sutherland: 'You and I may be in a minority of two, but will still be right in thinking that Francis Bacon has genius.'

The following year, from Monte Carlo, Bacon wrote a letter of thanks, doubting whether he would have sold anything if Sutherland had not promoted his work. Tired of London, he was considering a studio in Paris which they could use together, and asked Sutherland to spray a fixative over the painting of a grinning man beneath an umbrella surrounded by carcasses of meat against a pinkish-mauve background. Subsequently, *Painting 1946* was bought by Erica Brausen at the Redfern for £100 which she sold to the Museum of Modern Art in New York for £150 two years later.

I wrote to my mother, 'We went and saw Chagall the other day, who's as big and phoney a showman as Sutherland is not.'

Bacon was restless. When a UNESCO exhibition containing their work opened in Paris, he was shocked by the lack of immediacy and the way that even the Picassos were starting to look jaded. The curse of 'decoration' was contaminating everything. Yet he wrote to Sutherland that he felt he was on the point 'of doing something good'. This was disingenuous for he knew he had done something good with his *Figures at the Base of a*

Crucifixion a couple of years earlier, and Graham Sutherland would have known it too. John Russell described their impact when exhibited: 'Visitors tempted into that gallery by the already familiar name of Graham Sutherland were brought up short by images so unrelievedly awful that the mind shut with a snap at the sight of them . . . these figures had an anatomy half human, half animal . . . they were equipped to probe, bite and suck . . . two at least of them were sightless. One was unpleasantly bandaged. They caused a total consternation.'

Roger Berthoud wrote: 'If any one influence seems to have predominated at this stage [1951] it was Bacon's, though the traffic in ideas was not wholly one way. One possible deduction is that in some cases Sutherland seemed to be painting Bacon-like works on a given theme *before* Bacon himself tackled it.' Berthoud pointed out that Bacon was the slower worker and that Sutherland could have seen paintings in his studio which were never shown because Bacon destroyed them.

Seeing a splendid new painting in Tony Hubbard's house at Regent's Park Terrace, I exclaimed, 'That's a very odd Bacon. I haven't seen one like that before.'

'I'm not surprised,' said Hubbard. 'It's a Sutherland.' This was obvious on closer inspection, but Sutherland had used a number of Baconian tricks: the black reverse of the massive canvas; the horizontal line near the edge which suggested a cage; the same heavy glass and golden frame. The subject was Sutherland's – foliage and tree-trunks in his inimitable green – but the presentation had fooled me momentarily. The critics started to notice this as well: one wrote that Sutherland was beginning to owe 'too heavy a debt to Francis Bacon', and *The Times* thought he had been drawing 'uncommonly near in style and sentiment to Francis Bacon in one or two recent moments'.

Too nice a man to succumb to jealousy, Sutherland strove to match Bacon's soaring reputation by imitation, even if this was subconscious. When he faced the truth of this, it must have been excruciating. Berthoud wrote: 'As a friend, Bacon was now fading from Sutherland's life. Sutherland continued to admire his work, though later he thought it had become a shade too autobiographical. He came to find Bacon's drinking bouts tiresome, and also Bacon's denigration of those Sutherland admired like Picasso, Braque and Matisse.' Also, and this was an unexpected twist, 'Bacon was far from enthusiastic about Sutherland's growing friendship with Douglas Cooper who had turned against him.'

Friendship turned to rivalry as Bacon became an international artist selling in Paris, New York, Milan and Zurich. Graham's pride made it hard for him to accept that Bacon's prices were higher than his own, even though he had a prolific output while Bacon concentrated on a small number of oils. When Bacon was given his retrospective at the Grand Palais in Paris in 1971, the show was acclaimed as one of the artistic triumphs of the century and a London newspaper stated that this was the first time a British artist had been granted such an honour since Constable or Gainsborough. A few days later I was dismayed to read a letter from Sutherland protesting that he had been given an exhibition at a gallery in Paris, although he must have known that the scope of it was puny by comparison. Considering the numerous international exhibitions which had been held in

Graham Sutherland behind the bamboo reeds in the Var Valley in the South of France. These shapes appealed to him and became an inspiration for his paintings, but the twisted forms of Pembrokeshire were his first love.

his honour, there was really no need for such a correction. It was then I sensed the anguish which had torn Graham apart for the last twenty years.

Ironically, Graham had all the trappings of success. It has been suggested that Kathy welcomed the invitations to the smart parties, but he undoubtedly enjoyed them too. He was flattered by the Order of Merit which he received in 1960, placing him among a chosen few, selected to sit beside the Queen in the group photograph, and it must have been irritating for him to know that Bacon would have refused such honours with disdain. Bacon's work was comparatively unknown to the public, and to an astonishing extent it still is today, but Sutherland was a celebrity due to the Churchill portrait and the massive tapestry of Christ in the new Coventry Cathedral, although this was a failure on a large scale, a disastrous concept from the outset with Christ apparently dressed in white bloomers. Sir Basil Spence admitted to me privately that he wished he had commissioned Bacon instead.

His commissions made Sutherland rich but his sitters were famous for their wealth or social position rather than their achievement, and I was shocked when I saw a canvas he was working on to find that it was lined into a series of squares. In this way he eliminated the chance which Bacon twisted to his advantage – 'the interlocking of image and paint so that the image is the paint and vice versa'.

Always comparisons were made with Bacon, and they must have been odious.

I brought them together for the last time. Graham agreed to a reconciliation reluctantly, and although he envied Francis his nomadic existence in Soho he realised that this would be a treacherous setting, so we met in Jules Bar in Jermyn Street. For a moment they fenced politely, then they rejoiced like long-lost brothers. Indeed the reunion was such a success that Francis suggested we move on for dinner at Wheeler's in Old Compton Street. Graham looked at Kathy wistfully, for they had vowed to do nothing of the sort, and they accepted happily.

As we sat down and Kathy left for the ladies', I sensed that Francis's mood had changed and heard Graham remark, with the sweetest smile, that he had been doing some portraits and wondered if Francis had seen any. I flinched at the reply: *'Very nice if you like the covers of* Time *Magazine.'* I doubt if these were his exact words to Graham though he said them to me in an earlier conversation. Francis is rarely so cruel, but this was the gist and that was the end of it.

Towards the end of his life, Graham realised he had been 'missing out' and returned every year to the Pembrokeshire landscape, staying in a caravan at Sandy Haven where he welcomed the clear light of the estuary which seemed to bounce off the sides of the narrow inlet in contrast to the monotonous skies of Menton. Today the Sutherland Foundation next to Picton Castle houses Graham's pictures, a fitting tribute to the inspiration he received from Wales.

I returned to Menton in May 1972.

'How's the monster?' These were Graham Sutherland's first, smiling words as he greeted me. For a moment I was confused.

'Haven't you heard? He's dead.'

Sutherland's eager expression was replaced by dismay. 'Oh *no*. But . . . I haven't seen anything in the papers. Are you – '

'Who are you talking about?'

'Francis, of course.'

'Oh! I thought you meant John Deakin!' We laughed with relief.

The Villa Blanche was now palatial with floors made from marble brought from Italy, and the spacious rooms were lined with his paintings, yet it seemed an empty 'set' for a famous artist. He showed me his latest work but it did not have the shock to make me reel back and exclaim spontaneously. I sought for the right words and found the wrong ones. Graham and Kathy were as kind as ever, but the first rapport had faded and I am sure they felt a disappointment too. After I left, Graham drove into Menton to collect the English newspapers, the fate of so many expatriates.

I had been careful not to give too jolly an account of Francis's carefree existence, for Graham's life seemed desolate by comparison. I believe Graham Sutherland recognised that Bacon was the greater artist. Therefore Bacon was the stronger man, for, ultimately, the two become inseparable. Yet Sutherland was the foremost Romantic painter in Britain this century, loved as a man and respected as an artist. He died in 1980.

Five years later I received a card from Kathy Sutherland from the Connaught Hotel: 'So kind to write. G. told me to live here as it was so safe but I have had awful bronchitis and general breakdown and don't care if I live or die. All was only possible with G.S.'

Of all the painters I have had the luck to meet, Graham was the nicest. Perhaps that was the trouble. He was surrounded by sacred monsters which is why I include him here, but he was never one himself.

A Freudian Lunch in Mayfair

LUCIAN FREUD

Sacred monsters do not retire; they retain their capacity to shock. If Graham Sutherland lost his way because he lacked ruthlessness, Lucian Freud has the necessary single-mindedness. Throughout his life he has provoked strong reactions as a man you are passionately in favour of, or against. His enemies are legion and call him mad, bad and dangerous to know, yet the Queen made him a Companion of Honour.

Born in Berlin in 1922, the grandson of Sigmund who sent him Brueghel prints from Vienna, he was drawing obsessively by the time he reached England at the age of eleven. As a student at the art school run by Sir Cedric Morris at Dedham, he set fire to the building one night when he smoked in the studio. I suggested that it was forgiving of Morris to invite him into his home afterwards to continue his studies, and Lucian gave me one of his startled looks: 'What else could he do? After all, it wasn't deliberate.'

His accent is emphatic with a mid-European descant, each word meticulously poised before it is flung. It enhances his caustic wit. He is disciplined yet reckless, with a taste for danger, a man who collected guns. Edwardian England would have understood him better. He cultivates the aristocracy because he finds the people more interesting, yet belongs to the seamier side of life as well, often enjoying a bacon sandwich in a Paddington caff used by villains, after dining at Annabel's on oysters and grouse.

His single-mindedness was revealed when he told me that no one can take advantage of him, and I asked why. 'Because I only do what I want to do.' This applies to his work which is free from the fashionable strivings of the New York artists promoted by Saatchi: 'I am single-minded but I never know how it's going to turn out. I'm not sure I'd do it otherwise. I loathe the idea of self-expression. There's nothing burning I want to say. I think my pictures are easy to understand, they are a kind of diary, a record of myself. I haven't got a grand project and only go outside my circle occasionally.'

I met him first in the 1950s in the French pub where he was being addressed by a voluble and boring stranger beside the stairs. Finally, with lethal politeness, Lucian stopped him: 'I'd much rather *not* listen to your conversation because I find it so excessively boring.' It was one of the few times I had ever heard someone speak the *truth*.

Lucian Freud

Later I discovered how considerate he could be when I joined the Merchant Navy and he invited me to a party the night before I sailed. It was halfway through before I realised he had given it especially for me, and I was so astonished I scarcely thanked him although I did not forget.

We were out of touch after I retreated to Devon, and then reunited in 1988 on the eve of his retrospective exhibition at the Hayward, an event looked forward to with enthusiasm among his friends and glee among his critics. The knives had been sharpened already across the Channel where *Paris Match* described him as *'un dandy tragique nommé Freud'* – 'I thought that was rather nice!' – and the critic of *Le Monde* felt he needed a hot bath after seeing the pictures, and then a Turkish bath after that to free him from the contamination. 'I do hope that translation's literal,' Lucian told me, 'because I find that really stimulating.' As for the first salvo from Brian Sewell, known for his petulance, Lucian commented: 'He'll be really poisonous when he *sees* the show!'

It was hard to tell whether he was genuinely pleased by the savage reaction until he quoted a French philosopher who recommended swallowing a live toad every morning before breakfast to make sure that nothing more disagreeable happened for the rest of the day. Perversely, he is indignant when a critic praises him but gets a detail wrong. 'I have never painted a rubber plant in my life,' he protested about a complimentary piece. 'Nor would I if it was the last plant alive. It proves there is no God for he would never have created a rubber plant!'

Freud does not indulge in the mock modesty, or disdain, of pretending that he does not read the reviews of his work. Understandably, he is interested to learn what the critics think, even if he does not give a damn for their judgement, although he was shaken when he shifted from close-focus to a looser style which some of the critics mistook for a loss of concentration. It was wholly deliberate – as always.

Conversely, the one man who was absent from the receptions for the retrospective was Freud himself. This was interpreted as the calculation of a man of mystery, yet the explanation could not have been simpler even if it sounds disingenuous – he preferred to work. Also, he knows the penance of the crowded private view and dreads overhearing the banalities, such as 'I rather like that one over there.'

'I prefer to talk to the people I like. I can't suddenly be civil to someone I've tried to avoid for years. I'm not on exhibition myself. My life isn't interesting, I spend the best part of each day and night indoors painting. I would wish my pictures to be remembered, but want to keep well out of it myself.'

In the age of the self-publicist, such reticence is regarded as peculiar, in contrast to Hockney – 'who would put on a green and yellow sock to attract attention'. Lucian has guarded his privacy scrupulously, resisting the blandishments of the media. 'The luxury of being a painter is that you need never see anyone you don't want to, and part of the charm of living in London is the anonymity. I wander freely while I'm still vertical.' Surprisingly, he sacrificed this anonymity when he appeared on television in BBC's *Omnibus* when the exhibition was over, partly because the interviewer was the son of his close friend, the painter Frank Auerbach. I was away at the time, but a young painter told me, 'Lucian's blown it, he's blown it, he's lost his cover. He must be mad!'

Lucian has avoided the written interview as well, and it was another example of friendship that he agreed to have lunch with me when I was asked to write a profile for the *Guardian*. Lunch was certainly preferable to our previous meeting at Blake's Hotel at seven on a dark winter morning, which may be fine for creatures of the night like Dracula or Freud who slide into a room with an air of apprehension and a sideways glance in case a crucifix or ray of sunlight might suddenly appear, but it is not my finest hour after a night on the town. Even a luncheon with Lucian can prove fraught. You do not telephone him, although he enjoys talking on the phone interminably. You call his agent and then Freud rings you back. Only a few, favoured friends know his number or address, or are invited to his home near Holland Park where he has his studio. I suspect it is quiet,

Lucian Freud with Brendan Behan in Dublin

opulent, rather dark with reds and browns, more Vienna than Berlin, but this is guess-work.

After various vicissitudes, and the rumour that one newspaper was out 'to get him' due to a new relationship, we met in Mayfair in the posh ambience of a gentleman's club called Harry's Bar although the white front door was anonymous. The walls were lined with the originals of cartoons by Peter Arno which Lucian pointed out with wide-eyed admiration. We were served excellent Italian pasta by an inscrutable staff, and the bill proved so expensive that for the first time in my life I felt guilty over the cost of a meal. I should add that, although I insisted on paying at the time, Lucian reimbursed me afterwards. His attitude to money is ambivalent; he is only aware of it when he hasn't got any. Although he is stimulated by having large amounts of cash on him, this can reach a point where it makes it difficult for him to work. Only when he has lost this restraint through gambling, increasing the stake with each bet until it becomes calamitous if he loses, does he retain his calm. His horror is breaking even. His recklessness as a gambler is alarming and has led to trouble with bookmakers and casinos. It seems that he is excited by the danger of losing large sums of money as a form of catharsis, for after such a losing spell there is only enough to sustain him for a few horse-free months while he devotes himself to his work. There was a time when he was sustained by his share in the royalties of his grandfather's estate, but he gave these to his children and today his pictures have increased to a hundred thousand pounds each, compared to the couple of hundred which I paid for the portrait of John Deakin, subsequently sold at Sotheby's for the same amount when I put my collection on the market to pay my debts to the wretched brewers who leased me the Waterman's Arms.

Taking into account the length of time which Lucian spends on a picture, it came as a shock when the considerable output was assembled for the Hayward in 1988. Because he sells privately, as soon as the paint dries and sometimes sooner if he needs the money urgently to cover gambling debts, his work is seldom seen in public galleries and until then was largely judged by reproduction. The Hayward established him as our leading artist, next to Francis Bacon.

There was a time when I thought his portraits of women were pitiless, exposing them like raw meat in a butcher's window, and I asked if he was trying to shock. 'I try to be truth-telling but I hope my pictures disturb. A painting should, at best, outrage your sensibilities.' Today I notice a compassion that I missed before. I am not sure which of us has changed, the portraits or me. Certainly there is no point in looking for a likeness which can be obtained by a colour photograph. His achievement is to go further than skin-deep. I asked him whether his sitters become his victims.

'Only in so far as I am active as the artist, and they are passive.' His bemused stare implied that all this was irrelevant. Indeed, there is a simpler explanation for the look of pain on their faces – they are bored out of their skulls. When John Deakin sat for him, he was collected at dawn and driven to Paddington where he was force-drunk with retsina to keep him still. One lunchtime he staggered into the French pub looking ashen. 'It's that bloody portrait,' he moaned. 'Lucian has just decided it isn't going right and wants to start again.'

The finished portrait captures Deakin's fatigue while revealing more. I have seen countless photographs of Deakin but this is the honest image which sticks in the mind, revealing the vulnerability behind the bravado. When I asked Lucian over lunch at Harry's whether he agreed with my father who preferred 'hurt' people, he greeted this in silence. Later he surprised me by returning to it. 'No,' he said deliberately, 'I don't believe I do like to hurt people.' I explained the confusion, but Lucian's response was significant. Although he meant it damningly, another painter has remarked: 'I don't understand how Lucian could contaminate anyone, when everything he does is so *careful.*'

Careful? I doubt if the numerous women in his life would agree, unless his treatment of them is a refined sort of cruelty. Certainly, like most sacred monsters, he is an irresistible seducer. He has written: 'What do I ask of a painting? I ask it to astonish, disturb, seduce, convince,' and, although he may be more *careful* in his work, these qualities spill over to his personal life as well.

'Have you ever driven with him?' asked Lady Caroline Blackwood, his second wife from whom he was divorced in 1957.

'Yes,' I replied. 'I was so terrified that when he stopped at a red light, for once, I threw myself out.'

'Exactly,' she agreed. 'That's what being married to him was like.'

While his portrait was being painted by Lucian, the Duke of Devonshire confided to a friend: 'Thank God it was me and not one of my daughters.'

Lucian is kinder to men because he loves them less. Referring to *Naked Man with his Friend*, I asked if he views a homosexual relationship with greater objectivity. 'Very likely, it's to do with delicacy.' The muscular young man became so bored during the sitting that he asked if his friend could join him, and Lucian allowed the older man the dignity of doing so dressed in his pyjamas. In contrast to his portraits of women, caught in their nakedness in 'the milieu of the unmade bed' (to quote the memorable phrase of Lawrence Gowing), the finished picture has tenderness. Both men recline on a couch as if this Freudian prop enables Lucian to analyse. The younger man rests a hand on his friend's ankle: both appear to be asleep and probably were for Lucian told me it took six months to complete over a period of two years. When I replied that it looks spontaneous, he smiled and said, 'That's where the art comes in,' and pointed out that the portrait of Madame Moitessier by his favourite artist, Ingres, took sixteen years to finish. 'If the public knew the time and effort that went into a picture, they'd leave exhausted.'

In a rare moment which could almost pass for sentiment, Lucian asked the same young man, who had the stamina to pose for another portrait, if he would mind holding Lucian's pet rat which he placed alarmingly close to the young man's genitals. Lucian confessed that he gave the rat a sedative and felt extremely guilty when it made the rat ill.

In a BBC broadcast, I was asked if it helped to know Lucian in order to appreciate his work. Decisively, for once, I replied that it made no difference, that all pictures must speak for themselves. I suspect Lucian would agree, for, as he told me over lunch in Harry's, 'The result is the only thing that matters, how it comes about is private.'

'Has it ever been easy?'

'It's a day-to-day activity. I have my good days.'

'Is unhappiness necessary for an artist?'

'I hate unhappiness. It's the one thing which makes me tired and restless. But when it's measured against the fact of being alive, it shrivels up. Work is the only way out.'

'Hope?'

'You need that, absolutely. The future is the next picture. Courage.'

In the age of the second-rater, he is a rare animal. If he dissects his fellow-man without mercy, he does so without condemnation.

Unexpectedly, the last time we met was in the Coach and Horses in Soho, a few days after his appearance on *Omnibus*. Before I could stop her, the woman I was with forced her way through and informed Lucian gushingly, 'I've seen you on television, and some of your pictures and I do like them!' Lucian blinked, which he does only occasionally. Her male companion joined in, demanding to know why Lucian was not in Berlin where the Hayward exhibition had been transferred (with the subsequent theft of his famous portrait of Francis Bacon (1952) on loan from the Tate). Lucian swivelled round, his face expressionless.

'Why should I?' he replied. 'I like being here.'

'You've received reports?'

'No, why should I? I'm only interested in what I'm doing at the moment. That's the only thing that interests me.'

'Most people would want to be present at their own show,' said the man reprovingly.

'R-really? How peculiar. I can only be myself.'

And with that look of astonishment, as if his pet rat had run up his trouser leg, he glided away in seconds, after murmuring to me that he would phone the next morning.

'Oh, you are naughty,' cried the woman, giving my hand a slap. 'You've scared him away!'

A Surrealist Stretch in Wales

GEORGE MELLY

Sacred monsters are too preoccupied to be vain, and they are beyond mere conceit. Conversely, their egotism is worthy of lovers and their belief in themselves has a touch of arrogance.

Listing his heroes – Luis Buñuel, René Magritte and Bessie Smith – George Melly describes them as 'entirely true to themselves while most of us, myself included, compromise a thousand times a day. They go "the whole hog".'

His definition for sacred monsters, a different breed with the occasional overlap, is 'what *enfants terribles* turn into. Perfect example: Jean Cocteau. Others are Edward James, Douglas Cooper, Nancy Cunard, Jean Rhys and Bessie Smith.'

George qualifies for both categories. Like his heroes he is true to himself regardless of the cost to others, while he remains an *enfant terrible* in his sixties: 'I look in the mirror and see a middle-aged man with some startlement, for I feel like fourteen.'

One of the satisfactions of growing old is the ripening of long friendships, as it has been with Anthony West who co-founded *Panorama* at Cambridge and now lives near me at Barnstaple, since the death of his wife. The same is true of my friendship with George Melly.

I saw him first in the early 1950s in the sweat-sodden basement of Humphrey Lyttelton's Jazz Club at 100 Oxford Street where his wild gyrations on the dance-floor gave him the nickname of 'Bunny-Bum'. We met constantly in Soho afterwards and he was never too grand to get up on stage during his visits to the Waterman's Arms, contributing to the evening's entertainment with a gusto which earned him the title of 'Good-Time George'. I have heard another description, that of Renaissance Man. I am never certain what it means, but gather it harks back to braver days when men were expected to display a number of talents rather than excel at one. If so, George is a Renaissance Man personified. With the British suspicion of anyone who is unusually clever, his versatility is not fully recognised. Those who admire him as *the* British jazz singer, roaring away with 'the raucous charm of an old negress', to quote John Mortimer, may be unaware that others go to see him *in spite* of his singing, wanting to share in the fun but respecting him more in his role as film and television critic; for his knowledge of art; and above all for his brilliance as a writer, with *Owning Up*, one of the liveliest autobiographies of our time, followed by *Rum, Bum and Concertina* and *Scouse Mouse*.

John Chilton, the leader of the Feetwarmers, the backing group who support him in every sense, acts as the invaluable foil, convincingly so because, like many jazz musicians, he resembles a suburban bank manager, though unlike a bank manager he has George's interests at heart. 'Where is he?' he tantalised the audience at the Royalty Theatre in London, with a look of real concern. 'Where can he be? He might come running in from Kingsway or even Queensway, what's happened to him?' He looked at his watch anxiously as George descended from the ceiling in a gilded bird-cage which had been used by a stripper in a previous show. Nonchalantly, he stepped out, balloon brandy glass in hand, to a standing ovation.

When the Beatles swept in, George and jazz went out of fashion. By 1961 George and Mick Mulligan's Band, which he sang for, had disbanded. He admitted that he found it hard 'to walk up the queue outside the Marquee on my way to listen to Howling Wolf, and to be completely unrecognised by several hundred blues fans. You get over it.' But tides return and so did George, honing his cabaret act to a perfection worthy of Noël Coward, cavorting on the trembling stages of jazz clubs, universities and village halls as well as smarter venues, dressed in suits which would shame a zebra.

Aware of the element of absurdity in his performance, both elephantine and dainty, he sports the broadest leer which surpasses that of Max Miller or even Sir Les Patterson to whom he bears a disconcerting resemblance. He is back with a vengeance.

Surely, ask his critics, the grin conceals an inner tragedy? And this could have been true several years ago when George nearly sank from sight. 'I got through a bottle of brandy a night *apart* from what I drank in the day. For nearly fifteen years I was a drunk.' He relates the traumatic incident when he was staying in an unfamiliar stately home. Desperate to relieve himself in the middle of the night, he stumbled about in the darkness in search of the bathroom. The next morning he stared in dismay at the open drawer containing a sodden pile of expensive cashmere sweaters belonging to his hostess, and fled before he was found out. There were many such incidents. One night he grasped the microphone and slid slowly to the floor like a flag being lowered. John Chilton informed the audience: 'I am sorry but the Captain is no longer in command of his ship.'

The cashmere sweaters could be laughed away, but not the lack of professionalism. 'I was pretending to be twenty-four and drinking as if I was. However, the drink was killing me.' When his current girlfriend asked him point-blank, 'Do you want to be a serious artist or amuse people by falling down every night?', he decided to give up spirits. Ronnie Scott, at whose club he appears regularly each Christmas, says: 'Since he eased off the sauce, we no longer have to allow ten minutes in order to rouse him off the floor of his dressing-room before his act.' George himself is able to state: 'I do now think of myself as a serious jazz singer.'

It would be wrong to suggest that George is reformed and such a prospect would

George Melly, the fisherman, in wellies in Wales

dismay him. He regards himself as a teetotaller today, yet allows himself wine, port, sherry and Campari. 'Champagne?' I asked. 'Of course!' He looked at me with astonishment. It is an abstinence which would wreck the ordinary man.

His love life is equally robust, though he has the grace to appear bemused by the attraction he exerts on young, beautiful girls. 'I'm fat and fairly famous and they seem to find that inviting. I very much enjoy the company of young girls and like to know what's going on.'

In his younger days he admitted to flirtations with chaps, probably induced by his service in the Royal Navy, soon to be abandoned in favour of a torrid infatuation with a coloured snake-charmer called Cerise Johnson who was so sexually possessive that she used to beat him up if she suspected that he was unfaithful. For a long time, George seldom appeared scratchless. There was an uneasy moment when his wife, Victoria, returned after a long absence. Cerise was calm although she insisted that Victoria leave the next morning. 'I'm your woman. How she think she trip in here after three years and give you a tongue sandwich?' Victoria left and so, in time, did Cerise for a modelling job in Paris. George watched her departure from the airport with sadness and relief.

When he married his second wife, Diana, in 1963, he rejoiced in the contrast of family life. The tours with Mick Mulligan had been a punishment as well as a pleasure. 'On the road. Ten years of it. I seem to have spent a lifetime looking out of grimy windows in digs at backyards in the rain. Weeds, rotting iron, collapsing outhouses.'

Eventually, his life with Diana drifted into an 'open marriage' which enables George to have his flings on the side. For most people, the arrangement would seem bizarre, yet I have seen him at his happiest when staying at the thirteenth-century tower in Wales where Diana lives for most of the year while he is based in London. 'Diana fell in love with the place. She adores home-making and always wants to move, but this house is so magical she seems content. I go back to London in a state of delicious calm which lasts until I return.'

In spite of their 'open marriage', Diana is a constant presence. 'George's drinking was rather annoying,' she concedes, 'but he was living with someone else when he was at his worst. I wouldn't say George is selfish but he is blinkered.' She quotes the unhappy time when both her parents died of cancer. 'On Tuesday my father died and I was very upset. On Thursday we drove into Abergavenny to meet Philip Core and George went off with him to do some shopping which provided the opportunity to explain why I was sitting in the car in such a state. Over dinner that evening, my brother phoned to tell me about the funeral arrangements, and I started to cry again. Philip Core looked at me aghast and said, "What's the matter?" I asked George, "Why the hell didn't you tell him?" and he looked at me with genuine surprise. "The subject never came up."' To be that blinkered, you need to be a sacred monster.

Fortunately, Diana has an unusual sense of humour. 'I find it very funny.' At his most unconcerned, George says: 'Diana and my son Tom treat me as an utter buffoon, which restores my perspective.'

The family take their revenge with elaborate practical jokes, instigated by Tom who is an actor in his twenties. Seeing a photo of his father on the cover of *Home Organist*, an unlikely publication in the first place, Tom wondered, 'Is there *anything* he wouldn't do?' Enlisting the help of George's secretary and agent, he typed a request on specially printed notepaper with the letterhead of *Practical Moped*, a non-existent publication, asking George to judge a Miss Welsh Moped contest in Cardiff. The first prize was a new moped; the second an evening with George Melly. Persuaded by a colossal fee, George turned up at the appointed time to find his step-daughter posing with the appropriate Miss Moped sash and a spoof copy of *Practical Moped.* He had forgotten that it was his birthday and this was the start of the family celebration. 'George demands a lot of attention,' Diana explains, 'and the rest of the family work out their aggression with practical jokes. So everyone's happy.'

Tom sums up his father perspicaciously as 'knowledgeable yet incredibly naïve. He was heartbroken a few years ago over a girl and I'd never seen him cry before, but I think he rather enjoyed finding out that he could be so emotional. The reason he did not become an alcoholic is because he's too stable. He'd make a good Falstaff but a lousy Hamlet, the last person in the world you'd imagine going mad. He's a very contented man, and maybe that's his problem, that he has no hang-ups. The most un-neurotic person I know, always safe, always warm, always generous, like a well-banked fire.'

George is not so perfect as all this suggests, otherwise he would be insufferable. The naïvety to which Tom refers is almost disingenuous. George is more conventional than he likes to appear. The image he presents as the antidote to respectability was fulfilled when he hurled himself into the headlines during the trial of *Oz* magazine in 1971, although it seems to belong to another millennium now. At the first hearing when the magistrate refused to allow bail for the editor, Richard Neville, there was the proverbial sensation in court. 'As the hairies were being pounded in the public gallery,' says George, 'I was in the section reserved for the press.' At that time he was the eminent film critic for the *Observer* and, realising that in this position he could take the police by surprise, George rose swiftly to his feet and shouted at the magistrate, 'You senile old prick!' and made his getaway while he could.

As Neville was dragged to the cells, Melly and friends tracked down a judge who overruled the magistrate's decision to refuse bail for the offence of possessing a quarter of an ounce of cannabis and for publishing pornography, yet unproved. When they trooped back on the Monday morning, the magistrate gave George a quizzical look and asked if he could really afford to put up £2,000 bail, for when George is not attired as a Chicago gangster he can be a sloppy dresser. A cross-examination continued interminably as George's possessions were written down: a large house in Hampstead, a valuable painting by Magritte . . . and so on.

'Anything else?' asked the policeman.

'Well, an old pair of brown shoes.' Finally his security was accepted.

The publicity swelled out of all proportion. 'One newspaper quoted me as saying "a senile old blank", so everyone assumed I had called him a "senile old cunt".' Such words did reverberate through a trial which became increasingly surrealistic. Assisting the court with a definition of that far-fetched word 'cunnilingus', he recalled that in his days as an able-seaman it was known as 'gobbling' or 'yodelling in the canyon'.

Finally there was a classic clash with the prosecuting counsel.

'Do you swear in front of your children?'

'Certainly.'

'You would call your daughter a little cunt, would you?'

'No, I don't think she is one. But I might easily refer to a politician as one.'

Neville was acquitted and George Melly's name became synonymous with permissiveness. His views were quoted, his letters published in the papers, a protest march was incomplete without his attendance. It could be said that he did protest too much, for in his tilting against the establishment he exaggerated his case as much as Mrs Mary Whitehouse who represented everything he loathed. Inevitably they were cast as antagonists on TV chat shows and there was one peculiar incident in the hospitality of a TV studio when Diana appeared in a black leather mini-skirt and fishnet stockings. Mr Whitehouse was so overwhelmed that 'he looked at her like the clergyman in *Rain* when he first sees Sadie Thompson, the prostitute. Then, white-mouthed with rage, he made this extraordinary statement: "Fornication is as bad as murder."' George pointed out that murder was hardly desired by the murderee. 'Well it leads to it,' came the stern reply.

Yet both George and Mary Whitehouse enjoyed being shocked in their different ways and, like most people who set out to shock, George is far from unshockable himself. Surprisingly fastidious, he needs a certain order 'because of the possibility of chaos. I'm excessively tidy.'

'Is there any pornography you would censor?' I asked him once.

'I don't think so.' No one is that tolerant. If every man has his price, every man has his prejudice. George declares that he cannot do with people who fail to entertain. 'Humour is what I care about. I can't stand a pious person. I'm amazed by the energy the Festival of Light people put into trying to repress: they're mostly teetotal, they certainly don't smoke pot, they regard sex simply as a means of propagation. The idea of going down or anything like that appalls them. I like my humour laced with cynicism, love people who blow it, hate plastic saints.'

George revealed that he draws his own line when I asked again if 'anything goes'. He admitted that this was true to a point but was not too sure about sadism and masochism, or the use of excreta. He went on to list a number of aberrations which he finds joyless and therefore distasteful. The girl who was with him was outraged. 'But that's because you don't have those particular hang-ups. The people who do, enjoy them. They don't find them joyless, and good luck to them however way-out their fantasies carry them if they find someone else who shares them too.' For once George was abashed.

When I asked if he had doubts regarding the legalisation of cannabis after the tragic death of his step-son which involved drugs, his face registered such instant displeasure that I changed the subject at once. Neither, I suspect, would George take kindly to being mocked, as against being *teased* which he enjoys. George's *laissez-faire* attitude conceals the single-mindedness which is sacred to the monster and cannot be distracted. When it is time to end an affair, I expect it is George who ends it, regardless of the pain to himself.

Having said that, he remains the most generous-minded man I know. I realised this when I devised the art quiz *Gallery* which brought us closer than before.

Various 'hosts' were suggested, most of them called Kelly, but I insisted on George from the outset. His knowledge of art is extensive, apart from the surrealists whom he met when he worked for the Mesens Gallery in London. His taste is infallible, which makes his judgement so.

Gallery had the virtues of simplicity: a detail was shown and the panels had to identify the painting and the painter, followed by a discussion when the whole picture was revealed. It opened new frontiers for me as I travelled through Britain selecting the pictures which could be seen by the public, finding such unexpected treasures on our doorstep as the Goyas in Glasgow, a Van Gogh in Walsall, a Bacon in Huddersfield and a Brueghel in Banbury, as well as the fine collections in Aberdeen, Liverpool and Cardiff. Simultaneously, George used the daytime when he was on tour to visit the local galleries wherever he performed.

My fondest image is of George standing beside his river in Wales. Initially he took the house because of the fishing ('it's the one thing I insist on'), renting a stretch of the water until the owner of the estate died and his heirs decided to sell it in six sections. 'I had to buy it. Ludicrous to go further afield. So I went to the auction and the locals thought it would go for £12,000 and as the bidding soared I could see my pictures vanishing off the walls.' He had to pay £47,500, selling a Picasso drawing, a well-known Magritte and a Klee watercolour, rationalising that as they cost him only £200 in 1940 he had got a bargain. Some of his trendier friends were shocked that he should spend so much on 'some water'. 'Why?' he asked, indignantly. 'No one thinks it odd if a pop-star buys a Rolls-Royce, and the water gives me enormous happiness and equilibrium. I get more satisfaction from landing a two-and-a-half-pound brown trout than anything I can think of – apart from sex.' He paused for a moment, and added: 'I catch the trout less often.'

Diana gave him a large Ordnance map for Christmas, renaming the parts of the river after the pictures he had sold: Picasso Rapids, The Lovers' Secret (after the title of the Magritte) and the Klee Pool. When he was sixty, George declared: 'From now on I think of life as a series of *treats*!' Casting a line into Lovers' Secret will prove one of the best, for this is where he is truest to himself.

One Helluva Day with Trevor

TREVOR HOWARD

'Hell raiser' is a glib label applied to film-stars who drink too much, and although Trevor Howard drank that was one of the least interesting things about him. He was a lovely sacred monster.

Remembering him now, one impression predominates: that of his endearing, slightly bashful smile as he greeted one with his natural courtesy. When Vivienne Knight wrote his biography, she chose a title which could not be bettered – *A Gentleman and a Player*. The cricketing term reflected his passion for the game and for England. Yet his upbringing in England was odious, leaving him vulnerable for the rest of his life.

Trevor Wallace Howard-Smith was born in Cliftonville in 1916 and he sailed with his parents to Ceylon where his father worked for Lloyd's of London. Sent back to England, he was visited briefly by his father when he returned on home leave, but then the relationship faded. He was eight when he went to Clifton College in Bristol, while his mother and sister returned to Colombo. Trevor was deposited with strangers at unfamiliar boarding-houses during his holidays from Clifton until one of the masters took pity on him and invited him into his home. This could be one reason why Trevor left £100,000 to Clifton College in his will.

The loneliness of those years accounted for the shyness and a certain isolation which he masked with the bravado that contributed to the 'hell raiser' label. It explains his aversion to show-business parties, the competitive rat-race and the ceremonies where most film-stars are anxious to be seen. Instead, Trevor Howard remained an outsider, his genius consistently underrated, receiving none of the honours which he deserved.

His bravura coloured his roles only when it suited them, in such parts as Lord Cardigan in *The Charge of the Light Brigade* and Captain Bligh in *Mutiny on the Bounty*. It is a pity that he turned down the part of Gully Jimson in *The Horse's Mouth*, although Alec Guinness bore a closer resemblance to Gerald Wilde. Howard never resorted to Acting with a capital A, the 'look at me, I'm acting' approach which fools so many, but responded with his eyes, revealing pain with a minimum of movement. He avoided the use of heavy make-up or props. As his friend Robert Mitchum remarked, 'You'll never catch Trevor

Howard acting.' This talent was apparent in *Brief Encounter* for which he was paid £500, received no invitation to the press show, and was cut at the première by Noël Coward who failed to recognise his leading man. However, it established Howard as one of those actors beloved by the camera. The audience could *feel* him thinking. His voice had a glorious timbre, full of wistful promise, changing into a roar when he was off the set which made the walls and passing strangers tremble.

I met him first at Ken Tynan's small flat near Marble Arch and saw him on stage in *The Devil's General* with his friend Wilfred Lawson. I found it a difficult play to follow, for Lawson died in one act yet reappeared in the next, although I admired the spontaneity of the acting which was courageous for the time. When I described it to Ken the next day, he looked perplexed and asked, 'Are you sure you went to the right theatre?' As I told him more he giggled with pleasure and said, 'They must have been stinking drunk! You say that Lawson *died*?'

'Yes, in that scene when he *falls*.' Ken shook with laughter at such naïvety.

I photographed Howard on the set of *Outcast of the Islands*; and we filmed a television interview for my series *Something to Say* when I worked for Associated Rediffusion. We did not meet all that often but he was the sort of friend who remained so even when we were out of touch after I moved to Devon. A characteristic letter applauded this decision. 'Personally I'm sick of cities. I've had a month of New York, Chicago, Toronto, Boston, Phil., Washington, LA, San Francisco, and I'm bushed. I was doing a promotion tour for *The Charge*, and I surprised everyone by *not* talking about *The Charge* but singing with the Dixie bands *and* getting encores!!'

He continued, enthusiastically, about a forthcoming visit to Peter Scott's Wildfowl Trust. 'He says there are thousands of wild geese there and up to 300 wild swans which are recognisable by their faces and which all have names (how many names are there?!!!) and they've come 2,500 miles from the breeding grounds of Siberia . . . ' He was the least actorish of actors.

In September 1986 I took the tube to Arkley in Hertfordshire, one of those journeys to the outer suburbs which seem more arduous than the trans-Siberian railway. At my destination – I think it was the end of the line – I saw a solitary taxi driving away as I reached the top of a steep pathway. Walking into the high street, I entered one of those cavernous, converted pubs, full of deep carpet and formica, depressingly empty except for the rows of fruit-machines. After the usual vicissitudes with lifeless machines, I managed to phone Trevor's wife, the actress Helen Cherry, who told me to stay where I was and she would collect me. Probably she was accustomed to such calls. Throughout his career, Helen was the constant, indispensable support and a clause was inserted in Trevor's film contracts to the effect that she could join him on location anywhere in the world. When they met in 1943, appearing together at the Arts Theatre, there was an instant rapport: 'Marrying Helen was the best thing I ever did in my entire life.'

During my filmed interview, I had had the nerve to ask Trevor if he regretted not having had children, an intrusion which I now regret. In fact, looking after him was a full-time occupation, in which his wife's career might have suffered, and the responsibility of

Trevor Howard in the canteen, while filming *An Outcast of the Islands*

a family could have jeopardised their partnership. Trevor could be difficult: he was arrested in Vienna for conducting the band in a restaurant late at night, dressed in the uniform of a British major for his part in *The Third Man*, and he was arrested in Kenya and in England for drunken driving. 'I drink,' he explained, 'because it makes the world a nicer place.'

Helen met me with her usual cheerfulness, but her short absence proved disastrous. When offered a drink on my arrival at Rowley Green, I was so taken aback by Trevor's gnarled appearance that I accepted. I would have refused, as I had vowed to do, except that it was obvious that Trevor had been making the world a nicer place while Helen was away. She discovered later that he had trotted over to a neighbour earlier that morning and borrowed a bottle of gin.

'My old China-Chum,' he roared, embracing me. 'You silly old Chinese idiot!' He added, with a tortured smile, 'That's a term of endearment.'

I was especially dismayed by his condition for he was due to attend a party that night to celebrate the publication of his biography by Vivienne Knight on the eve of his seventieth birthday. In a whispered exchange, Helen assured me that his drinking was due to the prospect of the party and had nothing to do with my arrival. He shunned such occasions anyhow, but dreaded this one in particular as I discovered later.

Attempting to interview him, I asked what he considered was the best thing he'd done in his life. A fatuous question.

'Nothing,' he shouted. 'Nothing, nothing at all.'

'What about your marriage to Helen?' I ventured, archly.

'Oh, that might have helped,' he said dismissively.

She laughed. 'It's nice to get the credit.'

As words were proving difficult, I produced my Rolleiflex and an extraordinary transformation took place the moment Trevor saw the camera. Instinctively, he posed and preened, smiled and seduced the lens as he had done so often before. It was an astonishing performance. Then he passed out.

'Give me a hand,' said Helen, 'and we'll carry him upstairs.'

'Upstairs!' I gasped as we tried to lift him. 'We'll be lucky to get him on the sofa.'

Finally we managed this and he lay there prostrate while we ate an excellent if dainty lunch of poached salmon chatting with a gentility that contrasted oddly with the slumberous figure a few feet away. 'Of course,' said Helen, 'there's no question of Trevor making the party tonight. Even if he wakes up in time, he must not go.'

I managed to make the party, upstairs at the British Film club in Piccadilly, but there was an undeniable sense of anticlimax with the absence of the star. And, suddenly, there he was, grizzled but grinning, making his entrance. His faithful driver, David, had woken him in the afternoon and told him he must attend because people would be disappointed if he stayed away. We were photographed together and this was reproduced in the gossip column of the *Daily Express* the next morning. The reporter claimed that the evening 'ended sourly when the veteran hell raiser suddenly left a Piccadilly party in his honour . . . as old friends like the Duke of St Albans, Michael Denison and Dulcie Gray waited to chat to him . . . Howard stumbled out heavily clutching his actress wife of forty years, Helen Cherry. "Trevor has had enough and so he's going," she muttered. Further explanation came later from veteran writer and TV personality Dan Farson. "Trevor and I had lunch together. He was a bit the worse for wear and fell over and hurt his head. It's been one helluva day."'

I could not remember saying this, but 'one helluva day' it was.

Later I discovered the reason for Trevor's return to the bottle that morning. He had kept a secret and he dreaded its disclosure with the glare of publicity surrounding the book and his seventieth birthday. Years earlier, a well-meaning publicist claimed that Trevor had been awarded the Military Cross as a captain in the Airborne Division. In fact he was rejected by the RAF, joined the Royal Signals instead, and was invalided out

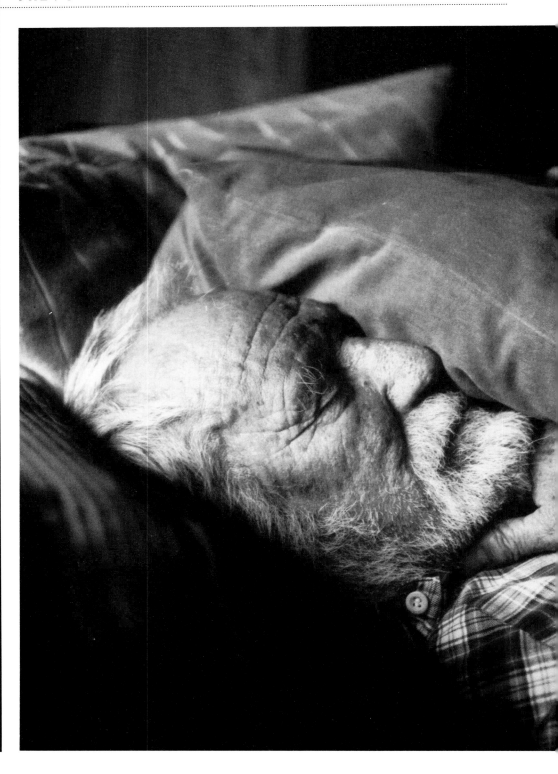

Trevor Howard asleep

three years later. The legend of his MC grew until it could no longer be easily denied, re-inforced ironically by his impeccable performances of gallant British officers in such films as *A Way to the Stars*. The lie festered over the years. If he was drunk in his local pub, the regulars would shake their heads sympathetically and remember his bravery in the war. If this was deceit, it was a small one, but Trevor Howard was too honest a man to ignore it and the secret haunted him increasingly with the likelihood that it might be exposed. Perhaps he was aware that the War Office told Vivienne Knight that if they read about the MC once more, they would have to correct the lie.

A lesser man would have shrugged it off, but Trevor was a man of principle and the pretence would have seemed dishonourable if revealed at this late stage. In fact it was a close-run thing, for a distinguished journalist approached me at that Piccadilly party, wondering if he should be the first to tell the truth. I urged him not to, and we agreed that Trevor should be allowed to keep his secret to the end. Now that he is dead, what does it matter?

Captain June and the Turtles at Iztuzu

In 1983, on my third visit to Turkey, I sailed on a yacht from Marmaris one afternoon and moored at Ekincek Bay. The next morning a caique arrived to take the yachtsmen through the slender entrance to the Dalyan Delta which was so shallow it could only be navigated by a flat-bottomed boat.

That was my first sight of the sandbar named Iztuzu. As we sailed past, I craned forward scarcely able to comprehend the curious formations of land and water, both beautiful and startling. The infinite beauty lay in the sweep of the curved bay with the sandbar of Iztuzu stretching for three miles, although little more than 150 yards wide at the northern end with a treacherous outlet to the sea. Inland lay the reeded delta with the ruined city of Caunus on the hilltop beyond and the modern village of Dalyan on the other side of the river, with Lake Koycegiz and the cotton fields in the far distance before the line of darker hills. The air on that May day was invigorating, but if it had been dull I believe I should have felt the same elation.

The element of surprise came from the shanty settlement shimmering in the early heat which rose from the sandbar. At first sight I was confused. Why did it look so extraordinary, apart from being unexpected? Then I realised that the huts were on stilts which explained why they seemed to be floating as if in some desert mirage.

Within seconds we were sailing up one of the labyrinthine channels of the delta, with multicoloured bee-eaters hovering on the banks and white egrets darting into the refuge of the bamboo reeds. I was captivated. Having hitched a lift on one of the yachts, I was able to stay on at the end of the day while the others were returned to their yachts by the ebullient Turk, Abidin Kurt, who owned the flat-bottomed caique and acted as the guide. Abidin became my closest friend in Turkey and I have returned to Dalyan every year since then, the last time in May 1988 to attend his wedding, but that is another, romantic story.

The following year I was impatient to see Dalyan again, wondering if my imagination had enhanced that sandbar beyond reality. It did not disappoint; until recently it never has.

Within a short time I established a routine. During the morning I would write at the Denizati Restaurant overlooking the river, while Ismet the waiter hovered happily around me, grinning all the time. Neither of us spoke the other's language, which made little difference to our voluble companionship as we resorted to mime. This spared us the boredom of the weather, football, television, or pop-stars, the mainstay of most conversation today. Ismet retreated from time to time to concentrate on a phrase book which baffled me as much as it did him: 'If John told you that last night, you can be sure he lied to you' . . . 'Helen needs a lot of money' . . . 'the doctor is drinking too much whisky'. What had they all been up to? I hoped that Ismet would never meet such a family in reality.

In the late afternoon I journeyed down the delta on Abidin's return trip to stay in one of his two huts on the sandbar where I jumped off while he continued to Ekincek. Incredibly, there were two restaurants, although that seems a formal description for the crazy, leaning wooden structures open to the elements apart from a makeshift roof. Yet, as I climbed the wooden steps from the sand, now cooling in the evening air, I thought this was the height of chic: to drink a glass of dry white wine and toy with a plate of octopus, the sea on one side and the brackish water of the delta on the other, an American thriller transmitted from Rhodes on a flickering TV set, unwatched by the owner, his child, his dog, or me, the only customer. One evening an elegant English couple rowed from their yacht in a dinghy and walked across the sand impeccably dressed as if for a soirée. Recognising me, evidently knowing that I was then the TV critic for the *Mail on Sunday*, the lady came across apologetically and said, 'Please forgive me for speaking, it must seem awfully rude, but I thought you'd want to know – Elsie Tanner has just died in *Coronation Street.*' After thanking her for the information, we had a few drinks together and they rowed back leaving me to the darkness and the sound of the sea, for by now the snowstormed TV set had failed and all was peace. Then Abidin would return from Ekincek.

I slept on the floor in the hut, washed in a bucket, and preferred the sea to the box-like lavatory outside. Luckily I had the wit to realise at the time that this was not primitive at all, this was civilised.

The next year I returned to Turkey for the whole of May, losing my job as TV critic during my long absence, though compensated with the pay-off which would help me 'buy' the plot of land beneath the Lycian tombs carved into the cliffs opposite Dalyan. I agreed on a price and paid a deposit but the owner changed his mind and I lost the land as well. Meanwhile the sandbar retained its incomparable magic and the loggerhead turtles returned as they do every year at the end of May, clambering out of the sea a few yards on to the sand where they lay their eggs, a hundred or more. Afterwards, using their flippers, they conceal the nests with sand and return wearily to the water. They are among the most vulnerable creatures left on earth.

One night I left Abidin's hut to look for the turtles with a torch and I was slightly relieved when I failed to find them for they hate the distraction of light and people. In the morning I looked again and saw that they had been there, leaving tracks like those of

Captain June dances with justified triumph on 'her' sandbar
at Iztuzu where the turtles wade ashore to nest

small tanks, one of them going in the wrong direction until it realised its mistake and headed back to the sea. Two months later, when the eggs hatched, Abidin would carry as many as he could find and place them in the water away from the scorching sand. Only a few survive but the mother turtles lay two or three times a season, so that is enough.

I should have known it was too perfect to continue.

It was on that sandbar that I met a kindred spirit and the last of my sacred monsters – June Haimoff, or 'Kaptan June' as she was known to the Turks when she sailed in ten years ago and saw that sandbar for the first time.

Captain June maintains the tradition of those indomitable Englishwomen who travelled in broad-brimmed hats in search of difference, whereas the tourist of today looks increasingly for the familiar. Knowing no fear in their wanderlust, they do not find it. 'Like Lady Hester Stanhope, I'm always moving east,' says Captain June. 'God knows where I'll end up. But I never forgot that first sight of Iztuzu and I vowed to return.' Like me she had found her paradise, but she made a home there and intends to stay unless something goes badly wrong, which could happen, as I shall explain.

In many ways, Iztuzu was meant to be her destination all along.

Her journey started in Essex where she was born many years ago. 'I was outrageous from the outset. I ran away from home when I was three to join the gypsies when I discovered that their children didn't wash or go to school, but they brought me back.' Perhaps they found her too much of a handful – I pity the Shiite who dares to hijack Captain June. At the age of seven, her father took June and her two brothers to Uganda, forming the sense of adventure which has never left her. 'I stayed in the bush for two years. Back in England I couldn't adapt to the classroom and studied dancing and singing.'

She made a disastrous début at the Wigmore Hall, singing to the accompaniment of Gerald Moore, but succeeded as a chorus girl at the Palladium and in nightclub cabaret. After a series of love affairs, including one with a Hungarian acrobat in Soho, she married an Englishman who exported herrings to the Middle East, and left him for an American-Bulgarian called Charles Haimoff. 'He was rich, for fourteen years I lived a jet-set life, I've done it all – top hotels, Ascot, a sixty-foot motor cruiser, yachts, a visit to Egypt every year.' When they separated, she bought a caique with her alimony and started to cruise the Mediterranean with her young Swiss boyfriend, and it was then that she saw the sandbar with the shanty huts on stilts, 'like floating pagodas, which appealed to my nomadic soul'. When the affair with the Swiss boy ended, she returned and sold her boat, drawing the plans for her own hut in the sand with a piece of driftwood. The following spring, the architect handed her the keys and the hut was complete. Running her life like a military operation, she conscripts every man in sight.

At first she lived there only in the summer; each year the stay grew longer. Sometimes she was the only person living on the sandbar, waiting several hours to hitch a lift on a boat to Dalyan to do her shopping. There were bad moments, when her dogs were kidnapped by a jealous suitor enraged by her various boyfriends, but the dogs were recovered and there was always the consolation of the solitude, especially in the evening when she drank her sundowners on one of her three small verandahs, and watched the sun fall into the sea. This was when she heard the cry of the turtle. 'One night I saw this shape. I had to keep a low profile, literally so for they dislike people standing over them, and I lay down a short distance away and watched. The eggs came out every few seconds like ping-pong balls, piled up in a pyramid, and every now and then she sighed. You feel for her, you know.'

With uncharacteristic sentimentality, Captain June explains why the turtles mean so much. 'If you save the turtles, you are involved in a sort of philosophy which ties in with the rest of nature. The mother turtles return to the beach where they were born and have been doing so for thousands of years. It's a primeval instinct. Kill them and you destroy the protection of motherhood.' Having no children of her own, apart from an adopted daughter who died a few years ago, she sympathises with the mother turtles.

As I have said, it was too perfect to continue, and disaster struck the sandbar in 1986 when the Turkish government decreed that all the shanty huts should be torn down. To add insult to this injury, the owners had to pay for the cost of their removal. To this day no one is certain of the reason for the dismantlement although Captain June admits that the settlement was becoming 'a bit of a slum'. There was another possible explanation: the German-Turkish construction project for a massive hotel at the far end of the sandbar, with 1,800 beds and a holiday complex for 4,000 people in the middle, where a channel would allow yachts to enter the delta, bringing their pollution with them. As Abidin told me with rare bitterness, 'Such a channel will bring rubbish boats with hippies and cheapies who will leave their shit and plastic behind them.' Of course he is prejudiced, for the transference to his caiques has made him rich. He has seven boats today and this is his livelihood, but he is literally correct about the shit, and the plastic which lingers interminably. Speedboats will follow, their wash disrupting the bamboo roots as they roar past, the noise disrupting the birds, the careful framework of the delta threatened.

The foundations of the hotel were laid in April 1987 and Captain June remembers the day with bitterness. 'A group of musicians with alp-horns were flown in wearing Bavarian costume, there were dancers dressed in leather, and officials sweating in their suits. They had their lunch and left the beach to the bulldozers. And no one looked at the sea, no one felt the wind, and no one thought of the turtles.'

This was when she started her campaign to save them, at least on the sandbar of Iztuzu, one of their last breeding-grounds, now to become a battleground with the danger that bulldozers would drive over the turtle nests deliberately. If there are no turtles left to protect, there can be no objection to the development. A terrible logic.

It is reckoned that less than 3,000 loggerhead turtles are left in the Mediterranean and the figure diminishes all the time as their breeding-grounds are encroached by concrete development. Their decline is one reason why these waters are becoming infested with jellyfish, which is part of the turtle diet. Three hundred turtles came to Iztuzu to lay their eggs, but this number is dwindling to fifty, as Dalyan becomes increasingly popular with the tourists.

Captain June received support from an unexpected source, from Germany where the influential Green Party was outraged to learn that a German woman MP had attended the foundation ceremony of the hotel, and applied such pressure that the developers agreed to limit the hotel to 620 beds with the lights of the hotel and tennis courts shielded at night. This is crucial, for when the baby turtles are hatched they are drawn to the sea by the reflected light and head in the wrong direction if confused. This compromise did not satisfy Captain June, however. 'Try telling that to the turtles. Anyhow, it's their beach.'

Turtles may be an emotive subject but the case against them was overwhelming from the Turkish point of view. Faced with a bonanza of tourism which would enrich anyone involved, the fate of the turtles seemed irrelevant. Indeed, the former Minister of Tourism let slip the tactless remark that 'development cannot be sacrificed for a few tortoises'. That is an observation he may live to regret, but he has a point when you consider that 1,000 beds mean $15 million in hard cash every year. Conversely, when asked if he wanted turtles or tourists, Prime Minister Ozal is alleged to have stated privately, 'Give me the turtles every time, the tourists are hardly an endangered species.'

Thanks to Captain June, Iztuzu had become a national issue, and this is when her own life became difficult, if not in actual danger.

The young men of Dalyan accused her of depriving them of their livelihood if she stopped the development of the hotel. She replied that the money would not go to them as they expected, that the tourists would pay their Deutschmarks in Germany, that the hotel would have its own shops, restaurants and ferry boats, even that the local youths could well be refused admittance as they have been at a smart hotel further up the coast. She had her supporters but local feeling went against her, and she was cut by former friends. 'There were no more "hellos" from people who had greeted me before.'

Then came the vilest slur of all: that she was a Greek spy because she went there so often. She pointed out that Greece was the nearest available country, but she made the mistake of ordering fifty T-shirts embroidered with a picture of a mother turtle and a baby turtle crying 'Help!' which confirmed the worst suspicions of her enemies when they saw the label 'Made in Greece'. She protested, 'My underwear is made in Paris, but that doesn't make me a French spy.'

Then the Turks took an exquisite revenge, as if to warn her to 'lay off'. The police impounded her passport, so she went to the governor demanding to know if other foreigners had been told to surrender their passports too. No, he admitted, but he promised that she would have it back within three hours. He was true to his word, but by then the villagers knew her real age, far removed from the teenage image which she conveys with such astounding success.

Captain June is nothing if not game, and continued her fight for the turtles undaunted. Delicately balanced as her position had become, it was aggravated by her voracious appetite for young Turks in their twenties. In a country of such morality that a bride can be returned to her parents after the wedding night if her husband discovers she is not a virgin, Captain June's behaviour was scandalous. One shopkeeper accused her in public of sleeping with every man in the village.

'Except for you,' she retorted boldly in spite of the hurt, 'I do have *some* taste.'

True to herself, she does not resort to guile. 'I have always had success with young men,' she declares unabashed. 'I have never had to coerce. They find me a good combination of maturity, yet still young. I keep myself in trim, wear trendy clothes, go to discos where I'm a good dancer. All this makes for a youthful image.' This did not prevent one irate Turk from dismissing her as 'that difficult English grandmother'!

She told me all this as we lunched at My Marina on the hill overlooking Ekincek Bay. When we arrived, they played a record of Dean Martin singing 'June in January' which made her momentarily tearful. 'We sang that at my engagement party here three years ago, when we exchanged rings.' The young Turk, now twenty-six, had just walked out on her, again: 'Without so much as thank you, in the clothes I bought him, the pockets bulging with the money I lent him, yet his friends take his side against me the worse he behaves.' Then she revealed the remarkable naïvety and blinkered self-deception of the sacred monster. 'I am afraid,' she told me, 'that my fiancé is one of the victims of the bad aspect of tourism, unable to handle the unlimited number of available women. He became obsessed and disappeared for nights on end, mauling a German hausfrau and then turning up at my door an hour later avowing his love for me! I couldn't take it.' It does not occur to her that she might be part of the process of tourism herself, which leaves the men dissatisfied with the innocence of the young girls they intended to marry.

'Are you a busy-body?' I asked her once. She rejected the idea indignantly. 'I love life and all that lives. That's what gives me the impetus.'

This philosophy and her undeniable courage enabled her to persevere despite the local opposition, and suddenly the tide turned in her favour. The channel through the sandbar seems to have been abandoned, and due to pressure from the Green Party fifteen German travel agencies declared that they would boycott the hotel if it is built at Iztuzu. Brigitte Bardot announced that she will discourage French tourists from going to Turkey, and David Bellamy urged the British to 'take nothing but photographs, leave nothing but footprints' on his return from Dalyan early in 1988. The developers also faced the problem of needing to drain the foundations which were flooded from the brackish lake near by: 'I hope that nature is taking her revenge,' says Captain June grimly.

Now there comes another twist in the story, that the turtles need to be protected from their protectors, from the conservationists themselves who descend with their camera crews, and from the tourists who visit Iztuzu at night in the hope of seeing the nests. 'I am not pleased with myself at all,' Captain June told me at one stage. 'I did not anticipate the bad effect this would have. But though the controversy is a double-edged sword, you find that most people leave the turtles alone if you explain the danger.'

If they are not left alone, they will lay their eggs in the sea and that will be the end of them.

Although the turtles are still in danger, there is a real hope for their survival as I write. Suddenly the turtles of Iztuzu have become a symbol to conservationists throughout the world. It is a historic moment in the corruption of tourism. With the opportunity to learn from the mistakes made in Spain and Greece, the Turkish government could be the first to say 'no' to development. This will not be wholly altruistic – nothing is when it has to do with tourism – but such a gesture would gain Turkey respect throughout Europe and enhance her application to join the EEC. Also, if Dalyan is allowed to remain unique, this could prove more beneficial to tourism in the long run, and even bring more profit.

After Abidin's three-day wedding, there was further cause for Captain June to celebrate. Her new house on the edge of Dalyan is complete, filled with her books and pictures and such graffiti as 'Good girls go to Heaven, bad girls go everywhere' and 'The rat race is over, the rats won'. The shanty hut she built on the sandbar has been resurrected in the garden. She calls her home The Peaceable Kingdom after the delightful American primitive painting by Edward Hicks which shows the beasts of the earth sitting together in harmony, while William Penn addresses the Indians in the background.

Her own peaceable kingdom consists of six dogs, of the small, cream-coloured Turkish variety; five cats, one of whom she rescued when the local children painted it blue and yellow; and the bear she keeps in a cage at the bottom of the garden. She rescued it when the mother was shot by villagers in the hills further up the coast and she found the cub being kept in wretched conditions. Now a splendid animal, the bear was given a Turkish name until Captain June learnt it was the same as the governor's and thought it more tactful to change it. Rechristened as Haydibay, the bear wrestles happily with Ibrahim, her caretaker, and a joyful rapport exists between the man and the wild animal although the bear will grow to twice its present size. Already, it could kill Ibrahim or scar him fatally with its long claws, but so far it is friendly. I fear for the animal's future: Haydibay was going to be presented to the Bear Park in Berne, where at least there is a lady bear of his own breed, but now there are export problems and it would be tragic if happy Haydibay ended in some wretched zoo. Ibrahim, of course, is determined to keep him. A charming, balding, middle-aged Turk, too old by Captain June's standards to become emotionally involved although he is her closest companion, Ibrahim is the guardian she needs. He disapproves of the young men and hopes to find a suitable husband for her, although this may prove harder than finding a suitable home for the bear.

'You are lucky to have him,' I told her impertinently.

'He is very lucky to have me,' she corrected.

'Hmm.'

At Captain June's house-warming, Nergis Yazgar, the lady who heads the Turkish conservationists, was adamant that there must be no development on the sandbar whatever. 'If you build at Iztuzu, then nowhere will be safe. Save the turtles and we save ourselves.'

The young man who represents Tourism and Culture in the area was present, and discussed the probability that the Dalyan Delta will become a National Park or Nature Reserve. He hinted that the government might stop the development and even reimburse the constructors their money, an act of foresight which would be blessed by future generations. It is the curse of tourism that tourists think in terms of next year, or five years, instead of a hundred years' time when such an area will be priceless.

In July 1988, Haydibay made a hole in the roof of his house and went off carousing in the neighbour's garden. 'It says a lot for the unruffled Turks,' said Captain June, 'that no one complained. Just a couple of anxious mothers clutching toddlers' hands.'

On my last day at Dalyan, I returned to the sandbar to find that a sign had been erected by order of the governor forbidding people to go there at night. Four guards will see that this is enforced.

'It's a triumph,' said Captain June. 'Not for me, for that would be too arrogant, but for the judgement of the Turkish authorities.' The latest news is heartening. The German financiers have withdrawn their investment in the project on the sandbar and the Turkish government has forbidden any development whatsoever.

Captain June has won. I photographed her dancing with delight on 'her' sandbar, to the cassette of a song she has written and recorded herself – 'Iztuzu Blues':

> Turtles used to come at night, and now arc-lamps light up the bay –
> So instead of nesting as they did, they panic and swim away –
> Singing the Iztuzu blues, just like you and me –
> Since that hotel started building, extinction is their destiny.

Now she will need to write a final verse to celebrate the conclusion, that the turtles of Iztuzu have been saved. What a triumph it will be if the turtles, who place themselves at our mercy, find that man is merciful at last.

A few nights later, I parodied Captain June's dance of triumph along the edge of another bay, so lovely that I dare not name it. I took a taxi from the nearest town at midnight to the end of the track where I had to continue on foot along the pebbled beach to the simple *pension* where I was staying, a farmhouse surrounded by geraniums, lilies, roses and pomegranates with their red, spring blossom. When I arrived that afternoon, a tortoise crossed the trickling stream and tiny, fluffy chicks pecked at the soil undisturbed by a scarred and lazy cat, while black baby goats, only slightly larger than the cat, skipped about in the field beyond where the family were planting potatoes. In my spartan room I noticed a huge, furry spider which looked alarmingly like a tarantula and thought of pointing this out to the family until it seemed irrational in such a 'peaceable kingdom'.

As I returned that night, my taxi-driver played Turkish music which was so glorious that I clapped my hands with delight and he flicked out the cassette and gave it to me when we stopped, refusing payment. Listening to it in England confirms it as the finest Turkish music I have heard, hauntingly evocative. I was only slightly drunk that night – I would call it invigorated.

As I made my way back, to the soft, gentle slurp of the water as it lapped the stones, I wondered why it was so light, for I had no difficulty in finding my way, and looked up expecting to see a full moon. There was no moon in sight, but a sky covered with a myriad of stars unlike any sky I had seen since my childhood in the north of Yugoslavia.

Memories came back as I thought of this book: Maugham with his lizard-look; Coward *uttering* his words rather than speaking them; my father's contentment as he fished the waters at Bohinsko; more recently, Captain June dancing.

I thought of the dinner at Putsborough Sands Hotel earlier in the year, to mark the sixtieth anniversary of *Tarka the Otter*. I had vowed never to go back because I thought it would be unbearable if I looked down on the trees that I had planted. However, because the Williamson family invited me, I accepted and it was dark, yet when I drove over the hill from Croyde the thing I recognised instantly was the smell of the sea. Absurd though it sounds, the sea smells differently there. When the speeches were over, I talked to the family: Henry's eldest son had come from Canada, and Henry's first wife, Loetitia, was present.

'You know,' I told them, 'Henry may have been difficult, but all I remember now is what a wonderful man he was and how lucky I am to have known him.'

That is true of all sacred monsters. They may be difficult, temperamental, occasionally treacherous, frequently drunk, usually unpredictable; this is their price for making life more interesting for the rest of us. They are worth the trouble.

In the course of writing this book, I realise how single-minded my own journey has been. I discovered some notes I wrote in Butternuts at Lake Geneva when I was evacuated to Canada; at the end of which I wrote this postscript, embarrassingly pompous even for an English schoolboy of thirteen: 'I have now finished my memoirs up to date, and I will now write a series of articles.' My God, I thought, was I at it even then!

There was a diversion when I became an alleged 'TV personality' and I still appear occasionally, the last time in the unlikely setting of the religious programme *Highway*, when Harry Secombe came to Bideford and I was asked to speak on Henry Williamson because he immortalised this part of England. There is a nice little boy at the local pub whose mischievous face appeared above the bar afterwards. 'I saw you on television,' he told me, 'and we got you on video but we wiped you out.'

Almost an epitaph: 'Was on television – wiped out'.

I escaped from television in time and tried to be true to myself, moving to Devon to find out if I could write. This is my twenty-second book and I am still finding out. I am starting to hope.

As there was no one to see me, I was inspired by the music and the raki to dance absurdly along the edge of the water that silent night, with the joy of being alive.

A NOTE ON THE AUTHOR

Daniel Farson has led an extremely varied life. The son of the American foreign correspondent, Negley Farson, he travelled extensively as a child and was evacuated to Canada and America in the war. At the age of seventeen he joined the Central Press, becoming the youngest Parliamentary and Lobby Correspondent. The following year he enlisted in the US Air Corps. He worked as a staff photographer for *Picture Post* for two years, then as a freelance journalist until he joined the Merchant Navy and sailed round the world. This journey was followed by a brief burst of 'fame' when he worked for ITV in 1956 and became a leading TV interviewer. His next venture was to run a pub of his own on the Isle of Dogs, the Waterman's Arms, with music hall entertainment. Since 1964 he has been a full-time writer and lives in North Devon.